MY DIARY OF DISASTER

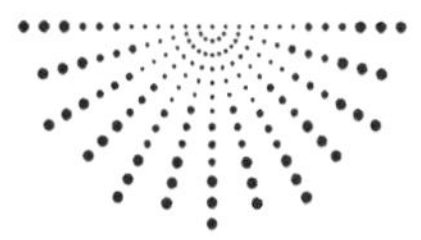

HOLLY MANNO

Edited by
JENNIFER L. ROOP

xo
www.fraudpress.hive

Paperback ISBN: 978-1-7337869-6-6
eBook ISBN: 978-1-7337869-5-9

ACKNOWLEDGMENTS

Dear Nanna (Geraldine Wheeler),

Thank you for taking care of my boy and for wearing my ass out with the thinnest switch from your tree.

Other souls who contributed to this book include: always my family, friends, former colleagues, a therapist or two, the anonymous women, the DD that Amish Guys Don't Call, Mr. L, Mr. C, the good sports at the gourmet book club, a bunny friend and Toto's mom who walks on the beach (advanced readers), a voice coach, a handful of bar flies, some jazz singers, that IG scribe, a few Willamette Writers, and a witchy godsend who introduced me to a Windy City editor.

For you Mother,

*The model of accomplishment & determination you exemplify
leaves the word formidable in monochrome. You have always defied
my imagination with your resolve & clarity. In many ways, you
are Evelyn Snow.*

And for all the women,

*May we stand together as the majority we are. United, we can
change the world toward the light.*

RULE #1 WHAT'S IN THE REARVIEW MIRROR DOESN'T MATTER (CANNONBALL RUN)

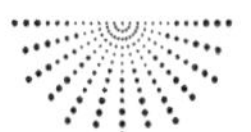

July 1994 – The First Time I Got Fired...

It's been twenty-five years since that day in the copy room, twenty-five years since Andy Nichols cornered me, and twenty-five years since Dad returned to the office earlier than expected. It's been twenty-five years since he unwittingly spared me from whatever his business partner at the CPA firm might have done next.

"All right, Evelyn, I'll be back after my lunch with Mr. Swanson. Please finish filling these," Dad said as he added another armful of Manila folders to the already tall stack at the corner of the table.

"Okay, Dad. Have a good lunch."

"I'll bring you something back."

"Thank you."

He nodded and proceeded out of the office, leaving me alone.

It was my third summer working at my father's office. Andy Nichols was Dad's business partner. His wife Natalie was their part-time assistant, but she couldn't work much during summer break because their kids were out of school.

That's where I came in. If I wanted to have new clothes and eventually a car, I was expected to earn them.

The copy machine whirred in the corner as I worked in the small records room. After a while, I heard the main office door open and I poked my head from the doorway to see if Dad was already back. It wasn't him, but his partner Andy. Instead of greeting him, I kept working and tried to be as quiet as possible. For some reason, I'd never been comfortable around Andy. He acted jovial enough, but there was something in his expression that made me edgy.

I was down to the last handful of files when I caught a whiff of stale cigarettes. I sensed he was behind me, standing in the doorway of the small, airless space. When I turned around, he didn't say a thing. Instead, he lurched forward until we were feet apart. I tried to speak calmly, though I wasn't.

"Hello, Andy. I didn't know you'd come back from lunch."

His eyes were glassy and his mouth rested in a smirk, "You didn't hear me? Funny, I thought I saw you poke your head out when I got in."

I didn't know what to say in the face of his confrontation.

He took another step forward and we were only inches apart. "You're such a good girl," he cooed. "Such a quiet worker. I'm thankful you can be here when Natalie can't."

His tone made me wary and there was no way out of the room unless I passed him. "Of course, Dad wouldn't have it any other way. Excuse me." I tried to brush past but he stopped me.

Holding my shoulders with his beefy mitts, he breathed, "What's the rush? You can take a little break. Charles isn't your only boss, you know."

I didn't like him touching me. His glazed expression confirmed he wasn't thinking clearly. I'd have to be diplomatic and talk my way out of the room. "Oh, I know, but Dad's due back any minute and I told him I'd finish copying the Branches file during lunch."

I tried to step aside, but he held me. "That meeting won't be over for at least another thirty minutes."

There was no choice but to remain in place. His sweaty hands crinkled the shoulders of my blouse and I considered my options. I could kick him in the shin, but that would be disrespectful. What if he was only joking around? But I knew he wasn't kidding. Even an innocent knows lust when it's holding her captive. I could scream, but that would be dramatic and no one would hear me. The copy room was at the center of the office and the walls between suites were soundproofed. I could grab the stapler and smash him over the head with it. "I need to use the restroom."

His tongue darted out of his mouth and back again, like a lizard reaching for a meal. "I've heard certain things are better when you need to go."

I had no idea what he meant, but he was no longer skirting around his desire as he bumped his lifted arousal at my hip. "Mr. Nichols, excuse me."

His fingers pulsed into my shoulders, kneading a warning as they dug. "Relax, Evvy, you have to learn to enjoy pleasure. Let me show you something."

He leaned forward until the heat from his sour breath warmed my ear. I was about to discharge a pointless scream when I heard the front door open. Andy heard it too. He jumped and pushed me away. I fell back into the copier and righted myself as my father arrived in the doorway. Andy strategically held a stack of files to cover the front of his pants and asked, "How was lunch with Mark Swanson?"

My father looked toward me. His expression flashed rage, then it went blank. His tone, as he replied, was professional and cool, "We had to cut it short but we covered the key points. I'll fill you in on the way to the Branches meeting."

"Great, well, I have some calls to make," Andy said and scurried from the room.

I'd yet to speak and Dad left no room for it. "Do you have the Branches file copied?"

"Um, just about. Give me five and I'll bring it to your office."

He stared briefly then said, "Fine. Your lunch is on the reception counter."

"Thanks, Dad." And that was it. If he noticed anything about my shirt or expression, we never spoke of it.

Later that evening, I was reading in my room when Mother came in. Antionette, as they said, had aged gracefully. At almost forty years old, she kept the shine of a much younger woman. Her smooth hair swung in a tidy upturned bob of strawberry blonde and her light eyes shone in the lamplight. "What are you reading?"

"White Noise," I replied.

She didn't hide the sarcasm in her tone. "Hmm, sounds interesting. Listen, I need to tell you something."

"Okay," I looked expectant.

"Dad doesn't want you to work at the office anymore."

My mind flashed back to the copy room and Andy's menacing boldness. I was about to explain when she went on.

"You made a mistake copying the Branches file so your father was unprepared during the meeting. He didn't have an important document and they had to reschedule." She patted my hand and carried on, "It's tedious work, the CPA business —maybe it's not for you. I know I couldn't do it."

My shame knew no limits as I absorbed her words. Was I banned from the office because of what happened with Andy or had I really messed up Dad's appointment? I'd never know, but my father's dismissal told me I was the problem. Maybe I was even guilty for Andy's advances. Had I done something, even by mistake, that led to that moment?

TODAY, I had a second session with my new therapist, Dr. Cord. I hated it. We touched on things I'd rather bury, things he believes are still affecting me. Apparently–I'm depressed and the key is in the depths of my childhood. I'm skeptical. I know what's happened and how fortunate I've been, even if my life didn't turn out as we'd planned.

I'm not new to upset. I've failed before and I've persevered. It's different this time; I'm different. Dr. Cord suggests it's something deeper than I've come to terms with. I disagree. I've had plenty of time to examine the circumstances of my life, but what can be done about the past? Yet, I can't stop my mind from circling around ancient history nor advance from the neutral purgatory I've paced lately. Yesterday is behind me and I refuse to ruminate. Stable people don't linger in trauma—they keep going.

It's just, I can't seem to move forward. For months the weight of anxiety has covered me like a lead apron. I used to hide in my work, but since I lost my job, with my reputation, I have no solace. I'm single and it's fair to say my relationships with men have been troubled. My only child, daughter, Athena, is starting her own life and I wouldn't burden her with my forlorn status. Mom and Dad are there, I suppose. We have a polite if superficial relationship. They know I've had problems, but not how deeply I'm affected. I can't show them the scars I've hidden beneath my carefully selected clothing. I'd never admit how often I cry, or that I can no longer sleep in bed. It's hard to admit that I can't pull myself out of this...

I've asked the doctor for help and he gave me an assignment with this explanation: "When you get things out in the open, however that looks for you, there is no longer anything to fear."

"But what does it matter now?" I asked, "Why waste time on the past?"

"Because the past is present until you face it. My guess is there are a lot of things you've never told anyone. You are used to holding darkness, Evelyn, but you've reached capacity."

So, Dr. Cord will get his way, and I'll open the door to forgone incidents. In the end, I agreed to complete the homework he prescribed. I'll write a journal, and I'll include certain milestones from the past—the hurtful or frightening things I'd rather not discuss. One thing to know about me: I do what I say I will. Welcome to my diary of disaster.

July 30, 1994

With all the free time that summer, I did exactly what my parents tried to protect me from. I got into trouble. One night, my school friend Julie Davies invited me to stay over, and to my surprise, my parents agreed. Mom dropped me off and Julie came bounding from the house. Her Sun-In blonde, curly hair, stood as if suspended in a perpetual state of readiness, announcing to the world, "the fun girl is here." She wore an oversized Def Leppard T-shirt and kilt-styled skirt, which likely shocked my mother, but she only smiled.

"Hey, look at you," said Julie as she studied my outfit. I wore sweatpants and a T-shirt, no makeup, and my hair pulled into a ponytail. "Ready for a cozy night of movies and popcorn?"

"I am." We hugged and I could smell the marijuana in Julie's hair.

I turned to my mother, who looked pained at the idea of leaving me alone with her. I didn't blame her, which was why I was especially sweet. "Thanks for the ride, Mom." I gave her a big hug and kiss. "I'll call you in the morning."

She wrung her hands and replied, "You two be good and remember, I'm just a phone call away."

"Don't worry," Julie called as she tugged me toward the house, "we'll lock the door behind us and my dad will be home later. Goodnight, Mrs. Snow."

"Goodnight, girls. Lock the door."

⁂

Colorful beams of light shot from every direction and silvery sparkles, like fallen stars, danced among them. The room vibrated with bass and the moving masses who swayed to Soul II Soul's "Back to Life," Julie and me included. The dance floor seemed to spin, or was I spinning? I couldn't tell. We drank brandy and Cokes and smoked pot before arriving at the underage dance club. It was my first time smoking or drinking, other than the sips my parents permitted on special occasions. I was moving faster or the ground was.

Julie grabbed my shoulders. Her eyes smudged from her black eyeliner. "Hey, you okay?"

I asked, "Can we go?"

"Say no more."

We walked arm in arm through the club and to the door. After a night of dancing, and the mile walk there, my feet throbbed in Julie's half-size-too-small heels. The Oakland air assaulted us as we stepped outside. I wished I'd worn my jacket, but Julie was adamant. Instead, I wore her skin-tight skirt and a scissored T-shirt from her collection. It was the kind of outfit my father would describe as "asking for it."

"Hey," an unfamiliar man's voice called.

Julie and I looked toward the car where the sound emanated. "Hey yourself, Brady Bower," Julie taunted.

"Need a ride?"

Julie didn't hesitate, "Yes we do!"

"Okay, get in."

Julie opened the back door of the Volvo station wagon and I slid in, then she hopped in front with Brady. "Hey," he turned to face me, " I saw you on the last day of school."

I remembered him too. In fact, I couldn't shake the memory of that day. He sat solitary on the railing near the bike rack and I was walking with my friend Vivien toward the parking lot where my mother planned to pick us up. He looked at me as if he knew me. His stare was unwavering as we made our way toward him.

"Hello," he had said, simply.

His voice was deeper than I'd expected and his eyes, ice blue. Embarrassed by his attention, I kept walking and looked down as I replied, "Hi." Flash forward two months and here I was trying to sound cool though nauseated and nervous, "Sure, I remember."

"I'm Brady."

"Evelyn."

Julie chimed, "But everyone calls her Evvy."

"Your place, Julie?"

"Yep. She's staying with me tonight."

He glanced at me through the rearview mirror and started the drive home.

Julie turned my way, "Brady knows my cousin Tommy. That's how we met."

Brady asked Julie, "Where's your pops tonight?"

"He's at his girlfriend's house in San Jose."

Their conversation dimmed as I rested my head against the window and tried to focus on the cool glass. The spinning sensation was ceaseless and when we finally arrived at Julie's house, I was grateful. I somehow got myself out of the car and into the house. Julie and Brady headed for the kitchen and me for the bedroom.

Julie's bedroom had its own bathroom which I quickly ensconced myself in. The pink wallpaper mocked my trashy-punk look. Seeing my reflection only made me feel worse. My stomach turned and the bile came. I kneeled over the toilet, retching the brown alcohol out. My guts and nose recoiled as I evicted the wickedness. When there was nothing left, I scrambled to stand. Running the water until it warmed, I washed the inky makeup from my eyes and lipstick from my mouth. I turned off the light and padded into the darkened bedroom. I could hear Julie and Brady talking, but I didn't have the energy to join. Instead, I crawled onto her bed and closed my eyes.

The teasing was lovely. Like puffs of air gently massaging my breasts. Soft as feathers, touches of gold traded off and I began to squirm. I smelled him before I tasted him. Liquor and desire warmed his breath while his caress betrayed me. The lightest glance of smooth lips pressed into mine then retreated. My breasts tingled with a new kind of energy and my lips shared the electricity. A coolness came and it was over.

My dream darkened and suddenly a strong force held me.

I willed my eyes to open and when I awoke, Brady was there. His hand was pressed firmly over my mouth, and he used one leg to hold mine down as he tugged at my panties. I wanted it to be a nightmare, but even in the dark, and haze of intoxication, I knew it was real.

I tried to push him off, but he climbed on top of me and used his shoulders to pin my arms. One hand covered my mouth, while the other worked below. I tried to wiggle free, to slap him away and even bite him, but he was heavy and he applied more pressure to keep me still. I could do nothing to stop him from tearing my panties off. A shock, like the stab of a knife, opened me, and with his forced entry, he took my precious innocence. My lungs were crushed by his weight. He moved rapidly and deeper with every thrust. One hand pinched at my breast and held me captive, while the other remained faithfully over my mouth. His grunts were pathetic and the more noise he made, the more pain I was in. Until, finally, he moved so quickly and deeply, I was sure I couldn't take another second. That's when he made the loudest sound of all, then collapsed his full weight upon me.

He stayed that way for an undetermined amount of time. Tears fell from the corners of my eyes. Finally, he raised himself on his elbow and removed his hand from my mouth. For the first time, his empty eyes met mine and he said, "You know something, for a hot girl, you sure are a dead fuck."

Without a hint of care, he yanked himself from inside of me, parting with one last slap of agony. After pulling on his pants, he wordlessly left the room and soon after, I heard the front door. My spot was throbbing. I got up and made it to the bathroom. Blood and a mayonnaise-looking goop dripped down my leg and I knew it was my fault. I shouldn't have lied to my parents and I shouldn't have left the house looking like this. I got what I was asking for.

Therapy - Session III – Read and Rewind

Dr. Cord studied me over the rim of his eye glasses. His long nose pointed prominently in my direction and was enhanced by the severe center part and ponytail he'd likely sported since the sixties. "Thank you for sending me the journal entries. Do you mind if I ask you a couple of questions?"

My pulse quickened at the mention of the diary. "I think that's what I'm paying you for."

His face softened and the crow's feet near his eyes deepened. "I know this isn't easy for you, Evelyn."

I let his comment rest.

"You've endured intense experiences. Looking back, how do you feel about those situations?"

I shrugged as the wounds I'd covered with layers of antibiotic cream reopened. "They have little to do with my life today."

A doubtful hmm escaped his throat, "What if those things happened to Athena? How would you feel?"

His questions struck a nerve and I had to stop myself from spitting a response. "I've done everything possible to protect Athena from things like that."

"Do you think your parents were protective?"

My response was nearly a whisper, "Yes, they tried to protect me."

"Do you think they could have stopped those things from happening?"

I contemplated this question for the first time. "No. I mean, how could they protect me when they had no idea something bad was going to happen?"

"Did you know something bad was going to happen?"

His question was asinine. "Of course not!" The moment I replied, I understood his logic.

"What about your father—what was he like when you were small?"

For an undetermined eternity of awkward breath, the room was silent except the rustle of my pants as I shifted in my seat and thought back in time…

Spring 1981 – The Stairs

I was three when we lived in the house with a giant set of stairs. Mom and I were in my bedroom playing when Father arrived at the doorway. Spring graced us with the first sunny day in months. Dad was restless to get started on the weeding that had been overlooked during the cold winter.

"Antionette, I'm headed out back to work in the yard."

"Daddy, can I help?"

I may have been too young to name his expression, but I sensed he was anything but thrilled to have me along. "Yes, but you have to stay out of trouble. I can't keep an eye on you so you'd better be a good girl."

"I will, Daddy."

"Fine, come then," he said as he marched out the bedroom door.

Mommy tugged at my arm, "Just a minute, sweetie. You need your coat."

I stepped from foot to foot waiting until Mom bundled me sufficiently. When she was finally through, I tugged away. "Hey," her voice admonished, "where's my kiss?"

I turned around and puckered my lips, and beautiful Mommy scooped me up and pummeled my cheeks with kisses until I giggled. "'Nuff, Mommy."

"Okay, now be a good girl for Daddy."

"Okay," I chimed and scampered for the door. As most

toddlers do, I ran toward the stairs. My patent leather shoes gleamed and as I rushed down the first few steps. I was so excited that I missed the handrail. My foot slipped and I launched forward. First my tummy, then my back, flip, flop, I went down the slick wooden stairs. Out of breath and hurting, I landed in a heap on the floor.

After a minute, I managed to stand. My leg was sore and also my arm. There were tears in my eyes as I limped through the kitchen and out into the yard.

When I made it to his side, Daddy was holding a rake and studying the flower beds. He looked at me. His eyes weren't warm like Mommy's. He was busy all the time. Daddy didn't like to play and he didn't like crying. "What's wrong with you?" he demanded.

I tried not to cry as I answered him, but that backfired. I sobbed, "I fell."

He looked me up and down and barked, "You're all right. Go back inside with your mother."

At the tender age of three, I already knew better than to question his directive. Holding my elbow, I limped into the house, but instead of finding Mommy, I sat on the other side of the glass door and watched him work. He was tireless, first loosening the soil with the rake and then pulling the errant weeds from the ground. His jaw clenched in determination as he moved. I wished I could be outside with him. If only I was a good girl and I helped, maybe he would have had time to play. Why wasn't I careful on the stairs? They always told me to slow down and I didn't listen.

"Evelyn?" Dr. Cord's tone was soothing.

"Dad was great. He was hardworking and home every night. He loves my mom and she's crazy about him."

He scribbled something down on his notepad and asked, "Shall we get into your work situation?"

I knew what that would mean and I wasn't ready for it. "Could we table it for another time?"

"Of course. Let's break for today and until our next session, why don't you have some fun?"

"Fun?"

"Yes, fun. See a movie, go on a date, try something you haven't done before. It'll give you new things to journal about."

I shook my head in disbelief that I was actually paying for this advice. "Okay," I rose, "fun it is."

2

HELLO (THE PRESENT)

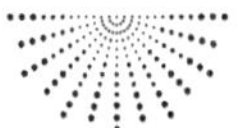

The windshield wipers swiped back and forth in their rhythmic attempt at clearing the glass. I blinked–trying to see through the downpour—and proceeded past a green light. My stomach growled so loudly that the sound filled the otherwise silent car. I'd spent the last two days helping my nineteen-year-old daughter Athena and her friends get situated into their new house by campus. With so much to do, there wasn't a lot of time to eat. Since no one was waiting for me at home, I made a quick decision to stop at a local restaurant. Pulling onto the street, I found a spot and parked. Rain drenched me as I hurried toward the entry.

The door's bell chimed and I found myself in a dimly lit space. I'd never actually been inside the restaurant. Though I'd eaten at the Thai place before, I always sat on the deck with Maggie, our Labrador retriever, and Sean, my former fiancé. Now Maggie was settled into her new house with Athena and Sean had left two years ago, taking the neighbor's wife with him. My thoughts were interrupted by the cheerful greeting of a server who acknowledged me.

"Hello. Dinner for one?" she asked.

I replied, "I think I'll take something to go, maybe have a drink while I wait."

She pointed to the left, "There's a bar just around the corner and you can order from the bartender."

"Perfect," I said and walked that way.

It was cozy inside, where floral prints and strung lights attempted to capture the spirit of the tropics. The ploy almost worked—almost. As I slid off my wet coat, I had a sarcastic chuckle knowing that the 40-degree January weather could easily continue through May. It was Oregon after all.

"Something funny?" The bartender's voice snapped me to.

I sat and replied, "No. I was just thinking I've never been inside before. I usually sit on the deck. It's very tropical in here."

His smile was easy. "You don't approve?"

"Oh no, I think it's cute, if a bit ironic." As if to emphasize, a few drops of water fell from my dark hair and landed on the counter between us.

"Yeah, it's pretty wet out there. Can I get you something to drink?"

"Hmm, I think so. Do you have a cocktail menu?"

"We do or I can make you something special."

"What do you suggest? Nothing too sweet, please."

"No problem. Do you like rum?"

I rarely drank anything except vodka or wine, but what the hell. "Sure, that sounds good."

With efficient moves, I watched as he dramatically poured a large amount of liquor into a shaker adding lime, mint and some other ingredients I couldn't identify. After a vigorous shake, he poured the mixture into a martini glass and floated a thin slice of blood orange at the top.

As he placed the drink in front of me I noticed his hands

were as immaculate as a surgeon's. "Here you are. I hope you like it. Let me know if you'd rather have something different."

"Thanks," I said and sipped gingerly at the full glass. It was blended so that the alcohol wasn't noticeable. "It's delicious."

"You like?" He asked as if he were fishing rather than double checking.

"It's perfect."

"Do you want to look at a menu?"

His eyes were shadowed under the vague light and I found myself wanting to see them more clearly, but I replied normally. "Yes, please."

He pulled one from a lower shelf and handed it to me. "I'll be right back to check on you."

I watched for a moment as he walked toward the end of the bar, moving with the ease of a man who lived in the present. I'd profiled him, of course, but in my experience most bartenders possessed this particular kind of flow.

Bringing my attention back to the menu, I skimmed the options and set it aside to concentrate on my cocktail.

A moment later he returned and asked, "What can I get you for dinner?"

"I'll take the papaya salad and the chicken satay to go."

"To go? You sure?"

I was a little surprised at his question. "Yes. I've been moving all day and I'm kind of tired."

"Moving?" he asked.

"Yes. Well, not me, my daughter. She left the dorms and moved into a house with friends. Though I may be next."

"I see," he said as he punched keys on his console.

I took another sip of the tangy drink and was surprised when he asked, "Why might you be next?"

"Oh, well, my house is a bit big for me and kind of expensive."

"You live in this neighborhood?"

I should have hesitated. Maybe it was exhaustion, but I answered before I could counsel myself, "I do, just up the hill."

"I'd love to take a look at your home," he said.

My expression must have been leery because he quickly explained himself. "Not only do I co-own the restaurant, I'm also a realtor." He extended his hand to shake. "Rye Cox."

I accepted and when our hands gripped, I felt the smoothness that was apparent as I'd watched him earlier. "Evelyn Snow but everyone calls me Evvy."

His voice was like a serenade. "Nice to meet you, Evelyn."

"You as well, Rye."

He released my hand and said, "That's quite a handshake."

"Ahh yes, a throwback from the past. I blame those years in corporate America."

His expression went green. "Corporate America, that's not for me."

I sniffed and spoke without hesitation, "Apparently it wasn't for me either." I cautioned myself to watch it. I was oversharing after only a few sips of the strong cocktail. Fortunately, I was only blocks from the house.

"Oh?" he tested as his eyes held.

I shook my head and tried to rebound. "I'm afraid that drink is gaining on me."

He chuckled and I got a better look at him. I liked the gentle creases at the corners of his eyes and the fact that he had a tan in January. It was a nice contrast against his dirty blond hair. The bell behind him rang, interrupting our moment, and he excused himself. Quickly he returned with my order, and after adding utensils, he placed the bag on the counter beside me.

"Thank you," I said and reached for my purse. "Can I have the bill?"

"No bill," he replied. "The only payment I'll accept is your phone number."

I felt flushed. Was it the drink or his statement? I straightened my shoulders and inquired, "Why do you want my number?"

"I'm a realtor, remember?" He handed me a business card with his name emblazoned on the front beneath the familiar logo I'd seen on almost every listing in the neighborhood. "If you're moving, maybe I can help you."

I was embarrassed by my mistake and ingrained paranoia. He wasn't interested in me. He wanted the commission he would earn by selling my house. I didn't have a realtor yet, so I made a quick decision. "Thank you, I'd appreciate that."

He pressed a tiny carbon copy notepad and a pen in front of me. I hesitated for a split second, then realized I had no reason to pause. Collecting the pen, I scribed my number and address beneath my name and slid it over to his side of the counter. "Thank you for dinner."

The corners of his mouth lifted, and he replied in a near drawl, "No, thank you. I'll call you tomorrow. Maybe we can have lunch?"

Was he flirting or trying to set up a business meeting? I was confused but responded neutrally. "Maybe we can. It was nice to meet you, Rye."

I felt exposed as he said, "The pleasure is all mine, Evelyn. Until tomorrow."

The front door opened aggressively, a result of my overcompensation with the troubled lock. Years later and I still hadn't figured it out. I chuckled for no one and proceeded over the threshold. I was alone. It wasn't new. I was accustomed to it now.

The aroma of food emanated from the bag, but I was no longer hungry. Two years of living alone, dining alone and waking alone had slimmed me down. I'd come to understand myself in this respite. I liked to eat with company, or not at all. Thus, the protruding hip bones and narrow waist.

My phone buzzed and I grappled to fish it from my purse. When I unlocked the keypad, a text message indication waited. I opened the app and saw a number I didn't recognize. It was Rye, from the restaurant. "Are you home safe?"

I settled myself at the base of the stairs and typed a reply. "Safe and sound. Thanks again for dinner."

His response came immediately. "Don't mention it. I'll reach out tomorrow before I pick you up. Looking forward to lunch."

I was definitely buzzed since I replied so cheerfully, "Okay, I'm looking forward to it too!" For good measure, I added a smiley face. No doubt Athena would lecture me, but before I could fall down that rabbit hole, I hit the send button.

The ringing phone was a relief. I needed a break from painting the living room walls. I stepped down from the ladder, tossed aside my gloves and plucked the phone from the table. Athena's face was on the screen.

Accepting her FaceTime request, I greeted her. "Good morning, sunshine!"

"Hi, Mom." The sound was a choir of voices and suddenly Athena's wasn't the only face on the display. Maggie and Shane, one of her housemates, smashed into the frame.

"Hi, kids. How was your first night in the new place?"

"Good," they chimed. "Are you coming over for the BBQ tonight?" Athena's big blue eyes implored.

"I don't think so. I'm going to leave you kids to your own devices."

Her mouth contorted into an adorable pout, "Aww, but we want you to come over."

My great luck didn't escape me. I knew most parents couldn't get their adult kids to visit with them at all. "You're so sweet, but I'm going to pass. I have a feeling the party will be a little wild for your old Mom."

"Ha, ha, very funny. You know no one ever believes you're my Mom anyway."

"Still, this is the first college party you're throwing and Mommy doesn't belong there, sweet as you are to ask." My screen flashed with a text message banner.

Athena heard it, and asked, "What's that? Is someone calling?"

It was Rye from last night, but I wouldn't explain that. "No, it's a text message from my friend. I'll get back to them in a bit."

"Okay, well, I'd better let you go. If you change your mind, stop by later."

"Thanks, honey. You guys have fun and remember, you're going to have to clean up tomorrow. I love you."

"Love you too, Mom. Byyyye."

We hung up and I took a minute to roll the tension from my shoulders before checking Rye's message. Normally I told Athena everything, but for some reason I'd hesitated at mentioning last night's encounter. Dismissing the thought, I clicked the message.

"Good morning, Evelyn. Are we on for lunch? I can pick you up. Will 1PM work?"

I looked at the time and it was nearly 11AM. I'd have to stop painting to get ready. My stomach lurched as my fingers hovered over the keys. For goodness' sake, Evvy, it's a realtor looking at your house, not a marriage proposal. I replied before I chickened out, "Sure, I'll see you then."

His reply was swift, "Great. Bring a bathing suit."

A bathing suit? What on earth…

3

STRAIGHT TO IT

It was ten after one when the doorbell rang and I stopped my obsessive tidying to answer the door. A flood of light from the unexpected sun glared at me, outlining Rye in a dark silhouette. I blinked and moved aside. Finding my voice, I said, "Hi. Come in."

He stepped over the threshold and faced me directly. "It's nice to see you, Evelyn."

With dark dots still nagging my eyes, I became flushed and hoped it wasn't apparent. "You too," I said and stepped back. "Would you like to tour the house? I'm painting the living room, so forgive the mess."

"Sure," he agreed.

I walked toward the kitchen. Although I'd designed it, and had lived with it for the past two years, I still felt in awe it was actually mine. "Let's start with my favorite part of the house."

"Wow, great remodel. Did you do this?" he asked.

"Yes, about two years ago. It was a fun project."

"Love the soapstone and the range."

I sighed my reply, "Me too."

"The lighting in here is amazing," he said as he walked toward the dining room. "These windows are huge."

I leaned against the doorway and watched as he discovered the beauty of my home. It reminded me of the first time I'd seen it. I felt as if the house were speaking to me, a silent urging that was hard to explain. "It's special, isn't it?"

His eyes met mine from the living room and he agreed, "Very. You've done an incredible job with the design. If I remember, it was built in 1940. Is that right?"

I was surprised he knew the age of my house and reminded myself he was a realtor, here on business. I rebounded, "That's right, though with the exception of the walls and the exterior style, the entire house has been updated. The plumbing and electric are up to current standards and I did a bunch of foundation work. It's a solid house."

"That's obvious," he agreed.

"Do you want to see the upstairs?"

"Please, lead the way."

Conscious that he was behind me, I walked up the flight of stairs and to the master bedroom. Daylight filtered through the sheer curtains, casting a glow along the oak floors. The four-post bed sat prominently like an elephant in the room. "Obviously, this is the master." I pointed, "Through that small door is a bathroom, and the walk-in closet is just over there."

He entered the space and I acknowledged the intimacy of the moment. I was overwhelmed by the way his every move seemed to permeate sensuality. A strange and sexy man was in my bedroom, where I slept, where I dressed and where—once upon a time—I used to have sex.

In silence he opened the doors and looked inside. When he was done, he leaned against the bedpost and said, "It's impeccable. Are you sure you want to sell it?"

I shifted as I worked to even my voice. "I'm not sure, just considering my options right now. There's one more room this way." I didn't wait and left him to follow as I walked down the hall. I opened the office door and said, "Please, go ahead."

He walked into the room and crossed to look through the French doors. When he turned back around, his smile was contagious and I knew he understood my adoration for the place. "You can see the river from here and Mt. Hood. This is fantastic. Did you add these doors and this dormer?"

"I did. It's been a labor of love. I'm glad you like it."

"It's a unique house. Very special."

"Thanks. We've had our ups and downs, but I knew it was mine the minute I walked through the door."

"It's not going to be easy for you to leave here."

"Yes, well…" I trailed off as I exited the room, not wanting to share the private details of my life with a man I'd met the previous night.

When we arrived downstairs, he asked, "Are you ready for a little adventure?"

I wasn't sure what to make of him and answered honestly. "I'm not that adventurous."

The lift at the corner of his mouth challenged me. "What a surprise. Come on, it'll be fun. Get your bathing suit and let's go."

"Excuse me but it's 42 degrees outside today. What makes you think I'd wear a bathing suit?"

"Trust me," he said and walked toward the bench at the entryway. Gesturing to my purse, he asked, "You need this, right?"

I looked at him, not sure how to take his command. "I suppose."

"And your swimsuit, is it inside?"

Between furious and intrigued, I leaned toward the latter and responded curtly, "It is."

"Perfect. Let's get going." He pressed a hand to my shoulder and guided me toward the door.

As I waited for him to reach the driver's side of the SUV, I questioned my judgement in leaving with the bossy stranger. Was I going on a date? Why did I need a bathing suit? At least I had verified his identity and nothing disconcerting showed up in the background check. He was a partner on several somewhat nondescript limited liability corporations and his broker's license was current. Fortunately, my profession still afforded me a few resources.

He climbed in and started the ignition. "Ready?" he grinned.

He was nice looking and had an easy manner. It was almost practiced, the way he lined things up. I noticed I wasn't nervous around him. My blood pressure was steady. I didn't feel the need to meet his challenge, but I realized I wanted to see something new. Maybe those therapy sessions with Dr. Cord were starting to pay off. "I am."

With that, he pulled away and in a few maneuvers, we were on the highway. After a time, he asked, "Are you from here, Evelyn?"

"No, my ex-husband and I moved up from Oakland fifteen years ago."

"How long have you been divorced?"

"A long time, over ten years now."

"How is that?" he asked.

"Jack and I are friendly enough. He lives in town with his girlfriend. What about you? Have you been married? Any kids?"

He looked over for a moment, and then back at the road, "No, not me. I don't believe in marriage and I don't want kids."

Hmm, interesting, but not really. I chastised myself for getting into the car with a virtual stranger. Was a pitch on polyamory on the horizon?

He continued, "It doesn't make sense, trying to hold on to someone. I've always had non-monogamous relationships."

I couldn't stop myself, and blurted, "Yeah, you and every other man on planet earth."

I felt his eyes on me and in a hushed voice, he replied, "Only I'm willing to admit it. A lot of guys are just like me, but they make promises they know they'll never keep and eventually, someone gets hurt."

I noticed his comfort behind the wheel. His relaxed defensive driving left no room for criticism, although his perspective on life certainly did. Emboldened by my silence, he carried on, "With me, you know what to expect from the start."

Nice how he waited until I was a captive audience to spew his unoriginal life mantra. My annoyance was apparent as I demanded, "Where are we going?"

His mischievous expression confirmed he reveled in having the upper hand and I knew my question would go unanswered. Though I didn't know him, for some reason I was unintimidated. We exited the highway and in two turns arrived at a funky resort on a winery. There were colorful hand-painted signs with arrows pointing to a spa, a tap room and a golf course. The turn-of-the-century hotel was made completely of brick, and large white pillars flanked wooden entry doors. To the side I noticed a garden area with rows of dormant flower beds and vegetation. It was a romantic oasis and a peculiar juxtaposition against the ideas shared by my "companion."

He pulled into the parking lot and eased into a spot. Looking my way, he asked, "Have you been to Evermore Lodge before?"

"No. I've heard about this place, but it's my first time."

That sure smile showed up again and he said, "Good."

It was like passing through a doorway to another dimension. We entered the spa and the chill from outside vanished. A buried memory of Star Trek and the transporter machine came to mind. Zen music was complemented by the sound of water as it dripped down copper chains shaped of bells. "Splunk, splunk, splunk" went the water as it landed in the pool below. A variety of bamboo and enormous bromeliads thrived in the atrium that doubled as a reception area.

A woman in a black kimono carrying an iPad approached us. "Good afternoon. What name is your reservation under?" Her monotone voice and translucent eyes played into the scene.

"Hello. Cox, Rye Cox is the name."

"Yes, I see your reservation for two. Welcome back, Mr. Cox. Please, this way."

He paused for me to go first and I followed as our host seemed to float over the slate tiles. She pushed the door and we entered a hallway. It was dim and lit only by candles that flickered along the floors. Pausing outside of another door, she turned to Rye and presented the iPad. "Please enter your code, Mr. Cox."

He typed something onto the screen and when he finished, the woman completed some steps and announced, "The door should open now. Would you please check?"

He tapped the keys on the door lock and it released. "Looks like we're good."

"Excellent. There are towels and the other items you requested inside the room. Don't hesitate to inform the staff of anything additional you need during your visit."

"Thank you," he replied and she promptly left us.

He held the door for me to go ahead and I entered tentatively. It was a compact room with a loveseat and a small wardrobe. Upon a side table sat a spray of white flowers and a bottle of champagne on ice. Muted light from the skylight and more candles from the hallway illuminated the space.

Rye followed me inside and quickly uncorked the bottle of bubbles. He poured us each a glass and handed one to me. His glass touched mine as he said, "To our adventure."

I was reluctant to drink to that, but tapped his glass anyway. "Cheers," I said and sipped at the wine. It was crisp and dry and lovely.

"Should we change?" he asked.

I looked around and didn't see a place for it. He noticed my bemused expression and said, "Why don't I give you a minute." Collecting his backpack, he headed for the door. "I'll be back in a few."

After he left, I twisted my long hair into a bun, securing it with a chopstick from my bag, and quickly changed into my black one-piece. The moment I finished dressing, there was a knock at the door.

I gulped the last of my champagne and called, "Come in." Rye entered wearing only swim trunks and I had to admit, he looked good. Before I could squash my thoughts, he whistled as he stared me up and down.

I couldn't help but smile at his childish compliment. After placing his bag on a shelf, he refilled our glasses. Handing one to me, he asked, "Shall we?"

I didn't know what was coming next, but anything was better than being half naked in the confines of that room. I agreed, "Sure."

"This way," he said and I followed him down the hallway. At the end was a glass door. He held it open and the frigid northwest air assaulted me. "Woah," I uttered.

He looked down and noted, "It's nasty out here today."

I couldn't agree more and again I questioned the logic of wearing a swimsuit in January. "Right through here," he said, and we turned the corner.

My breath caught as a splendid, tropical world unfolded before us. Mist floated above heated pools as water poured over rock falls. Lush foliage of misplaced species, like palm trees and birds of paradise, engulfed the area, giving the birds a getaway from the chilly weather. "This is incredible, Rye."

"Isn't it? Whenever the grey starts to wear on me, I come here to reset."

"I can see why," I replied absently as I looked around. We continued walking until we arrived at a set of lounge chairs under a cabana. A table rested between them and on each chair were towels and robes. Though it was beautiful and a well-thought-out scene, the cold was intense.

"Want to get in? It's heated."

I shivered and agreed, "Yes, please."

I followed him toward the largest of the pools. In the center was a small island and the water circled like a miniature river. After finding the stairs, we quickly got in.

It was gloriously warm as I submerged myself up to my neck. Rye dove under the water then floated like an otter on his back. The bluest sky framed the view and sunlight cut through the steam, creating fingers of light around us.

Paddling around the pool, we followed the tiny current and I felt at ease. The warm water and wine sated the bit of nerves I carried. My shoulders, which were tight from painting and helping Athena move, became supple with the heat. I breathed in the atmosphere and relaxed.

We moved in an amicable silence for some time. Occasionally he'd tap my hip and point to a beautiful bird or flower that caught his attention. It was easy to get lost in the beauty of this sanctuary. After several loops around the pool, he swam close and put his hands around my waist to stop me. His grip was softer than I'd have expected, teasingly so. He finally asked, "Ready for a break? I ordered us a snack."

Since my fingers were getting pruney and I wanted to escape the intimacy of the moment, I agreed, "Okay."

We got out of the water and rushed back to the cabana. When we arrived, he took a robe from the chair and wrapped it around me, pulling me close. His eyes held mine and for the first time I could see them clearly. They were the color of sage and sand. The lightest brown mixed with a golden-green that reminded me of desert dunes, making him all the more unreadable. He stepped away and pulled the second robe on.

Adjusting my focus, I tightened the sash and looked around the cabana. There was a platter of food and the bottle of champagne set out on the table and a heat lamp flickering between our chairs. The curtains were drawn except for the entrance, cutting the wind and giving us privacy. We sat and with glass in hand, I said, "Thank you so much for sharing this place with me. It's like taking a vacation in the middle of the city."

"I'm glad you're enjoying it." His eyes danced as he scooped some spread onto a cracker and handed it to me.

I accepted it and took a bite of the tasty salmon mousse. "Mmm, this is amazing." After a sip of wine, I ventured, "Tell me about yourself. Who is Rye Cox?"

He volleyed, "What do you want to know?"

"For starters, where did you grow up?"

"Between Northern California and Vancouver, BC."

"What brought you there—Vancouver, that is?"

"My Uncle Will. He traveled between those places for business."

"Your uncle?"

"Yes. He raised me after my parents died in a car crash when I was seven months old. Well, he and whatever woman he was entertaining at the moment. My uncle was the inventor of friends with benefits. He did have a favorite though, Rebecca. She stuck around for me long after she stopped putting up with him."

There were so many facets to this man. His easy manner and no-strings lifestyle didn't quite match up with the person who planned this date to precision or the one who'd shared—what must be—his deepest vulnerability. "Are you all still close?"

His eyes narrowed. "My uncle passed away a few years ago but Rebecca and I talk all the time. She's been my mom for as long as I can remember. She lives in Oakland. What about you? Where are your parents?"

"My story is pretty boring. I'm an only child. My parents are still married. They retired to Florida a few years ago."

He leaned forward and my eyes betrayed me as I lingered over his profile. I knew he'd caught me by his expression as he asked, "Are you guys close?"

I glanced ahead and said, "We are. We talk all the time and see each other at least twice a year. They adore my daughter, Athena. She's nineteen."

Our small talk was interrupted by a sweet voice near the entry. "Good afternoon, Mr. Cox. Your room is ready."

We arrived back at the doorway of "our" room and the woman turned to us. "Please undress and start facedown. Your massage therapists will be in shortly." She turned and floated down the corridor, leaving us in an awkward pause. Rye spoke first, "Go ahead, I'll be right behind you." He punched in the code and held the door for me.

I entered the room and noticed the quantity of candles had seemed to double in our absence. There was a light fragrance floating through the air; lavender and rose came to mind. Two massage tables were set up side by side. Though I questioned what I was doing in such a situation with a man I didn't know, I also admitted it was amazing. First that incredible pool and now this… I quickly undid the sash and hung the oversized robe on a hook and did the same with my wet bathing suit, then smoothed onto one of the beds. Before I could even pull the covers up, I heard the code at the door. He called, "I'm coming in."

I was naked with a strange man in the room. He entered and without ceremony hung the robe and his trunks on the hook. It happened so quickly, I didn't have the chance to avert my eyes before he turned around and I saw it. Oh shit, oh shit, oh shit! That was huge. No, I must be imagining things. It's dim in here and it was only a second. Mortified and thankful for a place to hide, I buried my face into the cushioned ring. A moment later, the knock at the door indicated our therapists had arrived. Rye responded, "We're ready."

"Good afternoon," their soft voices seemed to sing. "I'm Susanna and this is Laura. We'll be taking care of you for the next hour."

The ladies walked to our tables. Laura spoke softly near my face. I glanced up and noticed her delicate complexion contrasted against her black hair. Her eyes seemed to disappear under the candlelight. "What kind of pressure do you like?"

It seemed an almost indecent question for a Sunday afternoon, and especially after the ordeal of the past two years. I felt a surge of gratitude to her and the man at the next table who was presently making eyes at Susanna. "I'll leave it up to you."

The submission felt decadent. I liked knowing he was in the same room but it didn't alter my experience. My body acquiesced to Laura's talented hands. She stroked and pressed places I didn't know were tender. My errant ankle injury seemed a beacon for her healing adjustments. Warm oil assisted nimble fingers as she caressed each hidden heartache that my body had contained.

Time passed quickly and I felt heavy, drowsy even, in the cozy room. She assisted me to turn over then smoothed a rice-filled mask over my eyes. Her hands resumed with long strokes along my neck and applied pressure at my shoulders. Slow moves across my collarbone moved the fascia and opened my chest. A few last strokes along my forehead and her voice was in my ear. "Take your time in here. You don't need to go anywhere for the rest of the day."

What did she say? And suddenly the firm closing of the door indicated that Rye and I were alone.

I heard the rustling of blankets as his bed squeaked but I was afraid to remove the cover from my eyes. After a few seconds, the room was once again quiet. I sensed his proximity and before I could remove the mask, he did. Rye stood above me and thankfully he was wearing a robe. I was at a disadvantage since my robe was on the hook across the room. He knew it.

He reached for my face and his fingers danced along my cheekbone then to my temple. Unexpectedly, he removed the lacquer chopstick from my hair. My mass of dark hairs spilled out of the twist and his breath caught. I sat up, resting with my elbows behind and before I knew it, his full lips were on mine. The assault was pure naughty. First, his teeth held my bottom lip with the gentlest pressure as he suckled it swollen. Next, his devilish tongue coaxed an unexpected moan out of me. For a minute I forgot we were strangers. His hands moved down my back and as he tugged me close, the drape slid from my breasts. The situation came into focus and I panicked. "No, stop, stop."

He pulled back instantly. The look in his eyes confirmed we shared a mutual desire. Still, this was way too fast. "I'm sorry." I tried to steady my voice, "I can't."

His sharp intake of breath was simultaneous to him raking his hands through his hair. In a gruff voice he replied, "I'll leave you to change." He huffed and pulled his bag from the shelf before exiting the room.

We drove back in silence. I couldn't help but replay my reaction to his kiss. The tension was palpable, and though I couldn't wait to escape it, there was also a comfort in his proximity. As we pulled up to my house, I found myself a little disappointed our adventure was ending.

After cutting the engine, he unbuckled his seat belt and I did the same. He met me around the passenger side and we stood strangely for a time. Finally, he said, "It was a fun day. We should get together again. In the meantime, I'll compile a market analysis and some cost estimates in case you do decide to list the house."

His ending the day on a business note was confusing. Should I hug him goodbye or shake his hand? I decided on neither and instead rambled, "It was such a treat going to the spa. Thank you for showing it to me and for looking at my house."

His eyes bore into mine for an instant, but before anything else could happen, I scurried toward the house.

4

MY FIRST DICK PIC

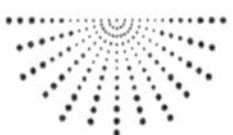

I sat at a table by the window, twirling my wine glass and waiting for a ghost from the past to arrive. Hal Schmidt was rarely late, so I arrived early. Taking a hefty sip of wine, I prepared myself for the inevitable questions he would pose. Although a year had passed since they fired me, every time I thought of my previous work situation, the anxiety still suffocated.

Glasses and dishware clinked as the pinot took the edge off. My mind drifted again and I found myself reliving the strange experience I'd had with the local realtor. It had been two years since anyone had kissed me. It surprised me how often over the past days I thought of his lips. He'd messaged me the next morning to thank me and to set up a time to review his financial analysis of my home, but I hadn't known how to reply, so I didn't. My thoughts were interrupted by Hal's presence at the table.

"Evvy," he exclaimed, "you look stunning as usual." His blue eyes creased and his bald head shone under the track lighting. The familiar tweed blazer he wore completed the look of a kindly older man.

I stood and gave him a brief hug. "So good to see you, Hal."

We sat down and a moment later a server arrived. "Would you like to order something?"

"Please, I'll have what she's having."

Her cheeks dimpled as she replied, "Sure, I'll be right back."

The second she left us Hal started in, "How are you really, Evvy?"

Although I knew to expect it, it didn't make it any less annoying. He was only being polite so I responded in that light. "I'm doing okay, Hal. It's been a rough couple of years, but I've just won a contract, so there's finally some revenue coming in."

He shook his head and pursed his lips. "Any luck with the recruiters?"

"Ha," I laughed aloud, "you have to be kidding. At least twice a week some new kid, wet behind the ears, calls and tells me how thrilled they are to come across my profile. Once I send them my resume and they 'float it up,' there's only crickets. No one wants to hire a woman who has been labeled an HR problem."

"I still can't believe they did that to you. What's happening with the case? Have you decided to sue?"

His indelicate line of questioning was the very reason I needed a head start with the wine. "It's still under investigation. When they respond to my complaint, I'll know more."

Our bubbly server returned with Hal's wine in hand. "Here you are." She smiled and placed the glass before him. "If you change your mind and want something to eat, just flag me down." With that, she turned and vanished into the back.

"Thank you," he called and leaned forward in his seat. "Any idea how long it will take?"

The man was relentless. "Not really. It could be weeks or months before it's over."

Hal shook his head, an incredulous look resting on his face. "It's impossible to believe that a company would act on unverifiable and anonymous allegations of a sexual misconduct…" His complexion nearly matched the wine as he continued his speech, "I hope they get theirs."

I couldn't agree more. With all of our experience in risk mitigation, neither he nor I had seen a situation like it. Hal's venom was the reason I remained friends with him. Though our perspectives could conflict at times, he was a person of integrity and it bothered him when someone—namely me— was unjustly attacked.

"Thanks for saying that, Hal," I reached across the table and patted his wrist. That's when I felt someone hovering over us. I looked up and was shocked to find Rye Cox standing at our table, a mocking expression on his face.

I stammered but managed, "Rye, what a surprise."

"Yeah, agreed. I came in to get a coffee and saw you here. Figured I had to stop over and say hello."

Remembering my manners, I gestured toward my companion. "Rye, meet Hal. Hal, this is Rye. Hal and I are former colleagues and Rye is a local realtor."

Hal stood and the two exchanged handshakes. "Good to meet you, Rye. Evvy, are you thinking of selling?"

Now I'd have even more questions to answer. "Just exploring the options, Hal."

"Evelyn," Rye's tone was direct, "can I talk to you for a minute?" He tilted his head as if to indicate outside.

Thinking it would be best to keep the exchange between the men brief, I agreed. "Sure. Hal, will you excuse me?"

"Of course," he replied.

"Good to meet you," Rye stated over his shoulder.

As I followed him outside, I couldn't help but feel like I

was in for it. I knew I should have sent him a response yesterday and because I didn't, things were going to be uncomfortable. Exiting the café, we continued to the side of the building. When we stopped to face each other, his strong arms zipped mine to my sides. The air between us was electric. His penetrating stare was brief and followed by a dizzying kiss. My first reaction was to escape, but a tenderness slipped through as his tongue teased mine and I forgot everything. That's when he let me go.

We stood a few feet apart as I tried to catch my breath. I noticed he too was shaking. His expression looked angry as he hissed, "To give you something to think about while you're having dinner with that old fart."

He squared his shoulders and turned to walk away. I should have let him, but something possessed me. I put my hand on his arm to keep him there. "Wait a minute," I huffed. "That's not a date. Hal and I know each other through business, and he's married, though I don't owe you any kind of explanation."

His jaw clenched with his reply, "You're right. I apologize for bothering you. It won't happen again."

My emotions were irrational. I didn't want him to leave upset, but why should I care? He already told me who he was and what he was looking for. Why waste my time? Yet, he did show me a lovely day and I wanted to be kind. "I'm the one who should be sorry for not responding to your message. Thank you again for the spa day. It was something else." I said it before I lost my nerve. "To be honest, I'm not sure I should keep talking to you. It's obvious to me we're pretty different."

His expression was unchanging as he replied, "You have a point, Evelyn. We are pretty different, but something tells me you could use a little different in your life. If you change your mind, you know how to find me."

As I walked home from the café, I replayed the events of the evening. Seeing Rye was surprise enough, but his nerve to kiss me as he did, and my reaction to soothe rather than slap him, was almost too much. Layered with the probing questions that Hal asked, and I felt drained.

The mockery of the situation didn't escape me. I'm meeting with a former work colleague discussing my alleged impropriety when an overbearing man arrives on the scene and practically drags me from the table. Once outside, he proceeds, unprovoked, to accost me with a passionate kiss. I chuckled and thought into the scenario. No, Hal, I was completely innocent of the accusations of having sex with my former colleagues. Meet Rye, the local realtor. We're just going to step out for a minute…conduct a little business.

That's when I realized that Sean's infidelity wasn't the only reason I didn't date. Although I knew there was no merit to the slanderous allegations I had faced, some part of me remained ashamed. I knew what happened and so did they, but the company wouldn't eliminate their entire sales staff. Mediocre or not, they'd been the constant.

My anger bubbled at the idea I could be attracted to any of them. I found them to be a sexist and generally offensive bunch. Plus, all but one of them was married and I'd never been one to get involved with taken men.

I knew it was wrong to let their lies influence my actions. As a single person, I had every right to kiss or sleep with anyone, but I finally admitted to myself I never wanted to be seen as promiscuous. Not only had their contrived attack made a deadly impact on my livelihood, but since it happened, I'd been traumatized into distrust. Who could blame me for not wanting to date?

I opened the front door and tossed my keys and phone on

the table, flipping on lights as I walked to the kitchen. I pulled a glass from the shelf and filled it with water from the refrigerator. After draining the glass, I resumed my mental waterfall. If Rye knew my situation, he would understand my reluctance to get involved in a "nothing serious" capacity. My cell phone rang and I walked to the hallway to get it.

Athena's happy face lit the screen and I answered, "Hey, sunshine. How are you tonight?"

"Hi, Mommy. I'm good. What are you up to?"

"Not much, I just got back from having drinks with Hal Schmidt. Do you remember him?"

"Umm, I think so. Random old guy who volunteered with us at the Humane Society event?"

I chuckled, "Yes, that's Hal."

"He was nice but Mom, tell me you're not dating him. You are way too hot for him. Unless you like him... Oh no, do you like him?"

"Honey, calm down. I'm not dating him. Hal's been married for over thirty years. He's a work colleague wanting to catch up."

"That's a good reason not to trust him. Have you heard anything new about the complaint?"

Athena knew of the situation, and I wanted her to. My decision to defend myself was for her and every woman. For years I'd tolerated poor behavior and was diplomatic when I didn't want to be. They pushed me so far that I had nothing left to lose.

I replied, "No, nothing yet."

"Well, you have to tell me as soon as you hear something. What else have you been up to?"

I was grateful if annoyed that my daughter was so persistent. "Not much. That contract is taking some time and after that I'll deal with the house."

"Mom, you promised me you'd start taking classes. I

really want you to take the jazz singing one I found. You have a great voice and people outside of the shower deserve to hear it."

"I'm still thinking about that. I'm not sure I could sing in front of people." She had no retort and I suspected from the background noise that I'd lost her. "Athena, are you there?"

"Yeah, sorry Mom. Shane and a few of the others just walked in. I should probably go."

"Okay, honey, I love you."

"Love you too, Mom. Bye."

We disconnected as a notification banner flashed across the screen. It was a message from Rye. I tapped the icon to open the message. Oh my god! Oh my god! Oh my god! He sent me a dick pic… a huge dick pic! It looked like he was in the shower and the caption read, "Care to join me?"

Holy shit! I'm forty-one years old and I've just received my first dick pic and what a trophy! I could barely take my eyes from the image of his engorged shaft with water running down it. The guy definitely had a few screws loose. I hastened to reply, "Wow, I don't watch pornos but I'm sure you could get a job. I'm not joining you and I have to tell you, this is the most explicit photograph I've ever received. There's different then there's polar. Take care, Rye."

I hovered over the send button wondering briefly if I could entertain having a fling with the man behind this glorious image. It was tempting and preposterous. Tap. The little green arrow solved the query. My response would shut him down.

5

SINGING NAKED (FOUR MONTHS LATER)

The bright yellow house converted to a music studio was steps away. I looked to my right and noticed an Irish pub. Hesitating past it, I pondered a pre-lesson spirit to loosen me up. Maybe after, I consoled myself. I took the last steps toward the entry and my heart sped. With damp palms, I turned the knob. The reception area was unoccupied and a sign indicated to wait for the instructor. I chose a chair by the window.

My phone buzzed in my purse. Since I was early, there was time to check. It was a text message from my former co-worker, Rob. He was one of the few people I kept in contact with from there. "Hey Evvy. Just wanted you to know they questioned me today."

Already I was a terrified wreck and now this… "Hi Rob. Thanks for telling me. How was it?"

His reply took only seconds. "Odd. They asked if you were flirtatious and if you dressed provocatively."

My stomach churned and I thought I may vomit. Why they would ask those things? "What? How did you respond?"

My pulse surged as I waited for his reply, which didn't

take long. "I said you dressed professionally and that I never saw you flirt with anyone. I also told them you were too good looking for the office."

It wasn't funny, but a sarcastic chuckle escaped my throat at the last part of his message. Although I wasn't the things they asked about, I could acknowledge the truth of his statement. I didn't blend in and with those leading questions, I wondered about the neutrality of the investigation.

A well of tears filled my eyes and I knew I should leave. This was no way to start my first singing lesson. I'd already paid for the session, so if I left it wouldn't matter to the instructor. I opened the email app and was about to send him a message when a man's bass-filled voice came through the walls. Tink, tink, tink, a few taps at the piano keys. "Okay, everyone, let's warm up with 'Climb Every Mountain.'"

I listened as the piano sprang to life and the walls began to vibrate from the sound of the well-trained choir. My eyes misted. The inspirational lyrics came at the right time and for a moment I felt a brush with divinity, as if the song had been sent to remind me to be strong. I'd forgotten the sustenance that music gave me. The freedom to feel and channel emotions into song was something I missed. The glee in their voices moved me, and though I was an unseen eavesdropper, I hoped they could feel my appreciation through the walls.

The waiting room door opened and a nice-looking man in his twenties stepped through. "Evvy?" he inquired.

I found my voice as I stood, "Yes. You must be Nick?"

"I am." He smiled, which created dimples in his cheeks. Clasping my hand, he gave it a shake and said, "It's good to meet you in person."

His handshake was firm and his clear green eyes unwavering. Though his reddish hair was messy—as if overdue for a cut—he was undeniably attractive. Great, I thought. It was already the most humbling time of my life and now I would be singing solo in front of a cute boy instructor.

He gestured, "This way."

Reluctantly, I followed him through the door, taking in the attention of the accompanist and choir as we made our way through the large space and into a hallway. My body vibrated from their sound. The pianist's fingers hovered over the keys, landing in time with the practiced voices of ten or so singers. Peaked ceilings painted bright white and thick rugs rested over wooden floors, creating the ideal acoustical design to showcase their harmonies. We passed a threshold and Nick closed the door behind me, which muffled the sound. "We're right through here."

I followed him into the small room that contained a piano and a chair. He closed the door behind us, vanishing any trace of the choir outside. I watched as he walked toward the piano and took a seat at the bench behind it. With an iPad in front of him, he studied the screen. "Please, have a seat."

I put my purse on the floor and sat at the stool in front of the piano. Pinpricks ran along my spine as I waited. Finally, he cleared his throat, "Okay, so Evvy, thanks for all of the information in your emails. Here's how we will work for today. I'll run you through some warm-up exercises and afterward we'll get started on your song selection. Does that sound okay?"

Nodding the affirmative, though I felt like running from the room, I agreed. "It does."

"Just one other thing before we get started. Why did you decide to take singing lessons?"

His question disarmed me. I should have been prepared for it, but I wasn't. Without thought, I blurted, "Because I need to get my confidence back. This scares the hell out of me. I haven't sung outside of the shower since I was in high school and I always preferred the anonymity of being a part of a choir. My daughter is gently forcing me to take this soloist class and there's a performance at the end. I thought a couple of lessons first might help. I'm really nervous, by the way."

There they were again, those damn dimples. His eyes sparkled as he said, "Evvy, there is no one in this room but you and me. If you need to close your eyes and pretend you're in the shower, go ahead."

His joke had the desired affect and I chuckled.

"Let's begin. I'll play and you start with O…"

And so, began my time with Nick. We connected in that narrow space where nothing other than the sound of his playing and my reluctant voice could fit. Embarrassment faded and instead of feeling naked, I felt a part of something beyond the confines of my skin, my mind or that room.

He stopped playing and said, "Evvy, your voice is strong. It's obvious you exercise it regularly. How much time do you spend singing every day?"

"You're too nice, Nick. Don't worry, you don't have to butter me up. I'm sold on taking more lessons."

"I'm not kidding, Evvy. This is what I do every day. Not many people have your range."

His compliment was kind and I wondered if he said that to all of his students. He wouldn't have much business if he told people they were hopeless. I replied doubtfully, "Thank you."

The rise of his brows teased as he said, "Now I can see what you were talking about confidence wise."

Pivoting, he instructed, "Get your sheet music ready. Let's run through your song before we have to end."

He started playing the monotone tune of Nancy Sinatra's "Bang Bang (My Baby Shot Me Down)," and I jumped in a beat behind. The first few lines were rough. I didn't know where to look so I focused on the lone window with a view of the adjacent building. I concentrated on the structure until I forgot I wasn't alone. The lyrics were like oxygen as her pain and mine converged. High notes followed the story and I imagined a dream wedding even as her love remained distant. Though anticipated, his abandonment still devastated me. My mind ventured to the moment when I returned home to find Sean's letter. His messy handwriting scrawled across the page, as if written in haste. I delivered the final verse, "My baby, my baby, my baby shot me down," and my voice went to gravel.

Nick played the last few bars and it came rushing back; the exhibitionism of singing gave me the liberty to feel without being exposed for my true vulnerability. Though sharing my voice was intimate, I didn't have to tell the truth. Except, I had volunteered a deep humiliation. Why else choose that song? In truth, I didn't pick it, Sean did. He liked the song and the lyrics were so telling, when I signed up for the course, I knew I'd sing it.

The room went quiet and soon, Nick's voice broke the spell. "Evvy, that was fun."

The hour sped by. As upset as I was at the beginning of our lesson, miraculously and if only for a while, I forgot my problems. "Thank you, Nick. It was fun."

I crossed the threshold and cool air hit my face. The high I felt after singing in front of a total stranger was blighted when I remembered the earlier message exchange with Rob. At the bottom of the stairs, I was confronted by the pub's open sign. I knew I had to duck inside.

The entry was as narrow as the tiny, aged restaurant. Dark ceilings and wooden walls were sparsely lit by votives at each scarred table. To the left was a miniature but well-appointed bar. On one end were a woman and a younger man playing a game of cards. At the stool nearest the window sat a man on his own. I chose the chair in the middle.

I found a hook under the bar as the woman a stool away said, "Welcome."

Hanging my purse, I replied, "Thanks. How are you?"

Before she could respond, a brunette bartender with a fitted t-shirt and snug Levi's arrived. "Hi. What can I get you to drink?"

"Hi, I'll do a vodka and soda, with lemon, please."

She quickly made the drink and asked, "Do you want to look at a food menu?"

"Sure, thank you," I said.

She set the drink down and handed me the menu. "I'll be back to check on you guys in a few," then vanished behind the wall.

I sipped the drink, letting the bitter alcohol balance my nerves. "Rough day?" asked the man to my left.

I glanced in his direction. Overcast skies glowed through the glass and it took a minute for my eyes to adjust. His hair was dark and his eyes blue. I'd guess him to be about my age. "I'm not sure if rough is the way to describe it."

"So how would you describe it?" He stared toward the mirrored wall that was adorned by floating shelves of alcohol bottles.

I took another sip of my cocktail and replied, "Like a roller coaster ride, I guess."

"Well, that could be good or bad depending on how you feel about roller coasters. Which was it?"

My eyes fell to the counter, unseeing. Which was it indeed… "Both, I suppose."

He turned to face me. "Sounds like there's a story there."

The woman to my right chimed in, "Stop bothering the

girl. She just sat down." Her mocking tone and admonishing expression gave us all a chuckle.

She extended her hand. "I'm Cindy and this is my nephew Ronnie." Her eyes crinkled at the corners as she gestured with her chin toward the man who had been questioning me. "Mr. Nosy over there is Scott."

"Nice to meet you, Cindy, Ronnie," I adjusted myself to face him, "and Mr. Nosy, I mean, Scott."

Everyone had a laugh in time for the bartender to return. "What'd I miss?" Her full lips imitated the perfect pout.

"Introductions is all," Cindy replied.

She gave a scowl and directed her question to Cindy. "Another round?"

"Sure, thanks, Nora."

"What about you, Scott?" Her arched eyebrow seemed to dare him.

"Yep, count me in."

With that she started mixing the drinks and directed her next question at me. "Did you have a chance to look at the food menu?"

"Um, not yet. I'll look now." Scanning the list, it was mainly pub fare. When in Rome… "I'll have the fish and chips."

Scott spoke up. "Excellent choice."

"Thanks," I replied.

Nora confirmed as she distributed the round of drinks, "I'll put it in."

The door chimed behind us and two men walked over. The taller of the two made his way to Cindy and gave her a sideways hug. "How are you today?" he smiled.

"Can't complain—besides, who would listen? How're you doing, Rick?"

"Good, just wrapped up a big project."

The other man moved toward Scott. "Hey buddy, what a

surprise to see you here." He was obviously kidding as they all appeared to be regulars.

"Yeah, long time no see, Matt."

With me sitting in the center, I realized I'd split the two friends. "Hey, why don't I move down so you two can sit together."

The men laughed, and Rick spoke for them. His skin was weathered but his blue eyes danced as he said, "You stay right where you are, young lady, that way we both get to sit next to you."

Nora's voice preceded her return. "Okay, guys, leave her alone."

Matt was quick to recuse himself. "Don't lump me in with this goof. I'm minding my own."

She didn't smile as she asked, "The usual, Matty?"

He nodded, "Thank you, Nora."

Her tone was admonishing as she asked, "And for you, troublemaker?"

"Seven and seven, sunshine." Rick's cheeky reply and the sparkle in his eyes hinted at the lothario he must have once been. She rolled her eyes and busied herself behind the bar.

"So, what's new, brother?" Matt inquired from Scott.

"Well, Char and I are officially on a break."

"What? I thought you guys were working it out."

I couldn't help but eavesdrop. The bar was small and I was sitting shoulder to shoulder with them. Scott answered glumly, "I thought so too, but for now we're on a break."

"Man, I'm sorry to hear that. I thought you guys were really into each other."

"We are, that's not the problem."

Matt ventured, "Is it the work thing? You couldn't figure something out?"

Using the mirrored wall to my advantage, I watched their exchange. Scott caught me looking and turned his chair my direction. Matt followed suit. Oh shit. "Sorry," I explained, "I didn't mean to eavesdrop. Close quarters." I waved my hand to emphasize.

"No need to apologize," Scott comforted in a slightly buzzed voice. "Maybe you can give me advice."

Here I thought I'd duck into a quiet pub, grab a drink and try to brush off the eerie feeling that settled over me after Ron's texts. "I'm not sure I should be advising anyone, but if you need to talk, feel free."

Matt joked while standing from his stool, "Oh no, here we go folks. He's found a new victim. Switch with me. This is going to take a while and I already know the sad story."

Whatever I expected to happen when I walked into that pub, the universe had different plans. I decided to go with it, hoping the distraction of his problems would give me a reprieve from my own. I removed my purse from the hook and, sliding my drink over, I sat next to Scott.

It was silent for a while and I sipped my cocktail. Nora arrived with a plate overflowing with French fries and fish filets, plus tartar sauce. The smell instantly awakened my listless taste buds and my mouth began to water. She set bottles of vinegar, ketchup and hot sauce in front of me and asked, "Another round?"

Without hesitation I agreed, "Yes, please."

I plucked a soggy fry from the pile, dipped it in the tartar sauce and devoured it. Remembering my manners, I ceased munching long enough to coax him along, "So, Scott, what's happening with you?"

My drink was replaced as I took the last sip of my first one. I forked a wedge of the crispy fish and gave it a dip. It melted in my mouth and I felt no remorse.

"It's a long story, but basically my girl and I are taking a break because we can't figure out what to do about work."

Curiosity piqued, I asked, "What does work have to do with it?"

"Everything," he took a deep sip of the brown liquor in his glass, "since we work together."

"Oh," I asked, "is it too much time together or something?"

"No, it's not that. Actually, we don't see each other or not often anyway. I manage a building a few blocks from here and she managed one in South East. Last month she got promoted and now she is the area director, which means she has all ten of the building managers under her. She's technically my boss."

The risk specialist in me had to start discovery. "Is there a company policy against it?"

He looked despondent with high cheekbones that seemed to press into his blue eyes. "There is but it's not very clear. We kept our relationship quiet because it's new and we weren't sure where it was going. Six weeks in, she got promoted. Now she's so concerned with how it will look that she wants to call it off."

I wondered if there was more to the story and my pause gave him room to continue. "Of course, it doesn't help that some of the other managers are saying she was promoted after having an affair with the Western Area VP."

I found my voice. "Why would they think that?"

"No idea, and I can't exactly defend her with myself as her alibi. That won't help her credibility."

My emotions ranged from superiority—of course, I knew better than to have a workplace romance—to rage, as I related to the wrongful accusation of her sexual favor causing the promotion, and finally empathy because I understood how difficult it was to meet someone. If they really liked each other the circumstances were a shame. "Yeah, you're screwed, Scott. She can't date you anymore, at least not publicly."

"It's so unfair," he huffed.

A surge of anger rose unexpectedly and I felt unraveled. "Unfair?" I spat. "Imagine how she feels. Not only is she so concerned for her reputation that she must end a relationship with you, but she's got to walk around knowing that everyone thinks her promotion was because of an affair."

"I know and she's a mom so this job matters a lot to her. I'd leave, but there aren't many companies like this one in the area and you have to be careful sniffing around. If they find out I'm looking, they could let me go and I live and work in my building, so it's tricky."

"That is complicated. I'm sorry." I took a slug of my drink, and felt even more deflated by his hopeless situation.

"Hey, enough about me. What about you? You were going to tell me about your roller coaster day."

I took a deep breath and wondered how to phrase my issue after his candid story. "Well, Scott, I've had workplace problems myself."

"How so?" He leaned forward and the smell of whiskey hovered between us.

Uninhibited by the healthy pour and my empty stomach, I replied, "I was fired actually."

His eyes went wide. "For what?"

"That part is unclear. Best I can tell it was for taking the wrong job."

"What did they say when they let you go?"

The entire bar was silent and leaned in to listen. "They asked me if I had sex with several of my employees."

Cindy gasped. I saw her wide eyes in the mirror.

Though I should've been mortified by my unfiltered statement, the flush that rose from my chest was out of anger. They all stared now; the pretense was over. I scanned the room, making eye contact with each.

Cindy was the only one brave enough to break the silence. "How did you answer their question?"

"Poorly, I guess, because although I denied it, I was without a job."

Matt braved to console me. "Well, I don't know what led up to that, but anyone can tell from one meeting you aren't the kind of person who would do things like that. Did any of the guys who worked for you stand up?"

I hissed, "They weren't really the standup type."

He shook his head. His large brown eyes were downcast and shadowed by dark lashes. "Well that's a shame. I treat my female co-workers like sisters. If I see anyone acting wrong, I set them straight like a big brother would."

Neither of us could have anticipated the fury his statement would awaken. I hissed, "News flash, Matt. Women don't want to work with their big brothers. We shouldn't need protection at work. We just want to work at work."

As I finished my statement, Nora placed another cocktail in front of me then started clapping loudly. Cindy joined in, adding a whistle for emphasis and I knew my troubles were shared.

6

SINGING OR THERAPY (ONE MONTH LATER)

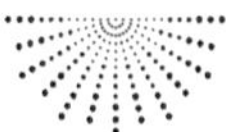

The gate lifted and I pulled through the lane, following the road to the entry of the parking lot. I took the first right and drove as close to the buildings as possible. I found a spot as the phone rang through the surround. Athena's number flashed on the display. I put a smile in my voice and answered, "Hello, darling."

"Hi, Mommy. Are you at school yet?"

"Just pulling in. I haven't been here in a while. I forgot how confusing the campus is."

Her sweet voice demanded, "Where did you park?"

"In the lot."

"Which lot? Look around. The buildings are lettered."

Pulling forward in the lot, I replied, "I'm looking at a beige building with the letter B at the top."

"Okay, good. You're not too far from class, but you better hurry, you only have 6 minutes. Look for the directory at the curb, you'll find it. Good luck."

I felt reluctant to hang up, but knew I could easily find the class on my own. "Thanks, honey. I love you."

There were six of us with the accompanist and our instructor. Syllabus in hand, I leaned forward and tried to accept what Professor Mitz was preaching. "I want you all to know you deserve to stand out and you deserve to sing. You need not be embarrassed or hold back in this space," she waved her arm to emphasize, "because no one is judging you here. We all want the same thing—to share our love of music. Believe in your voice and you will be outstanding." The spotlight cast her in an otherworldly tone, and her ashen hair faded into the white backdrop, enhancing the experience.

For a moment I felt like I was watching a play. The leading lady was comfortable in her skin as she commanded the stage with the flounce of her gown. "Before we get started, let's introduce ourselves, share a little about your musical background and what you hope to gain from taking this class. I'll get us started. I'm Leslie Mitz and I started singing before I could talk. There are pictures of me using a hairbrush as a microphone before my first birthday. Teaching this class helps me tap into the joy I discovered when I was only a child. My goal for this semester is to open the door to your singing potential and leave the audience with a memorable performance as our finale.

"If you didn't know when you signed up, our last class will be a live show at Cleo's, the city's oldest jazz club. Every year my beginners and advanced singers get together to put on an incredible event. I expect this year will be even better than the past."

If I wasn't already nervous, her mention of a live performance at the famed jazz club put me on edge. She waved her hand toward the pianist and said, "This is Michael Shae and he will be our accompanist this semester. Michael, would you introduce yourself?"

The lanky Michael pulled the glasses from his face as he stood. He started his talk while polishing the lenses. "As Leslie said, I'm Michael. I've been playing piano since I was five. I teach private lessons, lead a choir group and work with Leslie in the beginning and advanced classes. When I'm not doing one of those, I play in a band called the Broken Keys. My goal for this semester is to help you bring your best voice to light." The stage lights shone on his silky dark hair and he resumed his seat behind the piano.

Leslie waved a hand in my direction, I swallowed the ball of nerves at my throat and addressed the group. "Hi, I'm Evvy."

Leslie stopped me, "No dear. Please take the stage." Her eyes pointed out the stairway.

I felt unreasonably nervous as I stood but I was grateful that the class was small. My thoughts rambled; was I the same person who once addressed boards of directors? Mindful she was observing, I straightened my shoulders and took the steps, joining her on stage. Her affirmative nod egged me on.

"Hi, everyone. I'm Evvy. My singing experience is archaic at best. I haven't sung in front of anyone since choir in high school. Well, until last month that is. I'll admit, I took a few one-on-one lessons to prepare myself for this class. I'm painfully shy to sing in front of people, but I've always loved music." I stepped back and looked at Leslie.

"Thank you for sharing, Evvy. We hope you'll find this a safe place to expand your wings and find yourself."

She turned her attention from me and nodded toward the next student. We made eye contact and I couldn't help but smile as we passed on the stairs. I sat as her introduction began.

"Hello, everybody. I'm Marissa and originally from India where I used to sing in a band. I've got a husband, a three-year-old daughter and a full-time career, so there hasn't been much time for singing the past few years. I'm excited to step back into music and I hope this class will give me the balance I need to take care of myself along with my family." Her dark, Bette Davis eyes darted and I knew her simple statement was anything but.

Leslie stepped forward and took the microphone. "Thank you, Marissa. It will be fun to watch you reconnect with your first love, music." Marissa smiled in confirmation.

The next student stood and made her way toward the stage. Her long blonde hair and severe bangs matched a lean frame. Wearing skin-tight jeans and a faded, oversized sweatshirt was on trend with the younger women. If I had to bet, I'd say she wore it the first time and had yet to purge her closet. She grappled with the microphone and cleared her throat. "H-hello, everyone." Her voice was higher than I expected. "I'm Vera and my singing experience was as a lead singer in a band, a rock band. It's been fifteen years since we broke up and I've missed being a part of a group. I'm really nervous to take this class because rock and jazz couldn't be further apart. I only hope I can sing it."

Leslie placed a hand on her shoulder. "It will be like riding a bike, a new bike. Imagine that somebody modified your old bike, perhaps added a more cushioned seat and replaced the wheels with wider ones. We can't wait to watch you perform."

She nodded submissively and turned to exit the stage as the last person stood. If the high-heeled tennis shoes and blue streak in her hair were any indication, she was the youngest of the group. I thought of my daughter and smiled as she took the mic. "Hey, everyone. I'm Nikki. Most of my singing experience is in choir, but I've also done some voice-over work. I have a one-year-old son so I can relate to Marissa about trying to find time for herself, but it's more than that." She stared at her feet, "I'm going through a divorce. Jeremy and I have been together since high school and a few months ago, he told me he's in love with someone else, a man. I'm having a hard time with that. I never expected to be a single mother, so I'm taking this class for my sanity."

Leslie hugged Nikki and pulled back. Holding her at arm's length, she said, "Thank you for being so transparent with what must be a trying time in your life. You will"—she clutched Nikki's arms tighter to underline her statement—"get your legs under you. It's going to be a thrill to watch you put those emotions into your music."

It was impressive how she turned that bomb of an admission into something optimistic. Was I taking a singing class or group therapy?

"Everyone, join us on the stage. We will run through some warm-up exercises." We filed up the aisle and surrounded Leslie on the stage. At first the lights were blinding, but after a while I got used to the limits they imposed. When I looked forward or above, I couldn't see the floor. The "audience" was virtually invisible. That was good with me since I could hide from their purview, if only in my mind.

We started with arm and shoulder stretches, a talk about posture, breathing exercises and finally, the letters. Following Michael's keys, we recited our vowels starting with "a" using our nose, throat and belly voices. We sang at varying octaves until Leslie was satisfied.

Time flew and soon our ninety minutes were over. I saw the classroom door open. A few people filed in but took seats at the back.

"Great first day, everyone," Leslie complimented. "Practice the exercises I gave you and pick your song by next week. Remember, there are only six more classes until the performance."

"Thanks, Leslie and Michael," I said as I collected my bag. Pulling the knit cap and scarf from inside, I put them on and started for the exit. I was about to open the door when a rush of air came through along with a handsome stranger. "Excuse me," I said and scurried past him.

"No problem," I heard him say behind me.

It was late and I was tired, but there was no food at the house. If I wanted to eat, I had to stop by the store. After a fast tour around the store, I loaded a bag of impulse purchases into the back seat and got behind the wheel.

An SUV pulled up and was waiting for me to vacate the spot. I backed out and circled the lane; that's when I heard a honk. I stopped and looked around to find the cause. The person pulling into my spot was none other than Rye Cox. It had been almost three months since our strange encounter. He looked childish with a silly grin on his face and his head dangling out the window. He was mouthing something but I couldn't hear.

I checked the rearview mirror to make sure I wasn't holding anyone up and rolled down the window. "Hey there!" I called.

He wore a ball cap that didn't suit him, but who was I to judge? "Hey yourself! Nice to see you."

"Yeah, you too." A car came and I had to move. I waved, "See you around."

As I drove the last mile home, my thoughts were consumed by our meeting and I wondered, ever so briefly, if there was more to the fiendish man who got me naked on our first date. I had to smile. Our tryst was the most exciting thing to happen to me in years.

I pulled to a stop in front of my house as my phone

buzzed. Sliding it from my purse, I unlocked it. There was a message from Rye. Who could blame me for hesitating to open it? When I clicked it there was a picture of a stack of eggplants and the caption read, "Thanks for saving me your spot."

Wow. Guess that answers that. DP AKA Mr. One-track-mind strikes again. What's with this guy? I was at a loss to reply, so I didn't.

7

WE MEET AGAIN

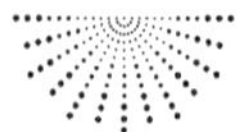

"Another round?" the perky blonde server scanned the table.

"YES!" Nikki replied for us all.

"Great, I'll be right back," she said and disappeared behind the crowded bar.

Marissa's voice rose above the sound system as she addressed the Thursday night singing group, "Okay, I know we said we wouldn't talk about it, but I have to ask, how is everyone feeling about our performance next week?"

I shook my head, "I can't believe it's already here. Two months never passed so quickly."

"Right?" agreed Marissa.

Vera's high-pitched voice expressed my nerves. "I'm not sure I can do it. Even with all the practice, I don't have the song down." She bit her lip and wrung her hands to underline her concern.

Nikki chuckled as she threw her hair for impact. "Who cares? It's going to be a blast. I plan on having some cocktails and giving it my best. If I blow it, so what! It's not like I'm auditioning for The Voice. Plus, I'm wearing this gorgeous burgundy dress that'll take all of the focus off of my song, if you know what I mean."

I admired her attitude. She was right. There was nothing to lose and we should make it as fun as possible. "That's a great way to approach it, Nikki."

Her expression went serious as she leaned in. "I have to look at it that way or I'll cry. Plus, one of the worst things I could ever imagine has already happened. My first and only left me for a man. I don't think singing in a club will break me if that didn't." She took a breath and expelled it audibly. "I've started dating."

"Good for you," Marissa declared. "I think it's healthy to get out and have some fun. Just don't jump into anything too fast."

Though I couldn't relate to her exact situation, I understood how it felt to be betrayed right under your nose. It humiliated me to speak of Sean's infidelity, but I wanted to be a comfort and maybe it was time to unburden myself of the shadows. I felt flushed as I dared to confide my story. "I'm sorry he did that, Nikki. My ex cheated too. It wasn't with a man, but it was with our neighbor. It was two years ago and I'm still trying to get past it. Be patient with yourself and listen to Marissa. Go out and have fun."

Her expression went angry. "I'm sorry, but how could he leave you for another woman? Was she a supermodel?"

Her comment disarmed me and I had to laugh. "That's sweet of you to say, Nikki. He was just unhappy and I knew her—she was too."

"Wow, what a low move," Nikki replied.

I was no longer shocked by their deceit, though the cycle of agony it took for me to get there was nothing to dismiss.

She carried on, "And so what if they weren't happy. Does that give them the right to fuck with your happiness?"

I knew her anger. It was once my own and it thrilled me

to learn that I no longer harbored those sentiments. "You know the old saying, 'Misery loves company.'"

Vera's soft voice chimed in, "Sometimes terrible things happen to lead us to something better than what we ever dreamed for ourselves." Her light eyes twinkled as she sipped her wine. "Trust me on this."

I shrugged noncommittally and steered the conversation. "Thank you, Vera. Now that I've bared my soul, can we get back to the topic at hand? Marissa, I believe you are the last one to answer. How do you feel about performing again after years?"

Her dark eyes were hooded by black eyeliner, enhancing a range of expressions. "Excited, yes, nervous, yes, but more than that, I feel grateful to be here now and to have met you three. It is like finding sisters as a woman. Thank you."

A choir of "Aww's" was interrupted by the return of our server with the drinks. When they were distributed, I held mine up in toast, "Here's to finally meeting our sisters."

"Salute, Cheers, Cin Cin."

As we sat there together, four women who all decided to take that class, I realized how much I'd found by being lost. It no longer mattered how the performance turned out because I'd gained something more valuable than a standing ovation. I found comfort in the chaos of my unraveling and the souls at this table were there to help me.

The evening waned and I was about to leave when Michael and Leslie arrived with two students from the advanced class. It was our first time meeting them though we'd all be performing in the show next week. After the greetings were complete, I made my excuses, "I've got an early morning tomorrow. It was great meeting you," I glanced at the newcomers, "and catching up, ladies. Good night, everyone."

Their goodbyes were followed by an admonishing

reminder from Leslie, "Keep practicing your song and don't forget to bring a copy of the sheet music next week."

I was embarrassed by her deserved poke. For someone who was once responsible for multi-million-dollar projects and the staff to go along with it, when it came to singing class, I was slipping. "Thanks, Leslie. I'll remember. See you all next week."

I wove my way toward the exit and was about to open the door when it was pulled from the other side. I hadn't seen him since the first class, and here he was, for a second time opening the door for me.

His blue eyes danced and brows rose as he said, "We meet again."

A nervous chuckle escaped my throat and I felt dumb. I replied simply, "Hello."

He came through the door and extended his hand, "Luke Anderson."

Mine was swallowed up in his as we shook, "Evvy Snow. Nice to meet you."

"You as well." He scanned my face. "You're not leaving, are you?"

"I am," I replied. "Early morning tomorrow."

"That's too bad but I understand. I'll see you next week, at the performance?"

For a second, I was lost in his blue-green eyes and I wondered why I had agreed to a 7AM conference call with my client. "Yes, you will. It was good to meet you, Luke."

His unabashedly sexy expression held as he replied, "To be continued…"

Seagulls called overhead as the gentle lap of water rolled against the shore. I dug my toes into the warm sand and took a deep breath. My pale skin was becoming pink from the hot sun. I was at ease.

Like a breeze, he came from behind and put his hand around my throat. The pads of his fingers dug slightly and I leaned into the pressure. Soft lips tantalized my neck and his short beard scratched delightfully.

To my dismay, the bird's calls grew more insistent. I wanted them to stop. They were ruining it. I opened my eyes and Rye moved away from me. A chill replaced his caress and, impossibly, he was gone. I was crestfallen. Where did he go and why did he leave? I was confused so I ran along the shore in the direction of the screeching birds…

"Bonk, bonk, bonk, bonk," the alarm clock demanded from the nightstand. It took a minute for my eyes to adjust and when they did, I saw it was 6AM. Unshakable guilt washed over me as I silenced the alarm and sat back against the pillows.

That was quite a dream, I admitted. There was no point denying the residual throbbing between my legs. Funny, I had neither seen nor heard from Rye Cox in months—wonder why HE appeared in last night's selection?

I recalled the night before and my second encounter with the cute guy from the advanced class. I laughed and thought it silly to have a crush on a man I'd spoken to for all of thirty seconds. Still, it would be fun and nerve racking to see him the following week.

Determined to redirect my energy, I tossed the sheets aside and went about tackling the day. There was a conference call and several important business matters to handle, none of which had anything to do with Rye Cox or Luke Anderson.

We chose the river path for today's run. The sun shone brightly against the lapping water and boats sped or sailed by as we pushed past the first mile. The dog's heavy breathing mirrored my sentiments. I never enjoyed running, but I'd done it since Athena started. Our bond grew deeper during these twice-weekly workouts. All the tough conversations happened over side bends and leg cramps. After five years, I'd settled into a love-hate relationship with it.

Athena's long legs—a gift from her father—caused more than one quarrel between couples passing by. Her lean physique was enviable and hard to overlook. What made her all the more spectacular was how unaffected she was by her beauty. She rarely wore makeup and spent most of her time studying, playing with Maggie or working out.

We jogged along the path and I could tell she was holding back for my benefit. I wouldn't raise the subject, though; I liked coasting more and more lately.

Her clear blue eyes scanned the river and came back to me. "Are you excited for Thursday, Mom?"

My pulse was already high and the mention of the performance spiked it further. "I'm really nervous."

"Don't be. You are a great singer. Remember, I've listened my entire life."

"It's one thing to sing in the shower, but this is kind of a big deal. There'll be a lot of people there and it's a swanky place. I hope I don't blow it."

She scoffed, "When have you ever blown it?"

My eyes widened at her question. "How about constantly? I'm not the best with romance, if you haven't figured that out, and let's not forget my employment status."

"You're great, Mom. That stuff was just life. You didn't blow it—you tried and things didn't fit. Look how you're doing now. It doesn't seem like you're having a tough time getting projects and you finally work for yourself."

At times she was wise beyond her years. "You're right, honey. It's not the income I once had, but there are benefits, like this midday run for instance."

"But what about your love life? When are you going to start dating?"

I turned her question over in my mind and finally said, "I think I need resolution with the case first."

"What does that have to do with dating? You know there was no truth to their complaints and you shouldn't let those liars affect what you do."

How could I explain the complexities of my feelings? Between Sean's exodus and losing my job in such a scandalous way, I felt…

There wasn't time to reply as a bicyclist called out, "Evelyn?"

He was coming toward us and slowed to a stop. Athena halted and I did too. I greeted, "Hi, Rye."

"Hey, good to see you." His smile was cheerful.

My eyes settled on his lips a beat too long. The dream came back to me and I was instantly flustered. Athena cleared her throat and poked my arm. "This is my daughter, Athena. Athena, Rye Cox is a realtor in the neighborhood."

Holding his bike in place, he leaned forward and shook her hand. "It's nice meet you, Athena. I certainly see the resemblance."

She smiled sweetly and replied with a tilt of her chin, "It's nice to meet you too. How do you know my mom?"

I jumped in. "Rye is the realtor who took a look at the house for me. If I decide to sell, he'll help me."

She looked suspicious and Rye contributed to her inkling. "We never set that meeting to go over my analysis."

I stared at my shoes. "Sorry about that. A few things have come together and for now, I'm holding off on selling."

"Understandable. What else has been happening with you?"

Athena instantly chimed in. "She's been taking a singing class. In fact, she's performing on Thursday night."

"Wow," his eyes trained in on me, "am I invited?"

Once again, my spirited daughter answered, "Of course you are. You can sit with me. It's at Cleo's at seven o'clock."

"You don't have to tell me twice. I'll see you both on Thursday then." His smile was disarming with an after bite of shit eating. With that he mounted his bike and rode away, calling over his shoulder, "Glad to meet you, Athena."

She smiled sickeningly and hollered back, "It was nice to meet you too, Rye."

Without missing a beat as she resumed running and simultaneously started in on me. "Mommy, why didn't you tell me about him?"

I tried for nonchalant, "Because there was nothing to tell. It was a business thing."

"That was not just a business thing to him and he is seriously fine. You haven't dated in two years. Are you crazy? Jump on that."

"Well, if you must know, my nosy, pushy daughter, the subject did come up when I met him, but we aren't a fit."

"You went so far as to determine you weren't a fit with someone and you never mentioned a thing about it to me?"

I did normally tell her everything, but this time was different. "You're right. I guess I kept it from you, but only because I knew it wasn't going anywhere."

Her tone bordered on snotty as she replied, "Not every date has to go somewhere and what made you think it wasn't?"

"He's kind of a George Clooney, lone wolf type. He likes to date, but he's never been in a monogamous relationship.

He made it clear to me that he doesn't want anything serious."

She laughed and pushed my shoulder. "For a smart lady, you sure are dumb sometimes."

"I don't disagree with that," I huffed, "but not in this case."

"Even George Clooney eventually stopped being George Clooney. He just had to meet Amal to change. Maybe you're his Amal or if things keep going the way they have been, maybe he's yours."

I wheezed a reply, "I don't know anything about Amal, sweetheart, but that sounds like a heartbreak waiting to happen."

She sped up a tic and insisted, "You can't get your heart broken unless you like him."

My protest was childish and exhausted me further, "I do not like him."

8

WHEN IT RAINS

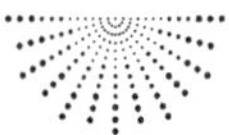

They'd practically shackled me to the chair and after an hour of primping, I squirmed. "Athena, I don't want to look like a member of Kiss."

"Stop fussing." She giggled, "You're almost done."

Shane returned to the room with the finishing touch. "I've got the hairspray. Close your eyes," he said and instantly began spraying the updo.

I gagged, "Okay, that's enough. Let me see what you guys have done."

I turned to look in the mirror, only it wasn't me. As I drew closer to the glass, I still didn't recognize myself. White wisps of glitter alternated with coal black eyeliner magnifying my eyes like a magic trick. Pale-pink matte lipstick swelled my mouth. The feline-siren look was finished by black platforms and an off-the-shoulder shift-dress in ivory silk.

"Just one more thing," Athena's eyes shone in the reflection. Seeing her in that floor-length strapless with her hair and makeup perfect, I wondered why I needed to do anything else in the world. I'd already contributed the most fetching and kind woman to the planet.

Unexpectedly, she placed a collar of shining gems that sparkled black and purple around my neck. They were cool against my throat and I hadn't seen the type before. "I made it for you, to celebrate you doing something you loved before you started taking care of everyone else."

My daughter's heart and talent defied imagination. "This is gorgeous, sweetheart. You didn't have to give me a gift but I'm glad you did. Let's not make too much of tonight—it's just a class."

"We are making a big deal out of tonight because it is one. I'm proud of you for doing this. I know how much it scares you and you're facing it. That's what makes you amazing, Mom."

Shane sniffed in the background, "It kills me to interrupt this moment, but I know you want a picture for IG and I've got to get to work. Chop, chop, now is the time."

"Yes, umm," Athena scanned the room, "over here."

I followed her to the fireplace and stood by her side feeling a strange sense of euphoria. Here I was, at one of the low points in my life, and somehow my daughter was proud of me. Though it placed more weight on me, I would gladly stretch to meet her impression.

Shane took several paces back and commanded, "Say cheers!"

"Cheers."

We pulled up to the curb just in time for the pre-performance meeting. I hugged Shane. "Thank you for driving us. Wish you could come."

"Me too," he agreed, "but duty calls. Athena's going to record it so I won't miss a thing. Break a leg."

I complained, "Great, now I have even more to think about while I'm up there."

"Thanks, Shane," Athena called and we got out of the car. A second later the horn beeped, I turned to look and he was waving for me to come back. I opened the door and in a stern tone he asked, "Forgetting something?" He held the folder containing my sheet music.

I shook my head. "What's wrong with me? Thank you again."

As we walked toward the red brick building, bile threatened my tonsils. I had to remind myself to breathe, hoping to settle my tormented insides. Why had I committed to singing at a club? I was never comfortable being the center of attention or on stage, and now I had to do it.

On the plus side, I was so made up that no one would ever recognize me. "Mom," Athena's sharp voice broke through my silent freak-out, "relax. You're going to be great."

I huffed in place of a response and opened the door. The entry was no larger than a closet. An emerald curtain hung in the doorway that led to the supper club. A small wooden podium and a singular light sconce were the only articles in the room. A nervous, slight man with beady eyes and thick glasses greeted us. "Good evening, ladies. Welcome to Cleo's."

"Good evening," I ventured, "I'm here for the performance."

"Wonderful. Names, please."

"Evvy Snow and this is my daughter, Athena."

He scanned the booklet and looked at Athena. "I see everything right here. Let me take you." He circled the stand and pulled back the curtain.

Athena gestured for me to go first and she followed quickly behind. We crossed the threshold into a firefly fantasy. Floor to ceiling windows highlighted the steel bridge and gardens that surrounded the 1901 building. Overhead were strands and strands of white lights and on every table, a spray of flowers highlighted by lit votives.

To the right was the stage and bar. I wondered about ordering a drink and reasoned I should find the class first. Our host led us, "This way, please." We followed him to a hallway. "Your group is inside. Miss Athena, please come see me when you're ready to sit."

She smiled oddly, "Yes, I will."

He held the door and I could see the instructor and accompanist inside. I ventured forward though every instinct told me to retreat. "Evvy, hello." Leslie's smile was wide as she greeted me.

"Hi, Leslie." I pulled Athena's arm, "This is my daughter, Athena. Athena, this is our instructor, Leslie."

Leslie's black sequins whispered softly as she took my daughter's hand. "So nice to meet you, Athena, and what a beautiful name."

"Thank you. It's good to meet you too. I'm so glad she took this class."

"Yes, I heard you had something to do with her being here."

Athena's wink was almost imperceptible. "I may have made a mild suggestion."

"Or twenty," I mumbled.

Leslie chuckled. "How's she doing tonight?" She directed her question to my daughter.

"After nearly vomiting on the way in, she seems to be settling down."

They both had a good laugh at my expense. "Well, we need to go over a few things with the group before the show. This is your chance to sync up with Michael and make sure your music is on point before you blow them away."

Athena took that as her cue. "I'll leave you to it then. See you out there, Leslie."

"Yes, you will."

I walked with her toward the doorway and was about to say goodbye when Luke Anderson entered. Our eyes met and he smiled. "Hi, Evvy."

I found my voice, "Hey, Luke. Good to see you."

His gaze was intense. "It's great to see you too."

Remembering my manners, I placed a hand on her shoulder, "This is my daughter, Athena. Athena, this is Luke. He's in the advanced class."

"It's nice to meet you, Athena."

She looked from him to me and back again. "You too, Luke," her reply was nearly a purr.

I knew where her mind was going and I needed no more pressure than I was already feeling. "I'm just walking her to the table."

"Break a leg," she called to Luke as I ushered her out. She giggled and teased, "Ahh, the plot thickens. Love interest number two."

There it was, the creative thinker I had borne was taunting me as expected. Until she said it, I hadn't thought of the meeting with Rye and I didn't expect him to show. "Honey, there is no number one and definitely no number two. I've said hello to the guy twice. That's it."

She held my shoulders. "Get back in there and say hello a third time. I can't wait to see your performance. I know you're going to rock it. Have a few drinks though," she hugged me, "I'm serious."

It was ten minutes before showtime and the room bustled with action. Michael sat at a tabletop keyboard making last-minute notes to sheet music. The other band members hovered in the corner, drinks in hand. Some performers were warming up their vocals or running through lyrics, while others chatted amicably.

Outwardly, I appeared calm, but that was the liquor talking. Thankfully, there was a private bar in the green room. For once, I followed my daughter's suggestion and after a cool martini, I was able to put my stage face on. That was until she burst through the doorway with the most unlikely company in tow.

"Hi, Mommy. Surprise." She waved her hands and my legs went liquid.

Beside her were my parents, Rye and Nick, the instructor from voice class. "What in the world?" I hugged my parents simultaneously, "I can't believe you made it!"

Mom's eyes twinkled mischievously. "Why, we've never missed one before."

"But Mom, I was in high school back then, not across the country."

Dad joined, "No matter how old you get, you will always be her baby."

Rye cleared his throat and I said to him, "Wow, I can't believe you made it either."

"And Nick, you've met Athena, I guess, and these are my parents."

"Yes, we all met at the table." He looked amorously at my daughter. "Athena overheard me mention that I was here to watch a student and she introduced herself."

She pulled her eyes from him long enough to sear me with a lecture. "It seems someone is omitting a lot of information lately. Why didn't you tell me you took lessons before the class?"

I wrung my hands and before I could reply, Leslie's voice commanded the room, "Okay, everyone, it's showtime.

Guests, I'm going to ask you to take your seats. Performers, front and center."

I turned to "my group," an odd medley it was, and I wondered how many drinks it would take for me to squelch the frenzied emotions twisting at my center. I was about to perform live. In the audience would be my parents and daughter sitting with a man who had sent me a dick pic. The hilarity of it didn't escape me and since I was already beyond my limit of embarrassment, there was nothing to do but go with it. "Wish me luck, everyone. I'll see you out there."

Athena's beaming smile filled the room, taunting me with her coo, "Bye, Mommy. I love you."

With that, they all shuffled out the door, all except for Rye, who made certain to get my attention. Our eyes met, a faint smile threatened the corners of his mouth and all sound disappeared. I blinked and he vanished through the doorway, leaving me to wonder.

"Oh, Evvy," Leslie's voice pulled me to the present, "care to join us?"

"Sorry, my parents surprised me," I said lamely to the room.

"Excellent," she announced, "now let us surprise them with a memorable performance."

As Leslie disseminated last-minute instructions, my mind wandered and I tried to envision what was happening at "my family's" table and Rye Cox sitting with them. Yes, I agreed with myself, this added twist called for another martini—make it a dirty one this time.

The stage was set against a brick backdrop and lit by a single spotlight. We lined up toward the back wall waiting for Leslie to start us off with the first song of the night. Michael took his position at the piano, followed by the stand-up bass player and drummer, both of whom I'd met that night. They waited patiently until Michael took the microphone. "Good evening, everyone. My name is Michael," the room perked with applause, "this is Tony on bass, and Terry B. on the drums." Terry B. tapped a rhythmic beat and everyone was awake. "It gives me great pleasure to lead the band, Leslie Mitz and the Paradise College singers. Without further ado, put your hands together for the very talented Ms. Leslie Mitz."

She swished past us in a rapid walk, her left hand raising the hem of her gown to assist. Peep toe shoes in black glitter scurried up the aisle and twirled the last few steps as she took the stage. Her red lips, and the final touch—added after the students were ushered out of the green room—a netted felt hat with a glorious ivory feather to one side, brought her drama game to the next level.

"Thank you, Michael and the Broken Keys band. Good evening, ladies and gentlemen," her voice was smooth and simultaneously breathy as she opened the night. "On behalf of myself and the Paradise College singers, welcome to Cleo's." Her remarks were interrupted by a round of applause. Friends and family were ready to show their enthusiasm. Her eyes went downcast as her hand raised to silence the room. "For those who don't know, I've been teaching this course for the past ten years." More applause erupted, this time louder as the students warmed up their vocals. "Thank you," her smoky voice soothed and told us to stop clapping. "It's been a terrific experience and tonight promises to be nothing less. What an honor it's been to work with the singers performing this evening. Each one has taught me as much as I hoped to teach them." A few errant whistles rang out followed by a wolf call.

"To break the ice, I'm going to start us off with an old love of mine, 'Summertime.' Whenever I hear this song it reminds me of my grandfather." She looked to the ceiling, "Gramps, this one is for you."

Her eyes met Michael's and she started a slow, rhythmic snap of her fingers. Mouth moving silently, she counted him in. I followed along, nervous because I had to do the same and hoping to learn any last-minute tricks before my song. The music came over us like a lazy wave, expelling slow rolling steps from the sidewalk to the heavens as Michael's sure fingers danced along the keys. The morose tune conflicted with the lyrics as Leslie's tone depicted the oppression of the era.

As moving as her rendition was, she didn't have my full attention. I couldn't help but fixate on what was happening at the table where my father was sitting side by side with Rye Cox. Why was he here?

The bartender shook a cocktail beside me. The ice crashed against the metal canister and I remembered I never got that second martini. I was tempted to break free from my fellow classmates to belly up. Out of politeness, I'd wait until the song was over.

Leslie wound down as she repeated, "Baby, don't cry." Athena looked over her shoulder and caught my attention. Her expression was cheeky and almost imperceptibly she tilted her chin my direction. I followed her gaze, and turned to find Luke Andrews was right behind me. He smiled down and gave a wink, just as Leslie's final, "Baby, don't you cry," landed us gently.

The podium style bar was poised at the corner of the green room, and now that I knew I was the second to final performer, I could either agonize the minutes away or get a healthy buzz. Making my way there, I was greeted by a man who dwarfed the counter. "Good evening, miss." He stooped to ask, "What can I make you?

I labored, chewing my bottom lip briefly. "I don't know, should I have another martini?"

He smiled and pinned me with his daring retort, "It will only make me look better."

I chuckled and felt the pressure back off a little. "Well then, another martini for me."

His moves were proficient. I watched as he mixed the drink, finally dribbling the liquid into a v-shaped glass. The succinct finish—three olives strung on a wooden stick—and he conspired, "Let's hope it works."

I snickered and slipped a tip into the jar wishing his bravado would rub off on me. "Thank you kindly."

Scanning the room, I saw Vera, Marissa and Nikki together and joined them.

"Perfect," Vera said. "Now that Evvy is here, we're ready." She raised her glass and we followed. Drinks poised above our heads, Vera's sweet voice toasted us, "To the night we've all been waiting for."

A consensus of rolled eyes was followed by a group, "Cheers," as we sipped our nerves behind.

"What's everyone's number?" Marissa asked.

"Five," Nikki said.

"That's two people away," I couldn't stop my response.

"Yes," Nikki replied almost unmoving.

"Are you okay?" I asked.

"I think so," she replied with the same stoic expression. "I'm trying to visualize the outcome I want."

I stifled a chuckle as Marissa redirected her questioning, "Vera, what about you?"

"I'm seventh," she said and took a gulp of her white wine.

I ventured, "Marissa?"

Her brows knit as she replied, "Number nine for me."

Expelling the air out of my lungs, I wondered what was worse, being at the beginning or having to wait until the end to get it over with. Yes, get it over with was how I felt about it. More than once that evening I had considered sneaking out the door. No one would notice my absence until it was time to perform and by then, I'd be home wearing fat pants and eating ice cream. "I'm after you," I replied, "number ten."

"Well," Nikki addressed us, "let's find a post. I want to watch the action." Her swagger was so on point I had to wonder if it was authentic or if she was so used to putting on a show it was now automatic. Either way, I wanted it to rub off.

"Let's go," I agreed and put an arm around her shoulder.

We found a spot at the back just in time to hear the roaring applause for Leo, a nineteen-year-old jazz and rap artist from the advanced class. His coppery curls had a life of their own as he took a bow and graciously introduced Beau, his father and fellow classmate.

He hugged his son and took the mic. "Good evening, ladies and gents." His rapid snaps united with his foot and we were launched into the music. Beau tipped his hat toward Frank Sinatra with his version of "The Way You Look Tonight."

The audience smiled and occasionally sang along to the well-known tune. He was a showman and more than vocal talent, he had a natural ability to control the crowd. He danced with the microphone, as his blue velvet lapels and patent white shoes completed the act. Drawing the last line out theatrically, he shut it a down with a final breath, "Just the way you look tonight."

His bow was as forceful as the chants and whistles that echoed against the windows, and his smile was contagious. For a time, I forgot why I was there, which was no small task given the impending chore before me. I sipped my drink as Beau said, "Thank you very much. Now I'm going to ask you to keep that enthusiasm as we welcome to the stage one of the newest members of the Paradise Singers, the smoldering Miss Nikki." He clapped vigorously and waited for her to join him.

"Go Nikki," I called and watched as she smoothed the skin-tight dress down her scandalous curves.

Teetering on four-inch heels, she sauntered her way to the front. Beau handed her the microphone and gave her a hug. Was it the meditation that did it? Nikki's face lit as she started, "Thank you, Beau. Wasn't he amazing, everyone?"

The crowed played along with another round of claps. Nikki bowed her head, which silenced the room. When she lifted her gaze, her expression was determined. "Tonight, I'm going to sing the song I couldn't resist. I hope you enjoy my version of 'Love for Sale.'"

Hiss, hiss, hiss, hiss, her count was matched by the drummer's snare. Michael commanded the ivories, taking us on a swirly ride of seduction and desperation. The music lifted her clear voice, as the telling lyrics laid bare her need to be kept. "Love for sale…" She purred the words and we were convinced by the total package and visual feast of Miss Nikki. Rapt with awe, men leaned forward in their seats and even the ladies loosened their shoulders when she smiled their way. As she slithered and paced through the number, something told me she was going to be fine.

Her finale was drowned out by a standing ovation and raucous round of applause. I scanned the upturned faces and looked toward my "family" table and all but Rye were looking at the stage. For some inexplicable reason, he was looking at me.

With a gap before Vera's performance, I decided to duck out to use the ladies' room. "Excuse me," I said and walked to the narrow, airless hallway. The alcohol I'd consumed wasn't sufficient to keep the nerves in check, but it was enough to fill my bladder. I used the facilities and washed my hands slowly, delaying the inevitable.

The gobs of makeup I wore masked my concern, but the pinpricks in my fingers and legs didn't. A sudden burst swung the door and Leslie entered. "There you are. I wanted to check on you. Everything okay?"

After watching Nikki and the others, I knew this would not kill me, but I was still unreasonably tense. My succinct reply was honest, "I'm nervous."

She walked to my side, rested a hand on my shoulder and addressed me in the mirror. "Were you nervous before Athena was born?"

Her question threw me, but it took little to follow her. "Yes, of course."

"And that worked out pretty great, didn't it?"

My nod was automatic and my reply cheeky. "Low blow, Leslie."

"Listen, you don't have to do this tonight. I hope you do, but you don't have to."

"Thanks for that," I said and her "take it away" tactic worked as devised, "but I'm going out there and I'm going make you proud."

Her eyes sparkled in conquest. "I have no doubt. Break a leg, kid," she said and stepped into one of the stalls.

He leaned against the wall, half blocking the doorway into the lounge. I drew near and Rye turned to face me. Against a backdrop of "Cry Me a River," he murmured, "How're you feeling, beautiful?"

His flattery was as disarming as his persistence. "What are you up to?" I accused.

His eyes darted then resumed contact with mine. "Let's save that for another time. Tonight, can I just say, I'm glad to be here? You don't need it, but good luck." Putting his hands on my shoulders, his lips whispered a peck on my forehead and he continued past me toward the men's room. The sweetness of his gesture was yet another perplexing twist by the indecent and assertive Rye Cox.

<hr>

Vera took the stage with the grace of a practiced entertainer. Her red poncho dress was trimmed in satin and flowed above the knee, putting her smooth legs on full display. Silence befell the audience as she started, one, two, one, two, three…

She chose "My Man," a Billie Holiday tune and it was perfect for the lilt of her chirpy voice. Naturally high, her sound raised the lows, finding joy in the wanting of a certain life. "What's the difference if I say I'll go away, when I know I'll come back on my knees one day, for whatever my man is, I'm his forever more…" Her eyes misted toward her dashing and well-postured husband who was obviously enamored by her.

The crowd roared to life and we joined in. Marissa and Nikki were beside me and suddenly Luke Anderson appeared. He clapped and asked, "How ya holding up?"

The absurdity of the evening was catching up with me. I'd voluntarily taken singing lessons and a course to prepare for tonight. Though Athena had nagged me, I committed. It was asinine to now act like I couldn't handle it. "I'm holding up. Thanks, Luke. What about you?"

He smiled and didn't have the chance to reply before

Vera's return. "Whew, that's behind me! Thank goodness!" she huffed.

"Girl, you were ah-mazin," Nikki chanted.

"Now that it's over, I want a shot. Come on, girls and you," she batted her fake lashes toward Luke, "this round is on me."

We entered the green room as the only visitors, which cheered the bartender exponentially. "A round of lemon drops," Vera exclaimed with a song in her command, reminiscent of a queen addressing her subjects.

We milled around waiting and Nikki chatted up Luke. "So, how long have you been in the group?"

Their conversation faded as Marissa elbowed me and Vera's glance followed. I shrugged in silent reply. "Here we go, ladies, and for you, you lucky so-and-so." The bartender was funny if a bit cheesy.

Luke raised his glass to toast. "To good luck," he said and looked right at me.

———

Marissa's haunting voice was gorgeous as she carried us through her take on "The Girl from Ipanema." She slowed the song a beat, managing the band with her leisurely pace. Her wild eyes fluttered skyward, framed by thick brows and deep purple eyeshadow the same shade as her halter. When she came to the end, she pored over the final phrase, lingering in the irony, "but she doesn't see, no she doesn't see."

The room was on fire. Hands over head, I clapped my approval and added a howl for good measure. After a gracious bow, the accolades were cut short, "Thank you, everyone." Her voice was breathy as she announced, "Next,

I'm proud to introduce my friend and classmate, the incredible Ms. Evvy Snow."

Sean was at the kitchen table, swirling his cup of coffee. My hair dripped onto the fluffy white robe and daylight streamed beside him. "Hey," I leaned in the doorway.

When he looked up, his eyes flashed sorrow then pity. "Your voice is angelic, Ev."

Though I loved singing, I was too embarrassed to do it around people. It had always been a problem for me. When I was a child, I began using the bathroom as my rehearsal space. It was a place where any missteps would fall on damp ears. Unknowingly at times, I still sang in the shower. "Thanks," I murmured.

"I know I've said it before," the sadness was replaced by a barely discernible spike of anger, "you should be performing in front of people. Won't you take that class?"

That moment summarized the great abyss of our relationship. I was dripping from the shower, hoping that he'd finally notice my desire, longing for reciprocity in his eyes, but what I found was a push. A reminder that I wasn't as good as I could be if only I tried harder, if I went out of my comfort zone and did something only for me. I didn't want to argue and I didn't want to cry, so I answered diplomatically, "I'll look into it."

He came and kneeled at my feet. His arms wrapped around my waist as he begged, "Do it for you, please, to remind yourself how great you are."

He left me the following week. In the letter he scrawled, "I never deserved you. You just didn't know it."

My feet knew the way, though my mind disassociated for a brief foray. Midway there, Marissa gave me a tight hug. "You were awesome," I whispered in her ear.

She dazzled me with a wide smile. "Go get 'em."

White lights almost blinded me, but not enough to hide the faces at "my" table. Athena looked happy as she perched beside my instructor, Nick. It was time to begin. Clearing the past, I emptied my lungs and dropped my head to begin a silent count. When I was satisfied with the beat, I looked at Michael and snapped the pace.

His fingers came to life and the band sat motionless. We'd decided on a stripped-down version of "Bang Bang (My Baby Shot Me Down)," using only the piano. As a result, there would be times when I'd sing acapella leaving no place to hide if my voice broke.

On cue, I began the tale of young love. The morose tone was magnified by the sedate tempo we'd arranged. The childish tale of make-believe evolved until enthusiasm was replaced by lost innocence.

As I navigated the twisted honesty of the song, the happy rising dragged by the lowest valley, her tragedy was my comfort. "My baby, my baby," I paused for what seemed an eternity, and that's how I exorcised the past. I rasped the last line and I knew he was gone, that all of them were gone and I was still standing. "My baby shot me down…"

It was good. Even I felt it and I didn't wish that Sean were there to see. Whatever I had to prove by doing this, it no longer had to do with him. My eyes gravitated toward the table. Rye's whistle reverberated and blended with the happy calls of Athena and Nick. My parents were hugging each other and everyone was on their feet. Guess I got that standing ovation after all.

Luke stood to the side, smiling and clapping vigorously. The ether wore off and I got on task. "Thank you, thank you everyone. Stay on your feet because our next singer will get you moving. Closing us out on a high note is Mr. Luke Anderson singing 'Fly Me to the Moon.'"

He tripped as he approached the stage and righted himself with my shoulder. The drummer thought it cute and added a few taps for comic relief. People were laughing and clapping. He took the mic, but held my shoulders. "Wasn't she incredible, ladies and gentlemen?"

Another round of applause and whistles came from the crowd. He pulled the microphone away and leaned to my ear. "You are bewitching. Tell me you're single."

The warmth of his breath and surreal clapping that surrounded us was intoxicating. His attention didn't hurt, but this wasn't the time. I cleared my throat and said, "Good luck."

With a half turn, I extracted myself and hastened to the back. Marissa, Vera and Nikki jumped up and down as I approached and engulfed me into a perfumed hug.

"Marvelous!" Vera cried.

"So good," Nikki declared.

"So, so good," Marissa confirmed. "We need a selfie for Insta. Come on, ladies, get close," she directed.

We surrounded Marissa, pushing in close. "Okay, say cheese, girls."

"Cheese," and the camera flash lit our faces.

She studied the photo and announced, "It's perfect. I'm posting it and tagging all of you!"

"Thank you," I replied, "now let's watch Luke."

Marissa's eyes grew large as she looked over my shoulder. I felt a tap, like a knock on the door and I knew it was Rye. He practically sneered, "Outstanding performance, Ms. Snow."

My response was steady, "Mr. Cox, are you having a good time?"

Wordlessly, he took my hand and led me into the hallway. When we stopped, his expression was pained. Biting his lower lip, he said the last thing I expected, "I'm not going to kiss you. The next time we kiss, it will be because you want it. I am going to ask you on a date. Will you please go out with me, again?"

Being asked out by two men inside of two minutes was an absolute first. It may have been a world record—it was one for me. I remembered his speech. According to his way of thinking, I owed no explanation to either person. I was free to accept both, either or neither of their advances. I replied in that spirit as Luke's practiced voice lifted to find us, "In other words, In other words, I… Love… You…"

"If I say yes, it's not because of the picture you sent me, but despite it." He almost smirked but held a firm line across his mouth. He nodded, "Understood. I realize that wasn't in the best taste. I'm sorry."

His transparency was the thing I most liked and equally despised about him. It fascinated me how he could be sincere and superficial. Maybe he had something to show me. My reply was dampened by the loudest applause of the night, "Then yes, I'll go out with you."

9

ONE STEP FORWARD

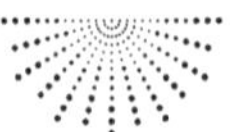

We stood at the trunk. Dad hefted their suitcase into the back and Mother faced me. Silvery hair framed her softening features. "Thank you for such a fun visit."

My eyes misted. "No, thank you guys for coming."

We hugged and before she let go, she teased, "I expect to be kept apprised of your dating life now that you're going to be juggling two handsome men."

Dad shook his head and announced, "I don't want to hear anything about your antics. Pick something and stick with it, Evelyn." He hugged me briefly and skulked around the vehicle.

Mother followed and replied in my defense, "If she were a boy you'd encourage her. It's a new day, Charlie, and women can have fun too."

Athena looked at me, a proud expression resting on her face, "What she said, Mommy."

I gave her a quick hug. "Love you, baby. Thanks for driving them to the airport."

"Love you too. I'll check on you later to see how the date with bachelor number one turns out."

At three o'clock on the nose, Rye knocked on the door and I took one last look in the mirror. The gauzy Spanish shirt-dress I wore covered the bikini he insisted I'd need. I opened the door to a gush of ninety-degree heat, and Rye wearing board shorts and a T-shirt. "Hello," he practically sang his greeting.

"Hi," I said.

"Do you have a bathing suit?"

What's with him and bathing suits? Dumb question. I replied, "Yes."

"Sunscreen, hat and a towel?"

"Yes, Mr. Checklist, I have them."

"Okay, let's go."

I felt like a child demanding how long until we get there as I asked, "Where are we going?"

"It won't take long," he replied as he opened the car door for me.

Knowing it was futile to ask anything more, I bit my lip and waited for the unfolding. If nothing else, life had taught me that control really was an illusion. No matter how much we think we've got it together, we are all just an incident or two away from the abyss of uncharted territory.

We took the road downhill and crossed the highway, finding a narrow street with houses on either side. He turned right and followed the road until it narrowed and finally went to gravel. The forest grew dense with white oak trees and with the sunroof open we moved under a canopy of green, serenaded by the calls of robins and jays. He veered left off the road and drove slowly through the semi-cleared path, coming to a stop by a wooden barn.

True to his word, it didn't take long, but where were we? Setting the brake, he announced, "We're here."

The area was secluded though not far from other residences. I scanned the grounds. There was a fire pit ahead, a picnic bench and up a flight of stairs perched a sun-bleached gazebo that had seen better days.

He quickly got out of the car and I joined as he marched to a barn. After a short scan through the options on his keyring, he selected the one that opened the deadbolt protecting whatever was behind the faded white doors. I had a fleeting thought that this wasn't the wisest decision, then remembered my entire family knew I was going out with him today.

The door opened with a creak as the rusted hinges moved for the first time in ages. He switched on the single light that illuminated the space. Inside were a myriad of items closely related to the outdoors. Chairs were stacked neatly, and tents and sleeping bags sat upon shelves, near lanterns and candles. On one side was a rack holding two kayaks.

He walked to the kayaks. "Give me a hand?" he requested.

I joined him and as he lifted one end of the kayak, I got the other. "This way," he said and I followed him through the door. We walked past the fire pit and turned right. The dirt path was well maintained and we didn't have to go far before we met the secluded beach that folded into the tranquil section of river. "Let's leave this one here and get the other."

That meant there would be one for each of us. I replied nonchalantly though I was leery, "Okay."

"Have you kayaked before?"

"No, I haven't," I admitted.

"Don't worry, the river is lazy here. I'll explain what to do. You'll be fine."

I think I believed him because I continued forward, holding my end of the vessel, hoping I wouldn't make an ass of myself. We placed it on the beach next to the first. He plucked a paddle from one boat and handed it to me. Pointing to the end, he explained, "Do you see the shape of the paddle, how it's wider here?"

I nodded, "Yes."

"The wide part is always on top."

It sounded simple enough. "Got it."

He pointed in the distance. "Do you see that island?"

"Yes. I've always wondered about it."

"That's where we're going."

It looked far and I wondered how strenuous an activity it would prove. I wouldn't let him know my concern and with a smidge of determination, I replied, "Okay."

"If boats come, avoid them."

I fired, "Avoid them how?"

"Listen and look for them, just like driving a car. The good news is they're noisy so there's time to react."

His instruction, though crucial, was making me second guess the outing. "And the last thing, when you come across a wake, don't turn. Head straight for it, otherwise you'll capsize."

A cool breeze kicked up and the water lapped gently against the shore. He pushed the first kayak until the nose was floating in the water and looked my way. "Ready?"

Even if I wasn't ready, I was doing it. I tossed my flip-flops into the kayak and climbed on board. He handed me the paddle and said, "Let me get mine."

He'd already explained how to paddle and what to do if a boat came. I saw no reason to wait. I wiggled my bottom while using the oar to propel from the shore. The paddle was lighter than expected and it took little to pull myself from the serenity of the beach and into the broader river. The water looked different from the tiny, powerless boat propelled only by me, more intimidating than it had from the shore.

The river became rough as I approached my first wake. Blue-green sets were headed straight for me. He explained it because it went against nature. Though instinct told me to follow the wake, his competent stance as he doled out the basics assured me what to do. I dug deeper with the paddle, hastening my meeting with the man-made wave. Up and over, a plop later and I'd successfully cleared my first wake without capsizing.

I listened carefully and heard no boat engines so I went for it. The simplicity of the action felt natural and I dared myself to make it to the island as quickly as possible. Digging in to the left then right, I moved steadily, adjusting my posture as I gleaned the nuances.

The powerful midday sun created thousands of dancing beams, reflections of the feared warming that consumes our globe. Today I enjoyed the heat and only the heat. Outcomes were not reasonable in the blink of an excursion. In that way I found peace.

Moored boats bobbled on the not-so-distant horizon as I drew closer to our destination. I slowed my pace and took in the surroundings. A row of river homes lined the eastern shore, each one with a private pier. An enormous broken branch sat submerged in the water, creating an island perch for a bald eagle. The forested beach ahead was desolate as the boats were anchored on the opposite side of the island.

Though he didn't explain what to do when I made it to the island, it was easy to surmise. I paddled until the nose of the kayak slid onto the beach and waded through the tepid river, tugging the boat onto the shore.

I scouted the vicinity of my "landing," enjoying the squish of my toes in wet sand. The trees were dense behind me and the birds' calls as varied as they were harmonious. Even their conflict sounded like love.

Rye pulled his kayak next to mine. The wind ruffled his feathered hair. "Seems you're comfortable in the water."

"I guess I am," I agreed.

He slid off his shirt, exposing his tanned abdominals, and I didn't avert my eyes as he pulled a backpack from his kayak. Carrying it over, he said, "I've got a blanket."

I found my bag and joined him. Technicolor was our filter as we lay upon a burgundy mat. The yellowest sun heated us and cyan water surrounded the fantasy.

I tossed my dress into my bag and fished out towels, a straw hat and a dozen chocolate chip cookies that I'd baked that morning after my mother's insistence. The cookies were in direct conflict with the black bikini I wore, but she overruled my logic with some sexist old school ramblings. I made the cookies under her constant supervision.

His smile was matched only by the pitch in his voice as he exclaimed, "Cookies. Are those homemade?"

It was as if a six-year-old had replaced the forty-something tomcat before me. "They are." I was embarrassed and had to clarify, "You have my mother to thank."

"Oh, I know. She told me you were really good at baking and she'd have you make your famous chocolate chip cookies. She works fast." He smiled with all the sex appeal he could muster, which was plenty. "Thank her for me," and he ate half of a cookie in one bite.

I shook my head in disbelief, but was I shocked that my clever mother had conspired with the likes of Rye Cox? To be honest, I wasn't. He gave the impression of being a nice guy, was easy to be around, attractive and funny—even when his sense of humor leaned vulgar. He was also the epitome of a bad influence and my sweet mom was a sucker for the Eddie Haskell type. My lack of reply resulted in a peace offering.

He pulled a cup from the thermos, unscrewed the lid and poured some milky liquid. "Trade?"

He handed me the drink and I gave it a suspicious sniff. Coconut, orange and vanilla came to my nose. "What is it?"

"Only one way to find out." He finished the other half of his first cookie and dug into the container to get a second.

It wasn't the tropics but the beverage and the seclusion of the island made me feel far from home. The creamy concoction, spiked with the perfect blend of rum and orange liquor, lulled me into the scene. "I love it. This is my new favorite drink. What's in it?"

"That's a secret. You'll have to pry it out of me."

I spat, "In your dreams."

His eyes locked onto mine and he didn't smile as he countered, "Sometimes my dreams come true."

The déjà vu instant struck an eerie chord as I recalled the dream of me on the beach and Rye at my shoulder. "Yeah, mine too. Like the other night for instance."

He leaned forward, and asked, "What dream did you have the other night?"

"I had a dream about a guy I went out with once, who then sent me a dick pic. The strange part was when he showed up at a family event months later. That was a real dream come true, for me."

His eyes darted left as he said, "You know, Evelyn, I'm a lot more than just a guy who sent you a dick pic."

His defensive reply made me wonder, had I hurt his feelings? Still, I couldn't imagine apologizing to him. Instead, I shoved him with my shoulder and took another sip of the heavenly drink. "This is dangerously tasty."

He rebounded quickly, and grabbing a third cookie said, "So are these."

The date was actually perfect, just as our first one was. He obviously liked planning fun excursions and was good at it.

This was the second unique experience I'd had by his side and I wanted to put us both at ease. "Hey," I pushed him again with my shoulder.

He looked over and asked, "Yeah?"

"I'm not going to ask why you showed up the other night, or what we're doing here. I'm not even sure you know the answer. I just want to thank you for taking me to this place and introducing me to kayaking."

"There's no need to thank me. I'm glad you accepted."

A pair of egrets glided by. The larger of the two held back constantly scanning the water and shore. His role was two-fold: to find a meal of surf or turf and to keep a watchful eye on the eagle, for they could cross wings in search of a feast.

Rye broke the silence. "Athena's amazing."

He'd found my soft spot. "Isn't she?"

"And your parents. Your mom is something else."

I chuckled then and wondered briefly what they discussed. "She is. I'm blessed to have the family I do."

"Do you mind me asking, what happened between Athena's dad and you?"

I inhaled as that familiar flash of the past came and left. Years later, I'd found acceptance that our love remained in the heart of Athena and whatever happened, it was over. "That seems like such a long time ago," I replied. "Nothing you haven't heard a hundred times before. Sam and I met in college, senior year, and fell madly in love. It was that devastating, can't stop thinking about him kind of love you read about in the romance books. We just knew." I paused wistfully. "The night we graduated, I told him I was pregnant. We were married the following week and our life began."

He interjected, "Sounds ideal. What happened?"

"It was gradual. I can't say I didn't feel the growing distance between us. I felt it. I just didn't know what to do, or maybe I didn't care to."

"One night over dinner he uttered the words that had been my silent chant for so long: I love you, but I'm not in love with you. Though I knew it too, the shock of hearing it aloud was like plunging into ice cold water. I remember feeling panicked."

He looked almost frightened as he asked, "How did you handle it?"

"It took some time, but eventually I saw the wisdom in a divorce. We'd stopped being a couple long before. We'd become a family without a foundation. Poor Athena was the mortar between us and aside from our love for her, we were a couple of unrelated bricks."

Rye asked, "When was this?"

"That was ten years ago. Things are fine between us now. It's funny—he's not a friend and not a stranger, but I don't know him anymore, if I ever did."

"Where does he live?"

"Here in town. He's been with the same woman, Jenell, since we split. She's pretty cool. I like her more than him. Athena does too."

"Did he leave you for her then?"

I shrugged the question away as I was once unable. "It doesn't matter. I never knew for sure if they were seeing each other before we split and I don't care. They weren't the reason for our end."

His expression was pained and his sincerity was apparent. "I literally can't imagine how hard that must have been. To have a whole family and pull it apart after years, that must have been devastating."

"We worked on that, making sure it was as peaceful as possible."

"Who is Sean then?"

That familiar lump came with every mention of his name. Wanting to hide from the full story, I replied with superficial facts. "No, Sean isn't Athena's dad. He was my fiancé after him, but we split up a couple of years ago. Why do you ask?"

He narrowed his eyes as if trying to recall, "Your mom and Athena said something."

Leave it to those two to bare my naked ass for a stranger. "What did they say?"

"Just that he hurt you. What did he do?"

Not only was this a painful subject to relive, but I wondered why we were discussing my history. With his life philosophy, what was the point? "That's a pretty personal question, Mr. Nothing-Serious."

Whatever conflict he had, his reply was smooth, "I want to be your friend and I'm trying to get to know you. If you don't want to tell me, I understand."

Resigned to answer, I wondered how to summarize my experience with Sean without sounding like a victim. "If I had to boil it down to one thing, I'd say we never had the melt."

His quizzical expression said it all. "The what?"

"The melt. You know, when two people meet and together they are like butter on a warm slice of bread, filling in all the cracks."

He smirked. "The melt, hmm. Not sure I believe in it, but not having it doesn't seem a reason to end things."

I flinched my reply, "Well, he did have the melt, but not with me."

"Ouch, sorry."

I admired his reserve at commenting further. If he were a real ass, now would be the time to make his point about monogamy not working. I was grateful that he didn't and was ready to turn the questioning around on him. "Yeah, enough about me. What about you? Have you ever lived with anyone?"

He hesitated then replied, "No, not really."

His answer was perplexing. "Not really?"

He shrugged, "Well, for a few months before my old girlfriend moved away, she stayed with me."

"When was that?"

"Three years ago."

His succinct replies forced me to keep grilling him. "What is the longest relationship you've ever had?"

"The girl that moved away, she was it."

I couldn't mask the judgement in my reply. "Your longest relationship lasted only a few months?"

His sharp intake of breath was all the answer I would receive. I tried to understand him, what his life was like and how he found the motivation to live each day. I spent the majority of my time thinking of others and that's how I felt worthy of taking space on the planet. I wondered how this man with no family or children found the spirit to tackle each day. What drove him? I had to know. "Don't you ever get lonely or feel disconnected?"

His brows rose and if he had any sadness about his choices, there was no indication in his expression. "I'm not immune to loneliness but I have a lot of friends, work keeps me busy and I have an active lifestyle.

"What helps me feel needed is volunteering at the Boys and Girls Club. A couple of times a month, I take the kids on outings. With the warm weather, lately we've been kayaking. In the winter we go snowshoeing or hiking."

Now more than ever, I found it impossible to comprehend this man. He didn't fit into any box that I'd ever seen. He had manners, loved planning dates, was interested and interesting, plus he volunteered his time for kids.

I was about to reply when his rapt focus over my shoulder caused me to follow his gaze. When I turned, I saw a large pit-bull dog headed our way. He looked quite at home on the island although his eyes frequently scanned the distant shore. I turned and was about to call him when Rye hissed, "Don't move."

Did he see something I didn't? The dog came nearer and was sniffing toward my bag. He probably smelled the salami stick I hadn't taken out. Rye stood slowly. The dog ignored him and continued sniffing the bag. The sound of a boat suddenly perked the dog's attention. He trained in on it, focusing intensely until it grew closer to the island. Its nearness must have confirmed his owner's return for he let out a howl and raced to greet it. I looked over at Rye. His fist was clenched like he was ready to fight. "Are you okay?" I asked.

"Are you?" he replied incredulous.

I was puzzled. "Of course, why wouldn't I be?"

"Do you have any idea how lucky you are? That dog could have eaten you alive."

"He was harmless." I stood and walked to my bag and pulled the salami from inside. "He was looking for this."

He fired, "That dog was starving. You could see his ribs."

I shook my head, confused. "All the more reason to feed him."

"You don't feed dogs like that. I love dogs but you never know. We're on an island and a large dog with a spiked collar and his ribs showing is nothing to tantalize. Don't do that again."

That was the first time he was right about something, but it had nothing to do with the dog. The concern on his face and in his stern admonishment, that he liked my family and my cookies, blended with the setting, and the simplicity of being with him. I did as he foretold when we last met: I leaned forward and kissed his frown away.

The first peck apologized, the second lingered and by the third, he was an active participant. We spent an undetermined amount of time on that beach, tangled in each other, our mouths and tongues intertwined in a sweet escape. His occasional foray to the crook of my neck tickled the memory of my dream, but I didn't waste time on that. For the first time in too long, I was kissing and being kissed. For now, that was enough.

Soon the sun was falling past the tree-dappled hillside, hues of yellow and orange burned against the shadowed skyline. It was nearly time to leave when Rye's statement threw me headfirst into an ice bath. His eyes weren't certain, but his voice didn't falter. "I've enjoyed this day more than I can tell you, Evelyn."

Without hesitation, I agreed, "I feel the same."

His eyes were downcast as he said, "I like you but I don't want to mislead you."

Until then, the excursion had been ideal. I didn't know why Rye felt the way he did, and I wasn't sure if I'd ever figure him out. I replied with the nonchalance that would keep things light, "Don't worry, Rye. I won't fall in love with you over a make-out session on the beach."

This rose his spirits and his eyes sparkled as he asked, "I'd love to do this again. Do you think we can keep seeing each other but keep it light?"

Not for the first time since he and I met, I realized that I'd never slept with anyone I wasn't committed to. Having been married young and with the time Sean and I had together, I'd really never dated until that point. As I examined my history from that angle, only one reply made sense. "I'm willing to give it a try."

Our pace was leisurely as we paddled wordlessly back to our starting point. Crossing the river against the fading light, the world looked the way I felt, subdued. Dusk fell over the water, as the birds raced against time in search of the evening's nesting spot. Soon we'd arrived on shore.

We navigated replacing the first kayak onto the rack and went back for the second when I saw the fire pit was filled with wood and a table was set to the side. It wasn't there earlier or I would have noticed. I carried my end of the second kayak and when it was set, with the barn locked, he finally spoke, "Well, how was it? Your first time?"

The suggestion in his voice danced in his eyes as he opened the car door for me. I climbed in and waited for him to come around. When he settled in, I replied with a smile and only the light I felt, "It was a perfect first time. I'd definitely do it again."

It was so fast that his flinch was almost imperceptible, and I had to wonder if we would do it again.

10

TWO-TIMING

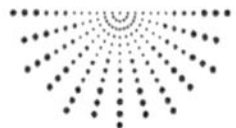

The ringing phone interrupted my weeding session, a welcome break from the monotonous task that had occupied the past hour. I stood too quickly and the blood rushed from my head. It took a moment but I forged ahead and collected the phone on the third ring.

"Hello?"

"Hi, Mommy," Athena chimed.

"Hi, baby. How are you today?"

"I'm good, but the real question is…how are you?"

I chuckled and knew there was no escaping her inquisition. "I'm well, sweetheart."

"And?"

I played coy. "And what?"

"Stop it and tell me what happened yesterday!"

It was rare that I had anything juicy to share and I still hadn't processed the experience. I replied honestly, "It was a beautiful date. We kayaked across the river and had a picnic on the island."

The doubt in her voice was stinging and her voice hitched. "You kayaked?"

"Yes, I did."

My miffed tone reigned her in. "I didn't mean to sound so surprised but you've never done that before. Was it fun?"

Within my sensitivity, I understood that I'd limited myself in the past. Sean and Athena both saw it. He left me because he thought I was too pedestrian, and Athena loves me although I can be. He tried to push me and she placed me in a box. "It was fun and easier than I imagined. I loved it."

"Wow, okay, so what about Rye? How was it with him?"

"It was easy. I think we'll see each other again."

Athena knew me too well, as her next question confirmed. "What are you leaving out, Mom?"

"First off, darling, I am not required to tell you every detail of my life."

She fired, "I know, but seriously, you haven't dated in years. I have to know what happened."

I tried to summarize the day and my feelings about it. "What happened was we had a long talk and we got to know each other a little more. In the end, he reminded me that he wants to keep things light, so that's about it."

Her voice was a near whine as she asked, "Did that hurt your feelings?"

I wouldn't tell Athena, but it did hurt my feelings. If as he's just getting to know me, I'm not enough to keep his focus, what would the future hold with a man like Rye? Still, I'd always dated with intention. Maybe it was time to lighten up and appreciate the moments. "It could have, but I didn't let it."

"How do you feel about him then?"

"Such deep questions for a Monday afternoon." I teased, "I feel open but I don't have any expectations. He's made it clear that he doesn't want a relationship and all the trappings. If I spend time with him, I know it's for fun. This will be my first time ever dating someone I know there's no future with."

Concern registered in her voice. "Don't take this the wrong way, but this doesn't sound like you. I'm kind of impressed, but also worried about your heart."

I willed a confidence as I replied, "I know I've been a bit reserved in life."

This got a guffaw out of her, but she didn't interrupt. "I see it's time I went for it. I mean, who am I walking the line for? You don't judge me, so why would I worry about what anyone else thinks. Women can be George Clooney too, isn't that what you said?"

Her voice was crystal as she agreed, "I did say that, Mom, and you are every bit as great as he is." Her tone softened as she admonished, "Be careful, though. I don't want you to get hurt again."

I mustered cockiness and dropped a grenade. "I have a date with bachelor number two on Thursday night."

"What? Woah!" Her reply was cute and annoying. "I can't believe you're really doing it. Grandma and I have been wondering."

I shook my head, knowing just how messy this could get with my parents in the loop. "Athena, it is highly unusual that a daughter be involved in her mother's dating life. Could you please keep the grandparents out of it? Don't I deserve a little privacy?"

She teased through the line, "You should have kept those boys away from us if you wanted that. What are you and McDreamy doing on Thursday?"

Great, he already had a nickname. "I'm not sure yet, dinner I think." It was time to turn the tables. "On another topic, I noticed a little something between you and my singing instructor, Nick. What's happening there?"

"Umm, oh shoot, that's my other line, an important call from my professor. I have to take it, Mom."

"A call from your professor and during summer break? Okay, little girl. I see how this double standard works. That's fine. I'll remember that next time you want to know about my love life."

She laughed, "I'm kidding, Mom. There isn't much to tell yet. He invited me to watch him perform on Saturday though. Maybe I'll know if he likes me after that."

I smiled and wondered briefly at the fates that brought me into Nick's studio. Athena's urging that I start singing assured our meeting. Wouldn't it be funny if...?

Late afternoon light beamed though the windows, like a spotlight. I studied myself critically, turning slowly in front of the mirror. I wasn't sure about the dress, but there was no time to change before Luke arrived. Besides, my bedroom already looked like a tornado had touched down with the dozen discarded choices strewn across the bed. Running my fingers over the scalloped collar of the black fit and flare, a pang of guilt overcame me.

I let the feeling in and quickly discarded it. Just because Rye and I had a lovely date, days ago—particularly since I hadn't heard from him, but for one vague text about doing it again, sometime—there was nothing to stop me. Luke's knock landed at precisely 5:15PM. It was time to open the door to my second date of the week.

We got out of the Uber and Luke guided me to a nondescript door underneath a black awning. He pulled it open and gestured for me to walk ahead. Even before I crossed the threshold, floating notes of piano blended with the straining sax as the snare smoothed them both in a melodious greeting. His hand upon my shoulder felt foreign and comforting as he silently instructed me where to go.

The supper club was intimate. Shaped like a U, one side was lined with six tables, each seat taken, and opposite was a bar. Straight ahead, the band was fitted into a compact space. Their shoulders nearly touched but no one seemed to mind. We stopped at the only vacant seats at the bar and were instantly greeted by a well-coiffed black woman in her late sixties. "Luke, baby, glad you could make it. This must be your somebody."

He blushed at being called out but handled it well. "Evvy Snow, meet Geraldine Wheeler. She runs the place and me from time to time."

Her voice started rocky but gained steam as she cautioned Luke, "That's right and don't you forget it or Nanna will wear your ass out, just like I did when you were a boy."

She turned her discerning gaze my direction. "Now let's have a look at you, Evvy Snow. That's a show name if I ever heard one and still not enough to do your beauty justice. You better praise GOD for those gifts, Missy. Praise GOD."

She was real and warm and it felt good to be there. "Thank you, Geraldine. It's a pleasure to meet you, and this place," I gestured toward the band, "is like a dream."

Letting out a whistle for the entire bar to hear, she complimented Luke, "Nice going, boy. I like her already. One thing though," she looked me dead in the eye, "you call me Nanna. Now, what can I get you all to drink?"

Luke looked toward me. I egged, "I'm guessing you make a terrific Sidecar."

"Little girl, you know it." She turned to Luke, "And?"

"Let's have two of those. Thank you, Nanna."

She nodded once and scurried to the other end of the bar to find the ingredients. Luke leaned close. He smelled of mint and lime. The coziness was unnerving. "Nanna took care of my kids when they were small. She also took care of me when I was a kid."

"That's amazing," I replied. "I didn't know you had kids. How old are they?"

"I've got twins, a boy and a girl, Darren and Nella. They turned twenty-one last month."

"Are they here in town?"

"No, the kids are in California for college. They're room-mates together."

"How nice. They must get along pretty well then," I said.

His teasing expression matched his reply. "Those two are either killing each other or killing for each other. They are the closest enemies I've ever seen."

The love shone in his eyes as he talked about his children. I asked before I thought it through, "And their mom?"

His eyes stared ahead. "She passed away three years ago."

Until he'd shared that, I had puzzled wondering why he was single. I replied sincerely, "I'm very sorry. That must have been hard on all of you."

"It was. She died unexpectedly from an aneurysm. She was mid-sentence, talking to the kids, when it took her. Nothing could be done."

The shock from his story was impossible to dance around. My hand automatically raised to rest on his arm as I replied, "How did you get through that?"

His tone became professional, analytical even. "My train-ing, for one. I'm an ER doctor. After I looked over the records, I knew there was nothing to be done and from what the kids shared, she didn't experience a moment of pain. That was a comfort."

The man beside me was virtually unknown and I found myself wanting to change that. I tried to relate to his tragedy. How would I feel if Athena watched her father die? I couldn't imagine going through a loss like that. It must have been overwhelming, yet he shared the story with a calm that demonstrated his acumen as a physician.

My reply was interrupted by the arrival of our cocktails. Nanna announced, "Here you go, kids. What about dinner?" She stared Luke down and demanded, "You having the usual?"

He nodded affirmative, "Yes, ma'am."

"And for you, skinny Minnie?" she solicited, "Fried chicken and mashed potatoes?"

It wasn't a question, but a directive. "Thank you, Nanna," seemed the only response. With that, she marched away to input the order.

Luke raised his drink in toast and said, "Here's to singing class."

My glass met his. "Salute."

The strong liquor and lively music loosened me up but Luke's candor had me spinning. He was raw and hopeful, which I admired. I responded in kind, sharing stories of my past and about raising Athena. He listened intently over platters of soul food as I stretched to relay a history I scarcely identified with. It was as if some other person had lived those years and I was an observer.

Remarkably, we'd nearly cleared our plates when Nanna set, unsolicited, another round before us. "Won't be long now. You two get ready. The way you're goo-goo eyein' each other, I'm expecting something fantastic up there."

She scurried away with our plates and I turned to Luke. "What is she talking about?"

He cleared his throat and squared his shoulders. "Well, if

you're up for it, and I hope you are, I've arranged for us to perform a duet tonight."

I demanded shrilly, "A what?"

He flinched. "A duet, 'All the Way.' You know it from Leslie's class, right?"

I did know the song. It was a favorite of hers that always pissed me off. The lyrics seemed to taunt me with their ring of truth causing me to wonder what my particular deficiency was and why no one ever needed me, 'All the Way.' "I know the song."

His eyes pleaded. "What do think? Want to give it a shot?"

That he'd organized a duet without my permission could have made me feel pushed, but I didn't sense that was his intention. Luke didn't know my history or hesitance for performing and why should he? We met at a soloist singing class. I wouldn't bore him with my fears. Instead I agreed, "I do want to give it a shot."

His smile was laced with desire as he held me in his gaze. "Thank you. I have feeling we're going to be great together."

The double entendre was well timed. When the band finished their song, Ray Shine, the pianist began our introduction. "Thank you, everyone. I have a surprise for you tonight. To finish us off, we are blessed to share the stage with our very own Dr. Luke Anderson and his somebody, Ms. Evvy Snow. They are going to perform a duet by James Brown, 'All the Way.' Let's put our hands together for these two lovebirds."

I sipped the dregs of liquor from my tumbler and set it on the counter before Luke whisked me to the stage. His hand was warm in mine as we hurried toward our impromptu performance. He took the mic and said, "Thank you, Ray, and ladies and gentlemen. Before we get started, I want to let you know, I sprung this on the lady. She wasn't expecting to sing tonight and we haven't rehearsed together so go easy on us, will ya?"

His announcement flooded the room with applause and even a few hoots. He touched my shoulder, "Evvy?"

I nodded.

"I'll start us?"

Another nod from me as I went over the lines in my head. I'd learned the song recently. It was a favorite warm up choice of Leslie's that I trudged through whenever necessary.

He counted and my foot involuntarily joined his snapping fingers. The music seemed to amble in reverse then to the stratosphere as notes "deeper than the deep blue sea" and "taller than the tallest tree" enveloped the room. His baritone voice added a thrill to the sincere song and I was not alone in my captivation. I dared scan the rapt faces of guests as each woman fell in love and each man raised his chest in silent challenge. He was a masterful singer and I suspected he'd learned the song as a child under the tutelage of Nanna Wheeler. Nope, I wasn't feeling any pressure.

A few beats remained before my part. I breathed intentionally feeling the ebb and flow of the music and on cue I began. The pace of the song matched my hesitance as I braved the hopeful lyrics. The tune challenged my range as I tried to convey the height of elation and the weight of their love. I wanted to be plausible, for any of it to be plausible.

I'd always thought the best relationships were based on want and not need, but as I sang the words, "When somebody needs you, it's no good unless they need you all the way," I knew it didn't matter. Whichever it was, want or need, the most important part was all the way. I'd never had it and I longed for it.

As I emptied my lungs over the last verse, "taller than the tallest tree, deeper than the deep blue sea," Luke's eyes met mine. I looked into those aqua pools and praise GOD the spirit moved me. I finished the song believing in all encompassing, too much, almost unbearable love, the kind that smooths all the nooks and crannies. Everyone was on their feet; a few even tipped chairs in their haste to stand.

Nanna made her way to the stage. Her lavender dress shimmered as she confiscated the mic. "Unbelievable! Everyone," she put a hand on her hip and looked our way, "Dr. Luke Anderson and Ms. Evvy Snow! Weren't they sublime?" Her voice was nearly a whisper against the worked-up crowd.

She held her hand up to slow the noise. "Listen, it's closing time so I need to get through these announcements. Number one," she held one pointy lacquered finger toward the sky, "do not forget to post your pictures and videos of tonight's performance on Instagram, tag Nanna's Place, Dr. Luke and Ray Shine. Number two," a second finger joined the first as her demands continued, "keep checking the website for repeat performances from these two. They will be back." The crowd broke the silence for a last round of applause. "Now go on, get your bills paid and skedaddle."

"Oh, oh, oh, wait, the third and fourth things, don't forget to show some love to Ray Shine and his band on your way out. The tip jar is at the exit. Thank you and get home safely."

She didn't mince words and she didn't have to. Geraldine "Nanna" Wheeler had a hot commodity and she knew it. The food, the music, and the crowd were without compare and as a result, there was rarely an empty seat in the house. "You two," she shuffled toward a side door, "come with me."

I did as she demanded and with Luke closely behind, we went through a doorway into a small office. The walls were paneled in scarred wood and an oversized desk flanked one wall. There was a tattered velvet sofa to the right and a tall ornate chair to the side. "Sit," she pointed toward the couch and we did.

Near the chair was a bar cart. We watched in silence as Nanna put ice and liquor into three glasses then handed one to Luke and me before taking a seat. Holding her drink up she cheered, "To chemistry."

It was a fun moment and we let her razz us. How could we contain ourselves after the way we sang together? "Cheers."

<hr />

I washed my hands at the sink and was about rejoin Luke for our ride home when I felt my phone buzz in my purse. I had to make sure everything was okay with Athena, so I fished it out. There were several messages: three from my daughter and one from Rye.

I clicked on Athena's messages. "OMG Mom, you're blowing up on IG. He's super cute. Not sure which one I like best… Will it be bachelor number one or bachelor number two?"

I shook my head at her silliness and hesitated over Rye's name. He wrote, "Hi Evelyn. I'm working at the restaurant tonight. Want to stop by for a nightcap?"

The sinking feeling of guilt came over me and I had to check myself. I was free to date and he was the person who made that point explicit. Although it was late, I sent a quick reply. "Hi Rye. Sorry, I can't come by tonight. Maybe another time?"

There, I thought, that was open but vague. I didn't lie but I didn't tell the truth either. Three dots formed by his name and I knew he was composing a response. Seconds later, his message came through. "Sure. Let's do dinner tomorrow night. Pick you up at 7."

I was miffed by his assumptive reply, but what reason did I have to be upset? Rye and I went on a date; four days later I was out with someone else. He's asked me out again. I can say yes or no. It is up to me how good I want to get at telling half-truths and balancing two men. The high from the liquor and singing with Luke emboldened me to accept. "Okay, see you tomorrow then."

We stepped out into the night and the streets were quiet. "The driver should be here in two minutes," Luke announced.

"Great," I said. "This was such a fun night. I don't normally like being surprised…"

His hands enveloped my waist as he held my eyes with his. "I'm going to kiss you."

I didn't have the chance to reply before he moved in. The whisper of his mouth against my lips was dizzying and any compunction I had about dating two men quickly vanished. He tasted of mint and bitter orange, a heady combination. His tongue was undemanding, almost lazy, like he had all the time in the world. I liked the way he tested and teased me.

Abruptly, a horn beeped and Luke pulled back. His forehead rested against mine and his expression was dazed. "That's us, I'm afraid."

As I followed him to the car, I let the questions in my head come and go. I reminded myself that one date did not constitute an obligation. I had done nothing wrong by going out with both of them. Still, a wary feeling came over me as I buckled in for the ride home.

11

WHO KNEW MY CAR COULD FIT A BIKE IN IT?

Amber liquid melded with orange slices as bubbles danced along the striped straw. The cheery cocktail stood out against the dim bar. I admired it, so I snapped a picture. I'd post it to Instagram later, or would I? After last night's video of Luke and me singing, since he tagged me with it, he may be following my account. What if he saw? The duplicity of dating two people was already making me uneasy. I recalled someone saying once, If it can't be out in the light, it isn't right.

A tap on my shoulder, timed with the beat of my heart, announced Rye's arrival. I swiveled away from the bar to face him.

"Hello," he huffed. "I'm sorry that I'm late. I biked and thought I had it timed just right."

His eyes were once again obscured as the late afternoon light shone through the windows at his back. "Hi." I replied as I stood, "Are you late? I haven't been here long. I didn't realize."

I leaned in to hug him, and he apologized, "It was hot out there; I'm a little warm. Should we get a table?"

"Sure," I said as I took my drink and followed him to check in. After a moment, we were seated at a table outside. The red and white tablecloth billowed softly as a warm breeze eased the heat of the northwest evening. I looked at Rye and couldn't help but wonder where he'd been this week. Then I remembered my own excursion and set that question aside.

Our server arrived and Rye ordered a beer. I sipped on my Aperol spritz and stared unseeing at the menu as I tried to stave off the heat that was both environmental and internal. I wasn't having an easy time sitting across from him after last night with Luke.

"Are you hungry?" he inquired.

At first, his question didn't register, but then I understood. "A little."

"I'm starved," he stated.

As I sat there, a distant observer in the scene, the oddest thing happened. Olivia Newton-John's voice singing the lyrics "You better shape up" played in my head. Obviously, my stupid thoughts were unfolding subconsciously.

Rye must have noticed my distance, as he asked, "Is everything okay, Evelyn?"

The formality with which he pronounced my name irked me and I snapped, "Yep, I'm great."

Thankfully, our server arrived with Rye's beer. "Here you are. Would you like to order anything right away?"

"Could you give us a few minutes?" he replied.

"Sure, I'll check on you in a while," she smiled and took her leave.

Rye took a deep sip of his beer. Setting it aside he leaned forward. "I'm going to ask you again: Is everything okay, Evelyn?"

What did I have to lose by telling him my thoughts? Without filter I blurted, "I'm not sure this is a good idea."

"You're not sure if what is a good idea?"

"Us, me sitting here, across from you."

He fired, "Does everything need to be a good idea?"

I thought briefly and answered him honestly, "No, I guess not, but it can't hurt, right?"

"Evelyn, what is it you want? What would make this a good idea to you?"

I hadn't bargained for his question nor was I prepared to reply. "Why do you care? You're not looking for anything serious, right?"

He demanded, "What does that have to do with it?"

A sudden, irrational impulse to toss my drink in his face was almost impossible to suppress. Instead, I put it as plainly as I could, "I'm not just filler, you know."

His gaze went downcast and his hands clamped the table's edge. "I don't think of you as filler, Evelyn."

"Really, what does that mean?"

He shook his head and stared, unresponsive.

"Here's what I think, Rye. You want it all. I think you like the idea of having me in the mix, but you don't know me, and you don't care to."

He flinched almost imperceptibly, and murmured, "You don't know me either."

"Whose fault is that?" I shot.

The server arrived, but caught the tone of our banter and retreated. "You can't handle the truth, Evelyn. You can't handle me."

"Yeah, maybe you're right. Why did you ask me to dinner then?"

His hand went to mine, and he said, "Because I can't seem to put you down."

The answer disarmed me and my anger was replaced with the sickly feminine instinct to lean in. "Then why do it?" I shot the question and immediately regretted it. What was I thinking? Did I like him? If so, why? Was it the undercurrent of dysfunction that caused it?

Rye's voice was calm as he replied, "Maybe we should call it a night?"

His retreat caused me to meet his stance, "Sure, that's a good idea."

He placed some bills on the table, and I rose to stand. He followed me as I hastened to my car. His words trailed, "So this is it then?"

Without a backward glance, I answered him, "You don't need to walk me to the car. I can make it on my own."

"Evelyn," his hand was firm upon my shoulder, halting my near jog to leave, "stop, please."

There was a vulnerability in his voice that I couldn't ignore. A range of emotions came over me, from anger to embarrassment. The guilt that had been simmering since I accepted the date with Luke had turned into anger which I now directed at Rye. I turned to face him and said, "I'm sorry. I don't know why I'm upset, or maybe I do. I've never been in a situation like this before. I don't think I'm ready for the dating world just yet."

His expression went from apologetic, to resignation and finally challenge as he hissed, "You seem to be doing just fine to me."

I puzzled, "What does that mean?"

He cleared his throat, "How was your date with Luke, Evelyn?"

Oh shit! How did he know about that? His question put me on the spot. Still, what right did he have to inquire about my dating life? He was the one who boasted his non-monogamous lifestyle. Though I had every right to see other people, some part of me wanted to put him at ease. "I'd rather not talk about it, just as I don't want to hear about your dates either."

He held both of my shoulders then, a steely look masking his face. "So, it would bother you to know I was seeing other people?"

Truthfully, I didn't know how to feel about any of it. We'd had that lovely day on the river and I wondered why he was so nonchalant about it. With everything he said, I guessed it was just another day for him, another date on the river of his life as a confirmed bachelor. What other conclusion could I draw, after his frequent reminders that he wants nothing serious? The intensity of our argument left me deflated, and I answered him plainly, "If it would bother me is irrelevant."

"Not to me," he replied.

I didn't have it in me to play games or dance around the topic any longer. "It does bother me. It also bothers me to date more than one person, but this is the way things are. I'm just following your lead."

He took a breath and when he spoke, the resignation on his face said it all. "I'm sorry, Evelyn. This is hard to admit, especially to myself, but I don't like the idea of you dating other people."

His reply inflamed my anger once again. "What a shock," I taunted. "You want to date me, and whoever else crosses your path. It doesn't surprise me that you don't want me to date—entitled men always want it all."

He implored, "Is that really what you think of me?"

"What else could I think? You're quite proud of your single status and all along have made it clear what you don't want. I'm following your rules, your concept, and now you're upset because I went out with someone else?"

He looked angry, but his reply was anything but. "Yes."

"Well, get over it. I don't believe in double standards. I'm sure there are plenty of women who will sit around on Saturday night hoping you'll fall in love with them, but I'm not one."

He sniffed and then laughed. I wondered what came over him. It was an odd reaction to our argument. When he stopped his guffaws, he said, "Truce. If I had a white flag, I'd wave one. Hands down, you won our first fight."

I shook my head and tried to let my emotions settle. Rye closed the distance between us and pulling me close, he said, "I'm sorry."

I had no idea what "I'm sorry" meant or if it changed anything, but I appreciated him saying it. I couldn't respond in kind, because of pride. I wasn't doing anything wrong according to his playbook, yet it didn't feel right either. "Apology accepted," I whispered.

He pulled me close. His lips near mine were an abyss of breath and anticipation. Everything was pushing in that direction. Without demand, he kissed me and I kissed him back. My lips and tongue said all the things I wouldn't.

His departure left me wanting, as he rested his forehead against mine. "I don't want to hurt you, Evelyn, but I don't want to let you go either."

Nothing he'd ever said contradicted his life choices. Even in that moment, his honesty was a force. I could even relate. Not only did I not want to be hurt, I also didn't want to cause Luke any upset. My thoughts were diffused as we stood there. He broke the silence first. "What do you say we start this night over?"

I wasn't sure how we would do that, but I agreed. "Okay."

"Good," he smiled and put his arm around my shoulder then guided me back toward the main street. His eyes creased as he continued, "I think we should try a different restaurant though. We might have raised some eyebrows with our tiff."

I sniffed and agreed, "Yes, I think our server was a little scared after her first check on us."

"There's a good wine shop down the way. Want to go there?"

"Sure," I agreed and we walked the couple of blocks in silence. His arm around my shoulder brought weight to the situation. Though our spat solved nothing, I felt closer to him after airing our feelings.

Quickly we arrived at the restaurant. Shelves from floor to ceiling housed bottles of wine from all over the world. After tasting a couple, we settled on a bottle of rosé then found a table on the patio. The moon was half full and strings of lights above our heads lent to the romance of the evening. After pouring wine in each glass, Rye raised his in toast, "Here's to our first fight."

Again, a fleeting thought to toss my drink his way came to mind. Still, I drank to it.

Soon the server delivered a basket of French fries so large we could have invited another couple to join and later she brought a board covered in meats and cheeses. For a long while, we sat eating and drinking and sharing small talk under the canopy of a night sky.

Our conversation had been light, intentionally so on my part, until he asked, "Tell me about your work, Evelyn."

That familiar rush of bile and nerves rose from my belly and twisted my insides. I hadn't discussed the demise of my corporate career with anyone but family and I wasn't sure how to approach it. "It's different now that, well, how do I explain?"

His eyebrows rose, and I knew I should tell him what happened. He listened intently as I relayed the start of my career after my divorce and some the experiences that led to my termination. When I shared the nature of the "anonymous" complaints, as inappropriate as it was, he burst into laughter. He caught himself, and quickly rebounded, "I'm sorry. I shouldn't have laughed, but as a person who has been trying to get into bed with you for a while now, I don't understand how anyone would believe you slept with the staff."

The wine and nerves from the earlier part of our evening caught up with me and I shot, "And you haven't seen the nasty selection of staff members whom I apparently couldn't resist." To emphasize, I aimed my index finger toward my mouth and made a gagging sound.

He shook his head, obviously perplexed. "How is that legal?"

"What?" I asked.

"What right does a company have to ask a woman about her sex life?"

"That was one of my questions when they pulled me into the HR meeting. Obviously, after I found my voice. At first, I thought I misunderstood what they were saying. It was one of the worst moments of my life. I felt guilty though their accusations were untrue."

"Why do you think it happened?"

"The company was going through a reorganization, which caused chaos among the leaders that trickled down to the sales team, mainly because my boss, Jake was friends with my staff, good friends. Whenever he was in town, he'd take the guys to a strip club. I always knew when they went out because they'd talk about it the next day. His worn-out line was, "You wouldn't believe how many young women I've put through college."

Though it was unprofessional, Jake's discretion was even less during their boys' nights. That's when he confided his job insecurity to the employees. As you can imagine, fear for their friend and the unknown future ruined morale and it caused the team to recoil against me. We all knew someone would be cut and I was chosen as the sacrificial lamb.

" When I told my daughter and parents what happened,

they were so upset, particularly Athena, that I knew what I had to do."

"What did you do?"

"I countered with a grievance. There is an investigation happening."

"That explains it."

I quirked my head, "What?"

"Now I understand why you are more afraid of men than a tough-looking stray pit bull."

His insight was unexpected. "It's funny, I recently realized that myself. When something like that happens, being besmirched in such a way, it impacts just about everything. As much as I didn't care for some of the personalities I worked with, I knew what I was doing in business. It was my constant, even if it came with intense challenges."

Rye's expression went unreadable. He stared off in the distance, and when he spoke, he apologized. "You went through all of that, then you met me and now I understand why you practically ran. I'm sorry I sent you that picture and if I treated you inappropriately. My sense of humor isn't always on target. I'm surprised you're talking to me at all, after everything you've shared."

I chuckled, and replied, "I can't believe I'm saying this, but don't be sorry about the picture. It was my first and only dick pic and though I'm not interested in building a photo album of men's members, it was one of the funniest things that ever happened to me."

He bristled at my comment and I rephrased, "Not that there is anything funny about your…"

He raised a hand to silence me. "I get it. Still, I feel like a jerk. Look, before we go any further, there's something I should tell you."

I looked expectantly at him as he fidgeted with his cutlery. He finally said, "Maybe this isn't a great idea."

It seemed as if he were working something out, so I remained silent. His eyes held mine and he said, "We should go."

Like an unexpected downpour, his words put a chill into the warm evening air. He stood and dropped some bills on the table, I followed. We walked silently toward the car and Rye remembered, "I have my bike."

"That's right," I replied.

"Maybe we can put it in your car. Do you mind giving me a ride back?"

"No, not at all," I agreed, "but I'm not sure it will fit."

We arrived at his bike then ultimately my car and like magic, he got his bike into my compact. The short drive passed quickly and Rye asked, "Will you drop me by the restaurant? I need to finish some paperwork before closing."

"Sure," I agreed. When we arrived, I got out and helped pull the bike from the back.

There was an awkward silence until he said, "This is probably not the best idea, you know."

Though our acquaintance was recent, I'd already found one certainty about Rye: he was anything but predictable. There was no chance to reply before his lips smothered mine. Demanding brushes raised my pulse as he pulled me near, ensuring I felt the evidence of his desire.

When he released me, I was lost for a moment. His voice was dust as he asked, "What are you doing tomorrow night?"

I tried to catch my breath, "Nothing really."

"There's something I need to show you. Pick you up at nine?"

I practically panted my consent, "Yes, tomorrow night."

He looked sad as he said, "I'm going kiss you one more time. Hopefully, it won't be our last."

THE CLUB

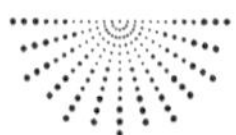

The phone buzzed on the table beside me and I stopped primping to read a text from Rye. "The driver is five minutes away. A black Camry will pick you up."

I quickly replied, "See you soon."

I studied my appearance with a critical eye, wondering if the red dress Athena had forced me to buy was "club" appropriate, but there wasn't time to second guess. The narrow straps and plunging neckline were less material than I was accustomed to wearing and the flared skirt was a little shorter, which was why I'd never worn it.

I glossed my lips and thought about what Rye had said as he'd kissed me goodnight. Why would it be our last kiss? And what was he going to show me tonight? I shuddered inexplicably as I remembered his answer to my question about what to wear.

"Think searingly provocative, without inhibition. We'll be at a nightclub of sorts."

We pulled up to the curb in front of a dimly lit double door shrouded beneath an emerald green awning. A line of people spanning a city block were tucked neatly along the sidewalk.

The car door opened and a tall, blonde model type—her eyes shadowed under the gritty lighting and the grey smudge of makeup—greeted me, "Ms. Snow?"

I said, "Yes," and got out of the car.

Her expression was a numb mask and her voice matched. "I'm Petra. Mr. C asked me to escort you. After you are inducted, I will bring you to him."

"Yes, he mentioned it in his text."

"This way," she waved her hand and we walked past the doorman and throngs of people waiting to enter. The screening room, as I'd later thought of it, was done in black velvet from the walls to the carpets and even the formal sofa, the only furniture in the narrow space. We walked up to a small podium upon which rested a laptop managed by a tall brunette woman with the straightest hair and bluest eyes I'd ever seen.

With her face glowing from the monitor, she addressed me. "Welcome to Club XO, Ms. Snow. May I see your driver's license?"

I handed it to her and replied politely, "Here you are."

"Before Petra takes you on the tour, I need to go over a few rules with you."

I was perplexed, and it showed in my reply. "Rules?"

"Yes, membership to Club XO requires you agree to the rules of conduct. The rules are in your favor. Almost no rules apply to women at Club XO, but we have to go over them with everyone."

This was getting strange. "Okay."

"Thank you, this won't take a minute." Her tone shifted and suddenly, I was listening to a well-tuned flight attendant preparing for takeoff. "First, no cell phones are permitted in any part of the club. You may not use phones for any reason while inside. If you need to make a call, or check messages, please exit the building to do so. Do you agree?"

Except for the times I had visited the FBI building and the data centers I'd worked in, never had I been somewhere my phone was banned. Now more than ever I wanted to know what was inside. "I agree."

"Great," she praised. "The next thing is safety. We have established a consent only rule, which means no one may touch you without your permission. You must also get permission before touching another person. We adhere to, 'no means no.' Do you agree to that?"

The rules piqued my interest. Though I hadn't been to a club since college, I'd never been to one when someone didn't lunge or press something unsolicited against me. "I do."

"Wonderful. When Petra shows you around, you'll see the rooms and different areas of interest. Keep in mind you may never open a closed door or curtain. Can you remember that?"

Closed door or curtain, what was she getting at? "I can remember."

"Excellent, and the last thing is, you may be anywhere in the club dressed or undressed to your liking, but men must remain clothed throughout the club except for the designated areas. If anyone is lingering or acting creepy in any way, get the attention of one of the employees. They will address the matter. We have security guards in force to ensure you have a fun and safe night at Club XO."

I can be dressed or undressed but men have to stay dressed! What the hell kind of place was this? Now I knew why Rye didn't escort me. He was probably afraid I'd walk out, and I would have, but it seemed dramatic in the face of calm presented by Petra and my flawless inductor to sin.

Petra lurched on six-inch heels toward a curtain in the wall. The heavy brocade pattern was raised against the dark fabric, hiding the curiosities on the other side. She pulled it back for me to enter.

I passed over the threshold into a glitzy world of light and color. An orange-hued bar flanked one side. The center of the room contained a dance floor with two caged platforms, inside of which scantily dressed women slithered temptingly. A second-story mezzanine lined with people hovered above. So far it was elegant and flashy but nothing I hadn't seen in other discos.

"This way," she waved me toward a hallway and stopped outside a curtained entry. I was confused—weren't we forbidden from opening closed curtains? "This room is for group connections. All are welcome to enter, but the other rules apply."

Pulling back the drape, I edged inside the darkened space. There was a center aisle and half stalls that looked like door-less cubicles made from red leather. Within each unit was a round bed and upon several, there were naked people in various sexual acts. An older couple unabashedly performed sixty-nine on each other as a young couple watched while screwing doggie style. To the side I could see a tangle of people, three or possibly four, pushing and whining to climax. My impassive outward expression was a show to hide my shock. I wondered, Is this even legal? A tap on my shoulder indicated it was time to move on.

In a trance, I followed Petra up a flight of stairs, where we found a row of rooms with glass fronts. She paused at each, allowing the different options offered to sink in. The first was unoccupied but contained two beds, which Petra explained was for voyeurs to share. The next room had only one bed, and another room contained an enormous platform upon which a gloriously fit biracial man was being ridden by a smoldering redhead. Her large breasts bounced seductively near his face. The last room, the one with the swing, was surrounded by onlookers. However, when Petra walked up, it was like the parting of the Red Sea. A gap in the crowd opened and she motioned for me to advance.

I peered through the glass in fascination as the couple inside were learning how to use a swing of sorts. She was pliant as he firmly planted her ass in the contraption. He reclined her with one of the straps and used the other to prop her up.

They were shadowed but I could clearly see his arousal as he dropped his pants to expose a hammer-hard penis. After tossing his shirt to a chair, he kneeled between her legs. Sliding his hands up her black skirt, he tugged, presumably to release her bodysuit. She squirmed and her head fell back as her mouth went lax with anticipation.

He buried his face and her arch was so strong it set the swing in motion. Large hands steadied her as he continued his oral assault. She was listless with consent, and he was bursting with need. He pulled back and pressed her to sitting, her face in line with his straining member. Just as she was about to take him in her mouth, like a slap, he shook his head and backed away.

Dark eyes narrowed toward the glass as his menacing stare pierced me. He marched to the window and dragged the heavy privacy curtains, shielding the crowd from whatever was happening next. His expression was hauntingly relatable as I stared at the drape wondering why I was there and what Rye expected of me.

We stood outside the closed door as Petra boldly knocked, three distinct taps. "Enter," his voice was a command.

She turned the knob and motioned with her chin for me to step inside. I did and the door shut behind me. The room was dim but well-appointed with a leather sofa to the side and a wet bar in the corner. Atop a luxurious Persian rug rested an ornate wooden desk, behind which Rye was poised. He rose to meet me at the center of the room. Standing feet apart, the silence was deafening and as I looked at him, I knew the person before me was someone new, somebody I hadn't met before.

The glint in his eye was neither daring nor assured, laying bare the vulnerability of his honesty. I had too many questions to settle on one and this moment was his to own. His voice vibrated between us, "Good evening, Evelyn. How are you?"

I said nothing.

"You've been through orientation."

Orientation. The word seemed an awful fit after what I'd seen. I remained silent.

"Do you have any questions?"

Was he serious? "Questions?!" I exclaimed, "If you think I'm going to have sex in the zoo, you're out of your mind."

He shook his head, "I'm not asking you to have sex in the club. I own it."

Was there no bottom to this man?

"Evelyn, will you say something?"

Amidst the colliding thoughts and questions exploding in my head, I found my voice. "I want to go home."

"I'll take you."

I focused on the road noises, wheels against asphalt, the

sound of the blinker and the bright red taillights ahead. He drove precisely following all of the rules—how ironic. Awkward was a scratch compared to the strange atmosphere that weighted me as I recalled the events of the past hour.

It was impossible to get the image of the couple with the swing out of my head. The expression in his eyes just before he closed the curtain—it was proprietary. She was his and his alone. At a point I'd have thought his actions protective, but tonight showed me a new truth. Men aren't protective of women; they are possessive.

We neared the house and he slowed to the curb. My hand raised to the door handle even before we stopped. He put the car in park and gripped my arm to prevent my exit. "Please, give me a minute."

I didn't want to give him a minute, not another second of my time. He'd opened the door to a world I never knew existed and even if I was tempted, curious, whatever you wanted to call it, there was a voice inside my head telling me no, don't go there. He's not safe and you'll just fail again. If you take this chance, it will be another mistake to add to the pile. We weren't compatible and there was no reason to belabor the point. "Rye, this isn't for me."

With a blend of sadness and stubbornness he snapped, "I know that. I know."

His hand remained snug around my wrist, "Then what is there to say?"

He exhaled and started, "You're amazing and so is Athena. I know I'm not for you. No need to explain why. I care for you, more than I expected, but I can't change who I am. Also, I don't participate at the club. It's a business to me and one that I've enjoyed over the years. You wouldn't believe how lucrative it is."

"Good luck with all of your business endeavors," I managed. "Please let me go now."

His reply was a steely whisper, "I'm going to miss you, Evelyn, very much."

Impossibly, his sparse words lowered my resolve to exit his life. For an instant our eyes met. Between us there was truth and war. I fled the car with a firm, "Goodbye."

13

GOSPEL BRUNCH

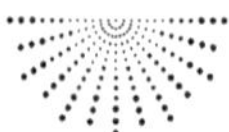

Morning came like an anvil to the head assisted by the open curtains and torturous summer sun. Though I wasn't hungover—in fact, I'd had nothing to drink the previous night—I felt it. Rest was impossible after everything I'd seen and how things had ended with Rye.

I stumbled to the kitchen for a cup of coffee and briefly considered lacing it with liquor, something I'd done only one other time in my life, on my previous birthday. Luke's invitation to gospel brunch had come before the weekend with Rye. I would have cancelled but I knew he had gone to a lot of trouble to get tickets. Still, how was I going to look at him, let alone listen to gospel music, after the night I'd had?

I drew a bath and settled into the lavender bubbles, breathing steadily and working to exorcize the relentless weirdness that shadowed my spirit. Flashes like photographs came to me, dim corners and lewd acts—or were they lewd? Did I even know what lewd was anymore?

The saying, blurred lines, was illustrated immaculately last night. On one hand there were rules and protections, and consent was mandatory. It sounded reasonable until I found myself standing at the center of live porno with people having sex for everyone to see. More unbelievable was learning that Rye owned the club, a sex club. Sex clubs exist. My thoughts were as disjointed as the legality of a members only den of iniquity fronting as a disco.

It was too much to conceive. Everything involving Rye had been tumultuous and disorienting. At first, I thought dating him was a good way for me to step outside of myself, but Rye wasn't a step, he was a base jump. The leap was more than I would take.

The water grew as cool as my sentiments toward Mr. C., and I toweled off, forcing myself through the getting ready process. I added an extra dab of concealer beneath my eyes and scanned the wardrobe for what to wear. After last night, white was out and so was red, so that left black and blue. If only I could find something with both colors, that would be most fitting. I settled on a beige wrap dress and pale pink flats.

When I looked online, I saw most people dressed up and even wore extravagant hats. To that end, I lifted the lid of a box that had sat untouched for far too long. Inside was the loveliest pink and beige, wide-brimmed hat. It was meant for a special occasion, but that day never happened. Sentiment seemed preposterous after last night. I wore the hat.

The effect of the outfit was demure, innocent even, an optical illusion that was as hollow as I felt. I'd seen the other side and watched things most only see on-screen. I huffed and wondered, was I drawing this kind of energy to myself? I didn't seek what I found, did I?

Luke's knock gave me a start. My pounding heart was relentless as I walked to the door. Daylight shone on his smiling face and he was as bright as the bouquet of roses he carried. "Good morning," he hugged me and gave me the flowers.

"Good morning." I sniffed the roses and relished in the citrus sweetness. "Thank you. I can't tell you how long it's been since there were flowers in the house. Let me put them in some water quickly."

"Sure," he agreed and followed me inside. The act of finding a vase was a good exercise that reminded me what a normal date was like.

He called from the living room, "What a gorgeous home, Evvy."

"Thank you. I have a soft spot for it myself."

I carried the flowers to the table as he said, "I can see why." His eyes were aglow in the morning light. "You look pretty."

The innocence of his compliment was almost too much. Was the universe mocking me? "Thank you. Should we go?"

"We should," he agreed.

Our table was near the front of the auditorium. A purple-hued stage, as yet unoccupied, glowed ahead. Rows of laddered pews, stacked one over the next, awaited the award-winning choir that would soon fill the space. The stage was set: drums, horns, stand-up bass, all would be represented in the morning festivities.

Luke raised his champagne and turned to face me, his shoulder touching mine in the close quarters. "To breakfast on Sunday."

As I tapped my glass to his, I wondered why I accepted Rye's invitation to dinner after our first date. Luke was sexy, a gentleman and he liked to have fun—plus he likely didn't own a sex club.

I knew comparisons were unfair, yet I checked certain boxes and my sanity at once. Rye was a superficial sex addict living solely for indulgence and thrill. Luke was a father, a doctor and a man with a history he cherishes. They were fire and ice, but maybe I needed water.

"Evvy?"

Luke's bass-filled voice shattered my mind maze. "What? I'm sorry. I didn't hear you."

His aqua eyes held. "Is everything okay?"

I put on a cheery smile. "Yes, wonderful. Why do you ask?"

He admonished, "You haven't touched your breakfast."

I looked down at my plate, and he was right. I hadn't tried a thing. Collecting my fork, I sliced into the eggs benedict and took a bite. "Mmm, it's delicious."

The hint of lust flickered across his face. He leaned closer and whispered, "Is it?"

His flirt should have hit the mark. "Yes," I agreed and took a sip of my mimosa. "How's your hash?"

He didn't answer and instead smiled devilishly toward my lips. As he leaned in, the lights were cut and the entertainers burst onto the stage, interrupting his progress toward my mouth.

The audience exploded with applause as the singers and band swiftly took their places. Without introduction, the orchestra played and soon the power of the choir took control in a demented version of Hozier's "Take Me to Church." The song choice was astounding, but the way they'd deconstructed, and shored it up, was divine.

It was probably exhaustion casting the aura of déjà vu and self-loathing over me, and it was unshakable. The lyrics were like golden lashes, their blows softened only by the molasses voices of the prophets. The operatic battering pinned me to my seat, exposing my darkness. They sang to me, to the filthy part inside of me that didn't look away.

The song ended and everyone leapt from their seats. My

ears rang against the uproarious applause. It was a welcome reprieve. Luke stopped screaming and whisper-yelled in my ear, "Amazing, right?"

"Definitely," I agreed as they launched into, "He's Got the Whole World in His Hands." The juxtaposition of the song lineup threw me as I'm sure it was intended. The words reverberated against the domed ceiling, and the image of a waterfall came to mind.

It was the first trip Athena and I took after the divorce. We went to Costa Rica and while in route to visit a volcano—helped by our assertive tour guide Poncho—we found ourselves on a narrow mud trail that led to the underside of a gushing waterfall.

Never before had I experienced that kind of vulnerability and trust, as we followed a man we didn't know and couldn't communicate with. He held Athena's hand and forged first along the path with no rail. I worried the ground might give, as the water below bubbled and churned from the impact of the aggressive faucet. A smashed wooden bridge was abandoned in place after an apparent flood had destroyed it. Fear overcame me and as we inched along, instead of seeing the beauty in nature, even in the destruction, I worried. Why are we walking this treacherous path? What if something bad happens? Who will help us? Somehow, Poncho's assured manner held my tongue.

Then GOD himself appeared and with him came the brightest beam of light as HE moved the clouds and took aim for our waterfall. We had arrived at the end of the path, and found the pot of gold. Our backs rested against the vibrating rock wall and as we faced the roaring water in its most rugged form. Sunlight pummeled the water as it spilled furiously from the ledge above, creating a screen of flashing rainbows.

Athena's face was ethereal as she glowed under the

miracle of nature. I didn't have to tell her she was safe, nor myself, for I knew it with the same certainty that came when I learned of her impending birth. We were protected even when we weren't because we weren't alone. An invisible force surrounded us with wonder and as I laid my concern aside, the presence was unmistakable. I wanted to draw on that memory, to have faith, but after last night, was I worthy?

Luke's arm rested easily over my shoulder—easily for him. I felt strange about the knowledge it presumed. He wasn't doing anything but acting companionably, yet the gesture seemed too intimate for the glimmering morning light. He hummed along softly and I saw things with an astounding clarity. He was courting me but I was dating him.

The song closed to another standing applause. He leaned in and said, "I need an intermission."

I tried for levity. "Might be the coffee and mimosas. I think I'll join you."

"Come on," he smiled and guided me from behind, his hand resting at the small of my back. The gesture was almost more than I could take. I nearly brushed his hand away but caught myself. I was acting crazy. Luke had done nothing wrong, nor had I. We'd been out once. I didn't owe him fidelity and I had no allegiance to Rye.

At the top of the aisle we parted for our respective facilities. "See you in a second," he smiled joyfully and walked the opposite way.

I felt sick as I made my way to the ladies'. Why did I want to freeze Luke out? I had to admit, Rye was a factor.

His grainy perspective touched a part of me that was born from trauma. I'd lived a conventional lifestyle and my enemies—as I could call them nothing less—painted me a temptress, slandering my character and confirming my perception that women must walk a straighter line for society. Dating him was like raising a middle finger at the world, and a way to say you have no right to hold me to a higher standard.

Luke was almost noble in his persona. He honored his widow and spent his life helping people. His appreciation for family and friends was evident and, from the little I'd learned about him, he wasn't afraid to show his heart. He was thoughtful and mannered and also, he was clear. I admired him from every angle. Why did I want to keep him at a distance?

Then it came: I wondered if I could be myself with him. He was ideal, but was I? My career was a scandal that would have to come out eventually. I was divorced and had a broken engagement under my belt. I had stories I wished I didn't. How would he feel if he knew my secrets?

I washed my hands and braced myself for the balance of the program. The door opened to a waiting Luke, and his boyish smile was almost too much. I tried for polite as I said, "You didn't have to wait."

He placed his arm across my shoulder. "I couldn't miss the chance to escort you."

His word choice struck a chord and I couldn't help but recall last night's escort. I squelched my thoughts as they were out of place and rude. We marched to our seats as the choir rearranged "Just a Closer Walk with Thee," most notably performed by Patsy Cline. Deep tones tiptoed to the highest peaks as they peppered even more soul into the pleading, faithful tune. Embarrassment and a peculiar exhaustion slapped me like the lyrics.

The show went on and I balanced my emotions between strong coffee and champagne. The grand finale was upon us as the group sang a song made immortal by Aretha Franklin, "Never Grow Old." The impossibly breathy piano keys and soloist, joined by the angelic delicacy of the whispering choir, raised hearts to the sky. Blues and hope intertwined and for the first time all day, I was at peace.

The room lit with screeches, hallelujahs and uproarious applause as the choir graciously received their accolades. Luke suddenly pulled me to face him and in anticipation of his kiss, I moved, causing his mouth to land squarely on my nose. He chuckled, "Awkward. I'll try that again later after I've regained some confidence."

Hat in hand, I willed a cheerful smile, "Ha, ha, sorry," I mumbled and followed the exiting masses toward the doors. We spilled out onto the bright sidewalk, baked by the midday sun and highlighted by the reflection of the parallel river. The unsheltered walkway was heated to unbearable. Finally, the hat was useful as I put it on to shade my squinting eyes.

He suggested, "Shall we take a walk?"

It was the last thing I wanted, but I politely agreed, "Sounds nice."

We walked along the railing. The few newly planted trees offered little reprieve from the blasting light. A flock of gulls dropped low as they flew one behind the next, scanning the busy waterway for any morsel of food. The warning bell from a bicycle rang to my left. Everything looked normal— why didn't I feel so?

I ventured, "Thank you for inviting me to the show. It was so moving that I was near tears a couple of times."

"I thought you'd appreciate it." He looked toward the river as he asked, "Is everything else all right?"

I don't know why I hesitated and ultimately clammed up, but it established a wall between us, a barrier of entry that assured our limit. "Yes," I lied. "I'm sorry if I seem distracted. I've got a work presentation tomorrow and a few sticking points to figure out before it's ready."

"I see," he said, but something in his tone hinted that he

saw through my excuse. "Well, maybe we should get you home then?"

I wanted to agree, to flee the date swiftly, but I lied again, "I have time for a short walk."

"Great," he said and asked, "What's the presentation about?"

I wanted to skirt the subject of my employment altogether and found the right response. "It's a little complicated and also confidential."

He did a double take and asked, "What is it you do?"

This I could explain, "I'm a risk consultant and a double agent for hire. Using technology like IT systems, surveillance cameras, access control and other investigative means, I help companies uncover and mitigate security, theft and employee issues."

He repeated, "A double agent for hire?"

I sniffed, "Sometimes."

"How does it work?"

"I consult with companies at a pretty high level. They tell me their concerns and I examine everything from security protocols, access levels, existing systems, policies and so on. Sometimes, I'm hired as a staff member where hopefully I learn even more. Every project is different, of course, and sometimes it's as banal as designing security systems."

He kidded, "Banal, designing security systems? I'm seeing another side of Miss Evvy Snow, the self-assured one."

I returned his chide, "This coming from the only ER doctor in the world without an ego."

"Hey," his cheeks rose to meet his glowing eyes, "you've got a point there." Even as he teased, he couldn't lie. The man didn't have it in him. He continued, "It does sound exciting. I didn't know that was a real thing, double agent for hire."

I didn't have the heart to tell him it was a new aside, something I'd marketed as a desperate attempt to differentiate myself from a competitor on the first project I'd won as a consultant. Time to change the subject. I asked, "So how are your kids doing?"

He blinked, but responded as if the segue were logical. "They're great. I spoke with them this morning. From what I could tell they were about to have a party or maybe they had one last night, or maybe they're having a party weekend." His eyes grew distant, "Summer vacation should be like that I suppose."

"Are you concerned?" I asked.

"No. They're good kids, reasonable in every way. I trust their judgment."

I wasn't sure if he meant what he said, and it was his turn to change the subject. "I talked to Nanna and she's determined to get a commitment from us."

I quirked my head, "What?"

"Relax, not that kind of commitment, though you need not look so alarmed. She wants us to perform in September and October. What do you think? Could we put together a set of, say, six songs by then?"

I knew it could be done, but we'd need to practice together. Still, I didn't know if it was something I wanted to do and the timeline concerned me. With how I was feeling today, could I agree to seeing Luke regularly for the next several months? "I'd like to think about it. Do you mind if I take a few days?"

"Not at all, just so long as when you get back to me the answer is yes."

I should have wanted to say yes on the spot. We sang well together even without practicing. He was the man mothers dream of for their little girls, yet something held me in reserve.

Luke's wristwatch chimed. He silenced the alert and checked the screen. "I'm sorry to cut this short, but there's an emergency at the hospital and they're down a few hands."

"Of course," I replied in wonder. We rushed in reverse along the familiar path and I was in awe of him. He saved people's lives and was good in every way. He deserved an equal and I didn't measure up to all that.

Each fact of my life confronted me. I'd opened the door to Rye in innocence and again after he showed me who he was, but I didn't do more than look and I wouldn't do it again. I'd forgive anyone that transgression—why not myself?

I was divorced and my fiancé had left me. These weren't reprehensible facts. My career was unblemished, even remarkable, until my time at the last company. Why was I mortified to share these things?

Thankfully, my house was in sight and a speedy exit was in the immediate future. He pulled to a stop and I turned. "Don't bother walking me. Just get to work safely." I pecked his cheek and scurried out of the car before he could say a word.

14

CHRYSALIS

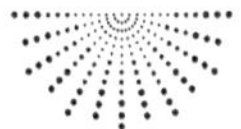

*I*t was 9:08AM and the Vice President of Human Resources at Base Productions in Hollywood addressed me over FaceTime. "Evelyn, as you are aware, we have a number of complex employment contracts in place with our actors. There are minute details we must follow to the letter not only for our permanent staff, but for the extras who work with us periodically. Can you assure the strictest confidence and discretion if you are permitted access to those documents, and commit that your consultation won't violate any, and or the sum total of those agreements?"

I'd anticipated the question and it was a fair one. My answer showed confidence but reality. "Laurie, I understand your concern and I share it. This was one reason I established a four-week lead time to prepare myself and define a plan with the many nuances of your obligations foremost. I understand the need to balance your legal requirements and the priority of finding who has been leaking your intellectual property to New Fish Broadcasting. The financial component of my proposal, which is outcomes based, should demonstrate my motivation. However, if something does go awry, I've agreed to meet the insurance provisions listed in your proposal request."

She admonished, "You realize we have clauses that require us to honor things like only green M&M's or no walking outside a trailer door during certain hours of the day. The use of surveillance equipment, even in common areas, can be a challenge. You've never worked in Hollywood. What makes you the person for the job?"

Another fair point from the powerful and legal-minded California HR VP. A flash, like a beacon at the corner of my screen, caught my eye. It was an ad for the writing academy in Los Angeles I'd researched a few days prior. The course promised students would leave the eight-weekend course with a completed screenplay.

Dr. Cord's diary assignment had rekindled my interest in writing. I'd studied journalism in high school and college, but that was the only formal training I'd had. Lately, the idea of writing a screenplay tugged at me. The Base Media contract meant living in LA for three months and I'd be working on a movie set as a part of my double-agent duties. The production was closed on weekends so I'd have time for the class. If I wanted it, I'd better convince the influential Laurie Sands of my competence as a risk consultant, despite my Hollywood outsider status.

"Laurie," I hoped my direct reply would hit the mark, "with all due respect, experience has shown me how to balance unreasonable demands and people. You have my word that I'll handle all aspects of the project paying strict attention to the boundaries. I can't deny I haven't worked in television before but I'm dynamic and research minded. My lack of familiarity won't be a hinderance; it may turn into an advantage."

She squinted, not unkindly, and the corner of her mouth

lifted just a little. "That's it for me. Marty?" she redirected to the CEO.

Marty Shaw replied, "How long before we have your amended proposal back, Evelyn?"

"No time at all, Marty. I'll make the adjustments you requested and have the revision back to you today."

"Good, and if we come to terms, how soon will you start?"

That should have been my question, but my feathers weren't ruffled. It was a tell. He was planning the project with me. "I'd start within the week and you can expect me in LA four weeks after I've received access to the pertinent standards and contract documents."

"That sounds reasonable," he said, but didn't smile. I couldn't end the call on that note. There was a lot riding on this opportunity. It distanced me from my recent dating excursions, the pay was incredible and I could finally try my hand at writing.

"Marty, if you trust me with this investigation, I'll get to the bottom of it. It would be an honor to work with your group. Is there anything else I can answer for the team?"

His brows rose as he scanned the room. The VP of Security, Bob Smith, waved his hand in dismissal, "I got what I needed." Next, he looked toward Bert Wells, Chief Legal Counsel. His dismissive tone left a chill, "Good for now. I'll review the updates in her proposal when I receive it."

Marty faced me once again. "Thank you for your time, Evelyn. We await your revision and will let you know our decision soon."

Before I could say goodbye, an email teaser from my attorney, Jack Robb, flashed across the screen. News from the other side. Can you meet today at 3PM, my office?

I signed off saying, "Thank you, everyone."

The screen went black and I clicked to open Jack's full

email. The subject was the entirety. I replied with the same brevity, Yes, I'll see you at three.

Before today, Jack and I had only spoken on the phone after Hal Schmidt referred him to me. As I pulled into the driveway of his office, I realized I'd passed it almost daily on my way home. I took a vacant spot in the front and made my way into a common lobby. The scent of must and stagnant air greeted me. To my right, a black velvet directory, circa 1970, hung solitary on a grainy faux-wood paneled wall. The listing for Jack's offices indicated suite #100. I followed the corridor until I found it.

The door swung into a time warp of green shag carpeting anchored by heavy wooden furniture and a vast wall of books that ran the length of the suite. Ahead of me was a set of stairs, a woman perched at a desk above. She furiously typed on a keyboard, but didn't miss a beat as she beckoned, "You must be Evelyn. Please come up."

The slatted stairs were covered in the same green shag that was rampant throughout the space. Dingy ivory walls, likely stained from years of cigarette smoke, complimented the balance of the furnishings. I had seen nothing like it since I was a child. The aged surroundings gave me pause and I wondered if I'd made the right attorney choice. I arrived at the top of the stairs and approached a woman with spiky pigtails and gum in her mouth. "Did you find us okay?" she asked.

She was fidgety, like a hummingbird. Her intensely long and manicured nails continued to tap annoyingly on the keyboard. "Yes, I did." I had to address the obvious and said, "This place is kind of unbelievable."

She smirked. "It's like working on a movie set without all the good-looking actors."

Jack's sharp voice cut through the intercom system as he demanded, "Florence, is Evelyn Snow here?"

"She is."

"Send her in, please."

Her brows rose as she pointed her garishly decorated index finger to a door across the way. "Thanks," I said and walked that direction.

The door was open and I poked my head inside. Jack Robb was tall, maybe six-four, and he rose from his seat with the speed of a sloth. I entered the windowless office as he came around the desk, his hand extended to shake. "It's good to meet you in person, Evelyn."

"You as well, Jack."

He gestured for me to take the chair opposite him, and as I sat, he took his position behind the desk. The walls were the same yellowed shade as the rest of the suite and the computer monitor he studied was another throwback to a foregone era. It was the size of an old television set and it dominated half of his Formica desk. The keyboard under his giant hands matched the console in age and discoloration.

"Ah," he spoke aloud, "here it is."

I nervously waited for him to continue.

"As you know, the investigation has been underway. They won't admit any wrongdoing, but there are some developments. What I'm about to tell you is confidential."

He spoke and I saw a cartoon. It is a moonless night. I am a rock adhered perilously to a cliff by the disintegrating soil. A branch from the tree above breaks. It lands squarely at my back, dislodging me from my teetering spot on the ledge. I fall mercilessly into the bubbling black sea beneath.

His voice droned on. "They don't believe you were singled out as a woman, but they did find other problems and a systemic connection to the leadership group at your former employ."

"What does that mean?"

"It means, you weren't the only one who experienced challenges and they found some financial mismanagement as an incidental outcome of the investigation."

His explanation left me perplexed. "Why haven't they reinstated me?"

"I asked about a rehire scenario and here's the thing, they don't believe you could adequately manage that team again. Since the complaints were filed anonymously, they can't address the staff. It's all a part of their non-retaliation policy."

My hand quivered with my voice as I said, "Then why aren't they ruling in my favor?"

"Don't get hung up on that piece," he stated as if I were hysterical over a broken fingernail. "Do you want the rest?"

I hesitated, "I guess."

"You'll be pleased to learn that your old boss was fired. The company would also like to enter into settlement talks."

"Settlement talks?"

"Yes, they've sent over an offer. It's straightforward: a lump sum settlement would be paid but the agreement has a stringent confidentiality clause, and some other tentacles you'll want to understand."

"Such as?" I inquired.

"Essentially, you can't speak of the settlement, or any of the problems that happened during your employment or slander the company in any way. There's also a two-year non-compete clause involved. They reserve the right to come after you for damages—unsubstantiated damages—if you break any of the terms."

"Damages?"

"It means they'll sue you and they won't have to quantify the loss because reputation damage is difficult to measure."

"They're worried about their reputation being damaged?" The nerve that a multi-billion-dollar company would include such heavy-handed language infuriated me.

Jack explained, "Yes, well with all the Hollywood hype these days, they're covering their bases."

His comment was like the wash of cola over a cavity. He clearly didn't understand my motivation for filing the grievance.

* * *

Dr. Cord's words from our last session rang in my ears, "This journal would make an incredible movie."

"My diary of disaster," I teased.

Dr. Cord stared intently but didn't smile as he replied, "That's a great title."

"You can't be serious."

He removed his glasses and began cleaning them with the corner of his sweater. "Do you remember what you told me when I asked you why you decided to fight it?"

"I do. It was for my daughter, for all the daughters. I got tired of trying to play myself down as a woman, of tip-toeing around my sexuality and competence. I got tired of being afraid. I want it to be easier for Athena, for all the women."

"That's a lofty objective, Evelyn, and one that will probably not be accomplished by a complaint. You're an engaging writer and you confided it was something you once loved. Maybe you should explore this."

* * *

I snapped back to the moment, but not before recalling my earlier pitch to Base Productions and the screenwriting course in Los Angeles. "If I accept their settlement, does that mean I can't write about what happened?"

He sneered through jagged teeth. His expression reminiscent of a grumpy old lion, "Not unless you want them to sue you for everything you have and more. Besides, you're not going to waste your time writing a book. You're going to put this nonsense behind you and find a new job."

That was the moment that changed everything. Jack's unwitting challenge assured my determination. There was no point trying to explain as his mentality matched the functional obsolescence of the furnishings. He was too outdated to grasp how deeply this would affect me. I knew it would require a more graphic illustration to penetrate his mentality.

A long time ago, I'd learned the importance of the pregnant pause. The only sound between us was the insistent whir of the fan from his ancient desktop computer. It sounded like the hard-drive was going to crash. It was time to leave. "I'd like some time to review everything. I'll get back to you with my questions."

"Do keep in mind, they've added a deadline for response and the sooner you agree, the sooner you can forget this whole thing."

It felt as if I were paying to be insulted. I rose from the rickety chair. "Thank you, Jack. I'll review the agreement and get back to you with my response."

The week flew by and I gave little attention to reviewing the settlement from my former employer. I'd avoided an earlier call from Jack and was about to listen to his voice message when another call rang through from Los Angeles. I answered, "Hello, this is Evelyn."

"Hi there, Evelyn. This is Marty Shaw."

My pulse quickened and the sensation of my heartbeat became overwhelming. "How are you today, Marty?"

"I'm well. I'm calling with some good news. We want to hire you for the project."

It was my first big win in years and I was elated to tears. "That's wonderful. I'm so excited. Thank you."

"You earned it. Even Bert voted in your favor, which is no small feat."

"Marty, your confidence means the world to me. I won't disappoint you."

"Laurie will forward the agreement before the end of the day and if possible, we'd like to finalize by early next week."

"That sounds reasonable. I'm wrapping another project now, so the timing couldn't be better."

"Excellent. Well I'm off, Evelyn. Have a good weekend."

"You as well, Marty, and thank you again."

The line went silent and I screamed out loud. Yes! Hollywood, here I come! The chime of an email received paused my celebration, but I was elated to find the contract from Base Productions. I scanned the particulars and again, I had to hoot.

My joy was interrupted by another email, this one from my lawyer, Jack Robb. Reluctantly, I opened the message. It was his reminder about the deadline. I was required to sign the agreement by 5PM today. I replied with the kind of abandon that was born of rage and insanity.

Good Afternoon Jack,

I'm afraid I can't agree to their terms. Please decline on my behalf as your final act of representation in this matter. Your assistance is greatly appreciated.

Regards,

Evelyn Snow

CALIFORNIA LOVE

SOFT LANDINGS

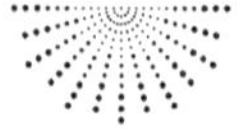

The afternoon sun beat down on us as we stood at the curb waiting for my ride. I felt flushed and tried to breathe through the nerves that had been building all week. It was no small miracle how everything came together. Without the kids' help and the obsessive-compulsive mood swing that had kicked in over the past few weeks, I wouldn't have been ready on time.

Athena held my wrist and spoke like a child, "I'm going to miss you, Mommy."

A strange sentiment came over me and it seemed accepting this assignment was like going away to college. Athena and I had never been separated, other than when she spent time with her Dad. I felt panicked thinking I wouldn't be able to visit her anytime I chose. Still, the change was the escape I needed. This town had become messy for me, particularly when you considered the added layer of my recent dating expeditions. I was appreciative for the excuse to vacate and that it would be temporary. Tears welled as I replied, "I'm going to miss you too, little girl. Stay out of trouble while I'm gone."

She smiled as Nick poked his head from the front door, "The driver is one minute away."

"Thanks," I called, then turned my attention back to my daughter. "I'm glad you and Nick are seeing each other. He's a good guy."

Her smile was delightful and proof she was happy. "He is and it's all thanks to you and that singing class."

"Not so fast—you were the one who kept pushing me to do it. If you hadn't, we wouldn't have met Nick."

As if on cue, Nick and Shane joined us on the sidewalk. He cheered, "Good for me Athena's persistent."

Shane exclaimed, "We need a picture to commemorate this occasion. Gather around, everyone."

The four of us crammed in close until we were all in the frame. "Say cheese!"

He snapped the photo as the driver pulled up. "I'm going to miss you guys. Take care of Athena for me and no parties tonight. The tenants arrive tomorrow."

Nick put my bags in the trunk as Shane pulled me in for a hug, "We'll take care of everything, don't worry."

Nick squeezed me next, "Good luck, Evvy. I hope it's a great trip."

"Thank you."

It was Athena's turn and as we held each other at arm's length, our expressions were a mirror of pride and longing. "I love you, little girl. I'll call you when I get to La La Land."

"Love you too, Mom."

Before I made a scene, I scurried into the car, waving goodbye until my baby was out of sight.

"Ladies and gentlemen, this is the final announcement before we land in Los Angeles. Please secure your seatbelts, place your seats in the upright position and stow your electronics for landing." I followed the instructions and tucked my laptop away then peeked out the window.

The area surrounding the airport was hued in shades of straw. The brilliant sun shone mercilessly on the city, blending every grassless yard and beige-toned building in a haze of smog. The scene was intensified by a lack of trees since the grid of streets and structures was built so closely together there was room for little else. The view faded behind me as we approached an unfolding tarmac and my destiny.

Buttery soft leather seats smoothed the commute as my driver, Tommy, navigated the harried traffic like a pro. He didn't take the direct route, yet according to the navigation system his maneuvers shaved twenty minutes from the ride. The world outside the window looked anything but glamorous, as we passed chain stores and fast-food restaurants galore. Soon we found our way to higher ground and a mega-mall came into view. Tommy made a few more turns then slowed as we drew nearer to my temporary home.

We crept through the neighborhood of well-cared for mid-century bungalows until he pulled into the driveway of a white home with emerald trim. It was set back from the walk with the entrance to the side and a picture window that overlooked the yard. He stopped and I surveyed my new surroundings.

The large maple tree that shaded the front yard was the only familiar thing I'd seen since landing in LA. Tommy came around to my side and opened the door. "Your home away from home, Ms. Snow."

I admonished as I exited the Lincoln, "Please call me Evvy."

He carried my bags and walked toward the entry. I waited at the landing as he fished keys from his pocket and opened the door. "This way, Ms. Snow."

"What's your last name, Tommy?" I demanded as I climbed the steps to enter.

He hesitated, "Smith."

"Thank you, Mr. Smith," I replied and crossed the threshold.

Textures of beige and cream greeted me. The space was flooded by light from the oversized windows and the living room unfolded toward the kitchen. A velvet L-shaped sofa and glass coffee table faced a fireplace that was out of place with the sweltering heat. A dining table sat beneath one window. At its center were a dozen or more white candles in all sizes and shapes.

"May I show you around?" Tommy asked.

"Thank you," I agreed.

He circled the sofa and walked down a hallway, flipping the light as he went. I followed. "Through here is the master bedroom."

I peered into the room and saw a large four-post bed, resplendently covered with white linens and throw pillows. French doors led to a backyard, which Tommy pointed out. "And around the corner is the bath."

He exited the room and walked down the hall. "Through here is the office."

This room was darker than the rest, with navy wall coverings and a dark wooden desk that looked through the French door. "Very nice," I stated.

He continued down the hall. "And in case you have visitors, this is the guest room."

One look inside and I knew Athena would love her home

away from home. The bed coverings matched the fluffy master bed and there was a reading nook under the window that faced—"a swimming pool!"

My comment elicited the first smile out of Tommy since he had collected me at baggage claim. "Yes, Ms. Snow, there is a swimming pool and barbecue in the garden."

He exited the room and circled back to the kitchen. The counters gleamed white and a large bowl of citrus fruits stood prominently at the center. "The refrigerator is stocked and you should find everything you need in the cupboards."

It was a first for me and I didn't hide my enthusiasm. "It is more than I need and I can't wait to try out that pool."

His straight face was relentless as he reeled off instructions for later. "You have some time before dinner with Marty Shaw and Clyde Parks. I'll come back to collect you at six o'clock. In the meantime, if you require anything, you have my number."

He walked toward the door and I called, "Thank you, Mr. Smith."

With the tilt of his chin he replied, "You're welcome, Ms. Snow."

As I watched him edge down the driveway, I let the doubts come creeping in. Was I worth all of this? What if I couldn't solve the breach? Then I remembered the swimming pool and decided I'd worry about that later.

After a winding drive uphill, we pulled to the front of the Castaway restaurant. A valet rushed to open the door. Tommy called, "Text me when things are winding down and I'll be back around to collect you."

"Thank you," I replied as I exited the car, squelching the nerves that had been building with every turn of the wheel. I smoothed my black pencil skirt and straightened my shoulders. Putting one foot in front of the next, I took the last few steps and a deep breath.

The restaurant was hectic and as I waited to speak with the hostess, I surveyed my surroundings. An ornate lattice wall in rich wood separated the entrance from the dining area. The gleaming marble floors, though glamorous, did little to dampen the noise. To the side was a wall of wine bottles the height of the twelve-foot ceilings.

It was my turn at the podium and a tall blonde with cornflower blue eyes greeted me, "Good evening. Welcome to Castaway. What name is the reservation under?"

"Shaw. I'm meeting Marty Shaw."

She perked at the sound of his name, "Certainly," she said and shined her pearly whites my direction, "this way."

Her halted walk—a runway habit she'd no doubt spent years perfecting—set the pace for our stroll through the swanky hot spot. I tried to match her poise as I sauntered past celebrities like Antonio Banderas and Susan Lucci.

We crossed the dining area and made our way toward a wall of glass. The door swung wide as we approached. She continued through and I followed in the wake of her bewitching fragrance until, finally, we arrived at a table on the edge of the patio.

"Mr. Shaw, your guest has arrived." Her megawatt smile could be seen from the valley below. Two men, Marty Shaw and presumably Clyde Parks, stood to greet us.

Marty addressed the svelte hostess, "Thank you, Melinda."

She nodded, "Mr. Shaw."

He turned. "Welcome to Cali, Evelyn."

"Thank you, Marty. I'm excited to be here."

"Let me introduce you to our producer, Clyde Parks."

The man circled the table and came to face me. His voice

was soothing and handshake firm. "Evelyn, it's good to meet you."

He was just over six feet with blond hair that had gone salt and pepper at the temples. His soft brown eyes were framed by oversized lashes, reminiscent of a cow. I found him unnervingly attractive, therefor my tone was deliberately crisp, "You as well, Clyde."

"Please," he gestured toward a chair by the glass wall, "have a seat."

I sat and took in the dusky sky as the sun fell behind the darkening range. "The view is incredible."

"I'm glad you like it," Marty stated from the seat next to me.

"Champagne?" Clyde offered and pulled a bottle from an ice bucket.

I reminded myself I was in Hollywood and champagne on a Sunday evening for no celebratory purpose was probably rote for them. "Thank you," I agreed.

Clyde filled three flutes then raised his glass in toast, "To Evelyn, our double agent."

Marty chimed, "Hear, hear."

I was unsettled by the pressure of their salute, but held my doubt at bay. As I sipped, the effervescent bubbles tickled my dry throat and tasted divine. "Thank you both for your confidence in me."

Clyde opened the conversation, "Evelyn, have you decided on a pseudonym yet?"

"A pseudonym?" I inquired.

"Yes. What have you come up with?"

I'd need to think fast as I should have considered the ramifications of using my real name in the era of Google. "Would either of you like to do the honors?"

Marty cleared his throat and I turned to face him. He was a slight man, with thinning hair and beady blue eyes that darted across the table to Clyde. "What would we name her if she were an actress?"

Clyde's attention was disconcerting, but I kept my back straight under his scrutiny. "Let's think about it. This little warrior is going to find our leak and when she does, it's going to be explosive."

Marty studied me as if I were an animal in the zoo. "Agreed."

Clyde continued talking like I wasn't there. "I say we call her Truth Nadine Tuesday."

Marty's sparse mustache twitched and he agreed, "TNT! It's perfect and Tuesday is my favorite day of the week."

I shouldn't have admired Clyde's dimples as he smiled in my direction and raised his glass, "To Truth."

With a shift of my shoulders, I swallowed my new name and the tasty wine.

Now that creating my alias was done, Marty suggested, "Shall we look at the menu?"

I quickly surveyed the options and set my menu aside. Marty and Clyde did as well, and in an instant, a server in a bow tie and vest inquired. His tone was almost superior, "Are you ready to order dinner?"

The men looked at me. "I'll have the short ribs, please."

Marty was next, "Salmon for me."

And it was Clyde's turn, "Short ribs as well."

"Very good," the waiter replied. "Is there anything else you need at the moment?"

Marty replied, "That will be all for now. Thanks."

With the introductions and ordering behind us, I thought it was a good time to get into the project plan. I pulled a notepad from my purse and started in. "I hope you don't mind, but I've got a list of items I want to review with you."

"Not at all," Marty agreed.

"First, I'd like to check that the IT department received

my instructions for the email audit of all employee messages over the course of the past two years. The parameters were outlined in accordance with your Acceptable Use Policies."

"Yes," Marty replied, "I spoke with Jim Gage about the audit last week. They started the process late Thursday, so we should have some data by next week."

"Thank you. Will I be able to meet with Jim, or should I limit my communication with him to email and telephone calls?"

Marty's intake of breath and downcast expression told me he was uncomfortable. "For now, we should keep you at arm's length from everyone except the executives and Tommy, of course."

"All right," I agreed. "What about the enhancements to your surveillance system? Have those been implemented?"

Marty nodded. "They have and you have been given full access to every feed on the lot, including the covert cameras."

"Thank you. I want to be frank with you: Since your writers use laptops to work remotely and they aren't required to use a secure VPN to log into your network, this could take a more personal approach."

"How so?" Clyde inquired.

"Well, depending on what anomalies to your AUP we find, the next steps might require access to the actual computer, face to face interviews and even physical surveillance."

Clyde questioned, "Physical surveillance?"

"Yes, there is a contingency to hire additional staff to follow suspects."

Clyde's expression showed a combination of humor and faux fear. "I'm sorry," he chuckled. "You are not exactly what I expected."

I had to ask, "Meaning?"

"Please don't take this the wrong way, but you look like

you could be one of our actresses, yet you're this badass, super smart investigator and it's throwing me."

Marty shook his head, and apologized, "You'll have to forgive Clyde. We don't let him off the set much."

I laughed at them both. "Shall we continue?"

"Please," Marty insisted.

"Before we go to the lengths of surveilling anyone, we need to collect computers and audit the actual hard drives to verify that no external USB or cloud storage has been used."

Clyde asked, "How would we explain that and what is that going to cost me? I need my writers to be productive and they can't write without computers."

"Understood," I assured. "That step, if necessary, won't be for a couple of weeks. We'll send a notice to the entire staff with instructions for an upcoming software update. To keep productivity up, we'll stagger the process so only one computer is being audited at a time. That will limit the downtime."

"Sounds reasonable," Clyde agreed but his expression went stern.

"Listen, I know this is unpleasant, but you have a traitor on your crew. Once we find the leak, you'll be able to move forward with confidence."

"I know," Clyde stated. "It sounds like you've got a solid plan."

"Thank you. Now, may I ask what to expect on my first day? I want to be a convincing Production Assistant so I need a crash course."

Clyde's cheeky smile came alive. "Well, for one, it's a movie set and though you look like an actress, your job is mostly grunt work. People, including me, will be barking orders at you all day." He raised his hand and swept it my direction, "Don't dress like that."

"Got it. Denim it is."

He nodded.

Marty spoke up. "We've got a trailer set up for you where you can do your work when you're not on the set."

"Excellent," I said.

Clyde addressed Marty. "How do we explain her?" He glanced my way. "No offense but PAs are usually kids fresh out of film school."

I was certain butterflies exited my mouth before the words did, "That won't be a problem. I'm actually taking a screenwriting workshop while I'm here. Why don't you say I was referred by the school?"

"Wait, let me wrap my head around this. You are a techie, a double agent, a security expert and a writer?"

I was suddenly flushed. "No, I'm not a writer, but I like writing and I thought it would be a good cover."

Clyde looked at Marty and said, "Stay tuned, she may write our next feature and find the rat in our midst."

DUAL AGENCY

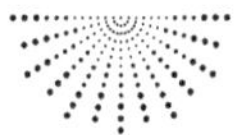

*J*awoke and was surprised to find an envelope had been slipped through the mail slot in the night. It contained a badge with my picture and a credit card, both issued under my new name, Truth Nadine Tuesday. Per protocol, I wore the identification card as I left the house. Presumably, this bit of identification would open the gates to the world behind Hollywood's most popular daytime television show, Twist of Fate. The irony of the show's title didn't escape me as this assignment was also a twist of fate for me.

My temporary home was under a mile from the studio, making it easy for me to walk to work. The early morning greeted me with near quiet and only a few early birds' calls could be heard. I used the commute to remind myself of the things I needed to accomplish today and in the coming months. The first day at a new job was always nerve racking. Today I would start two jobs at once.

After a short walk, the wrought iron gate came into view. Taking the last few paces with focused breath, I approached the booth and a security guard addressed me through a hole in the bulletproof glass. "Good morning. May I see your identification?"

I removed the ID and handed it through the slot. He scanned it and after a moment said, "Have a good first day."

With that, he slid the badge in my direction and released the pedestrian gate for me to enter. "Your orientation will begin at building six. Follow the walkway until you reach craft services and take a left. It will be the first trailer on your left."

"Thank you," I said and pressed through the heavy door. I followed his instructions, soaking in the terrain as I went. I'd been given a studio map and blueprints as a part of my onboarding, but it wasn't the same as seeing the lot in person.

I followed the walkway and took in the early morning activity. The stage crew huddled around an unseen director who disseminated today's objectives. A crane moved slowly to my left. At the end of its chain dangled a set of stairs, beneath which were six gloved men, ready to assist in placing it on the set. There were rows of trailers with actors' names emblazoned above the doors. Quickly, I arrived at the craft services tent and after taking a left, I found trailer six.

The metal stairs swayed as I took the last few steps into my new role. Before opening the door, I made a silent plea, *Please, let this work.*

"Good morning." A young woman behind a counter greeted. "You must be Truth."

The name sounded foreign, if silly, but I confirmed, "I am."

Her curly brown hair moved excitedly as she said, "I'm Bernice. Welcome to the set of Twist of Fate."

"Thank you, Bernice."

"I have a few items for you to review and sign before your tour. Here's a clipboard and the forms I need you to accept.

You can have a seat over there and come back up when you're done."

I followed her directions and took a chair at the corner. After a quick perusal, I swiftly executed the documents as I'd already authorized them once, but under my real identity.

Returning to her station, I said, "Here you are, Bernice."

She commented, "Wow, that was fast."

"Yes," I explained, "I'm somewhat of a speed reader."

"Terrific, that could come in handy around here." She studied her screen and announced, "You've got a fantastic assignment."

"Oh?" I played coy.

"Yes, you will be working directly with our Senior Producer, Mr. Clyde Parks."

"Exciting," I replied.

"I'll say. It's the assignment everyone wants. You'll be the envy of all the PAs."

"I'm honored."

She stood and circled the counter. "Let's get you to the staff meeting, so you're not late for your first day."

I followed her outside and as we walked, she pointed to different sections of the lot. "As you came in, you saw where the refreshments are. The restrooms and a gym are over here," she waved her hand left, "and the different sets are along this path," she waved toward a row of modified warehouses, with rollup doors pulled open. I peered inside and saw real-life versions of the places I'd watched on screen as I boned up on my daytime television preparing for the job.

We arrived at the last warehouse and she said, "The staff meeting is in here."

I followed her inside the combination lounge and storage room. Half of the space was filled with oddities such as a clown costume, lamps, tables and assorted furniture. On the opposite side was a long table with a couple dozen chairs, around which stood a variety of cast members and crew. I noticed several vaguely familiar faces that had yet to see "hair and makeup." We approached the group and Bernice cut through the crowd to find my new boss.

"Good morning, Mr. Parks."

He replied, "Good morning, Bernice."

"Allow me to introduce you to your new PA, Truth Tuesday."

A near smirk played at the corner of his mouth, but he kept it together. "Welcome to the team, Truth."

"I'm honored to be here, Mr. Parks."

"Call me Clyde. You too, Bernie."

"Thank you, sir," Bernice replied. "Well, I'd better get back," she stated. "Check back with me after the staff meeting. I should have your computer and other items from IT by then. Oh, and Mr. Parks—"

Clyde's raised brows had her sputtering, "I'm sorry, Clyde, the new trailer you requested is ready. Here are the keys."

He accepted them, "Thank you, Bernice."

"Of course," she said. "I'll see you soon, Truth."

"Thank you."

His sharp whistle got everyone's attention as the director, Ron James, swept into the space. He was slender and gaunt in the face. His bald head shined under the florescent lighting. "Good morning, everyone. Let's get started."

He made a beeline for Clyde as the balance of the group quickly took their seats. "Who do we have here?" he asked as he approached.

"Ron, meet Truth Tuesday, my new PA."

He chuckled, "Truth Tuesday, huh? That sounds like a stage name. You're not an aspiring actress, are you?"

Clyde answered on my behalf, "No, a screenwriter."

Ron nodded, "Aspire away, just not on my dime. You've

got an important and demanding job here. If you want to keep the PA spot, you'd better hustle."

"I'll do my best."

"Fine, take a seat."

I settled in next to Clyde as Ron brought the meeting to order. "Good morning, everyone."

The group chanted, "Good morning."

"Before we get started, let me introduce you to our newest slave, I mean PA, Truth Tuesday. Don't get nervous about the name, she's already assured me she's not an actress in disguise. She's assigned to Clyde's team."

A few of the staff waved, or said "welcome."

"Truth, would you like to say anything before we begin?"

It was a dreamlike moment as I addressed the famous actors and professionals who thought I belonged. "Thank you, everyone. I'm happy to be here and please let me know how I can help."

Ron sneered, "Don't worry, they will. Okay, let's get going."

He was commanding and efficient as he reeled off the day's objectives. "Today's schedule is as follows: We'll start with the hospital scene, then move to the breakup between Rebecca and Manny. After that we're filming the cave act and to finish us off—ha, ha, ha—the suicide attempt."

A few staff members chuckled, but most sat silent and sipping coffee. He scanned the table. "Are there any issues we need to deal with before we tackle the day?"

A man raised his hand. Ron demanded, "Chuck, what is it?"

"They're setting the stairs as we speak. It may make sense to shift the scenes around to give the team a little more time."

I looked back at Ron and saw his jaw clench. "Unacceptable, Chuck. You of all people know the time crunch we're under. Why isn't this done?"

"The crane broke down and we didn't get a replacement until early this morning."

Ron shook his head, obviously disappointed by the explanation, and studied his laptop. "Okay, let's move the breakup scene to last position."

A miffed sound emanated from one actress, Mandy Rowe. "Sorry, Mandy, I know you've got the little one at home. If you need to bring him on set, I'm sure our new PA can keep an eye on him for you."

She looked doubtfully in my direction. "Thanks, but I'll ask my nanny to accompany him. Please get her clearance set."

"Done. Truth, handle that."

"Sure," I agreed and made a note in my tablet.

He asked, "Anything else, people?"

The silence confirmed there were no other problems. "Great, get to it." With that Ron stood and marched toward the exit and the balance of the crew followed.

Clyde hung back, as did I. When the room was empty, he addressed me, "Nice job so far. Come find me at the hospital set after you've finished with Bernice."

"I will," I said and we parted ways as I backtracked to the administrative office.

I opened the trailer door and Bernice practically leapt from her chair. "How was your first staff meeting?"

Her cheerful demeanor was overwhelming, but I tried to match her enthusiasm. "It went pretty well. Ron James is kind of intense, huh?"

"Oh yes, but you have to understand the pressure he's under. We're in a battle with Big Fish Productions for the number one daytime TV spot and he doesn't like to lose, nor do the executives."

"That makes sense. I don't mean to gossip, but it seems like you know everyone here. What can you tell me?"

Her eyes danced with excitement. "Let's just say, Twist of Fate isn't only the title of our show. There's enough inside drama here and no script required."

I pressed, "Really? How so?"

The phone rang behind her. "I'd love to dish, but duty calls."

"Of course," I said.

"Here's your computer and walkie-talkie. There's also a headset in the bag."

"Thanks," I said and I remembered my first official assignment. I grabbed the Post-its from the counter and scribbled, "Mandy Rowe needs clearance for her nanny and child to visit the studio today."

Though Bernice was already on the call, she nodded and gave me a thumbs up. "Lonnie, I apologize, but could you hold for one moment? Thank you," she said in a sugary tone.

"I'll take care of this for you."

"Thanks, I owe you."

And she waved me off simultaneous to resuming the call.

I slung the laptop bag over my shoulder and made my way to the hospital set, wondering what Bernice could tell me. I decided a girls' happy hour might help loosen her lips.

"Quiet, quiet on the set," a man in black jeans and a T-shirt called. Mindful not to make noise as I approached, I came to stand near Clyde.

He looked down and placed his index finger over his lips to signal silence. I nodded and turned my attention to the set. A medical monitor beeped steadily in the background while a faux nurse adjusted the fake IV drip and exited the room. A grandmotherly woman sat beside the unconscious patient with a tissue clenched firmly in her hand.

"My darling Beau, you have to wake up now. You've had enough rest and I can't do this without you."

I'd caught up on the latest episodes and knew that Beau was in a coma after falling down a flight of stairs. What his wife, Sally, didn't know was that their adopted son, Thomas, had pushed her husband during a heated argument. Thomas had dependency issues and Beau refused to give him more money, which infuriated the young man.

On cue, Thomas arrived for a visit. "Hi, Mom," his tone was somber. Suddenly, the machine beeped more rapidly.

Sally stood slowly, using the bed's railing to hoist herself up. She shuffled toward her son, then fell into his arms with a sob.

"There, there, Mom. It'll be okay."

She pulled back and sniffed into her tissue. "I hope you're right," she said and cried more.

"Is there any news from the doctor?"

In true daytime television fashion, Doctor Taylor knocked on the doorframe. "Good morning, Mrs. Hotsworth."

"Good morning, doctor," she managed. "This is our son, Thomas."

Dr. Taylor extended his hand to shake, "Hello, Thomas. I'm Brian Taylor."

Thomas's earnest expression was chilling, given his act of violence. "What's the situation, doctor?"

"Well," he flipped pages on his chart, "his brain activity is improving, but the swelling is still a major factor. We've done everything we can. I'm afraid the rest is up to him."

The machine's beeping became erratic and a group of nurses rushed into the room.

"Thomas, Mrs. Hotsworth, I need you to leave."

They both stared at the unconscious man in the bed. "Thomas," the doctor barked, "get her out of here."

The son reacted to the doctor's orders and spirited his mother from the room.

"And cut. Great scene, everyone."

"Let's get moving with the nurses, quickly. We're shooting again in five."

I watched as makeup artists touched up the actors' faces and adjusted their hairstyles. The prop team was busy moving equipment. The reception counter was replaced by rows of chairs as they designed a waiting room. When they were finished, Sally and Thomas took their places.

Ron shouted over the action, "We're starting with the patient, then we'll move to the waiting room. Places, everyone."

It was fascinating to see everything come together and in no time, they'd shot the other two scenes. The drama continued as the father remained in a coma and Dr. Taylor shared the news with the family. Finally, Ron called, "That's a wrap. Crew, take thirty then I'll see you at the cave."

Clyde addressed me. "We have a few minutes. Why don't we go find your trailer?"

"Sounds good," I agreed.

The lot was heating up both in temperature and activity. It seemed almost everyone we passed had something to say to Clyde. He was polite and engaging but steadfast in keeping us on track. After a short walk to the back lot, we arrived at a trailer with the name Tuesday on the door.

"How do you like that?" He asked referring to my fake name.

"It's great," I joked. "Wait, how did you get that done so quickly?"

His smile almost made me swoon. "This is Hollywood, Evelyn. Things move fast here."

"So I see," I said as he held the door for me to enter.

I stepped into the trailer with Clyde closely behind. It

looked new and modern. There was a large television mounted from the ceiling, a white leather sofa beneath a window and a small table to the side. There was even a micro kitchen.

"Check this out," he crossed the room and tapped a wooden wall. When he did, a hidden door opened and a desk unfolded, behind which was a monitor. It was powered up and all twenty surveillance cameras streamed live.

"Nice," I said as I took command. I checked a few settings and adjusted the views per my requirements while Clyde opened the mini-fridge and pulled out a bottle of water. He took two glasses from the shelf and poured water in them.

I tried to focus on working with the video system, but the intimacy of the tight quarters was a little distracting with my handsome new "boss" so near.

"Find anything yet?" he asked as he set a glass beside me.

"Sorry, I don't work as fast as you do, but with a few tweaks, at least the lot will be more secure."

"I hate to show you this and drag you away again, but we're due at the cave set. There will be a lunch break before the afternoon sessions. You can take your meal here. I'll cover if anyone asks where you went."

"Okay," I said and rose, "thanks, Clyde."

"You can leave your things, but bring the headset and walkie-talkie. You need to look legit." He handed me the key as we made our way to the cave.

"And, cut! Nice work, people. Let's reconvene at 1PM for the suicide scene," Ron's voice called to the already departing crew.

He came to where Clyde and I were standing. "How are the writers coming with my next episodes?"

"They're coming," Clyde commented without inflection. Did I sense some tension between the two men?

"I'd like to see some pages tomorrow." It wasn't a request.

"You'll see the script when I'm satisfied with the plot. You've got two weeks of taping before you need the next episodes so cool down."

Ron's eyes darted to me and he commanded, "Would you give us a minute?"

The air was thick with unspoken frustration and though I should have wanted to observe their dynamic, I was grateful to obey orders. "Certainly. I'll see you both at the next taping. I've got my walkie-talkie if you need anything before then."

"See you shortly," Clyde replied.

As I left for lunch, I knew if I wanted to get to the bottom of their breach, I needed insight into the set politics. On my way to get something to eat, I decided to pop in for another visit with Bernice.

I opened the trailer door and she was wrapping up a call. "Thank you. We'll see you then."

"Hey," I called, "busy day?"

"Nothing unusual," she replied. "How's your first day so far?"

"It's been interesting. I'm heading to lunch. Do you have time for a break?"

She looked worried toward her work station but said, "Sure, I can take ten minutes."

As we walked to lunch, I asked, "So, what do you think of Ron James?"

Her brows rose and she looked over her shoulder. In a conspiring tone she said, "He's tough but brilliant. Though lately, he's been even more intense than usual."

"Really? How so?" I asked, but we were in proximity to the lunch area and I saw her hesitation. "Why don't I ask you again later? Want to get a drink after work?"

She looked relieved and excited. "I'd love that. There's a good place just a few blocks from here. It's kind of divey."

"That sounds great," I said. "I'll come get you when we're done for the day."

We took our lunch quickly and with frequent interruptions as Bernice introduced me to a number of grips and electricians who worked on the set. I'd yet to meet any of the writers or actors and I wondered where they were.

"What about the actors and writers? Don't they eat lunch?" I asked.

"Yes, of course, but they take meals at their trailers or in the writers' room." She glanced at her watch. "I'd better get back, but I'll see you later, right?"

"Looking forward to it," I agreed.

After she left, I made my way back to the trailer and buried myself in the CCTV system. My first order of business was to tap into the feed that recorded Ron and Clyde's encounter today. Perhaps the tension between them was normal, but I had a duty to check it out. I forwarded the footage until I found the part where I'd exited and watched their exchange as a voyeur. Though there was no audio in the feed—I couldn't utilize microphones and adhere to most of the contracts between the actors and the studio—I could tell from their body language the conversation didn't go any better after I left. At the end, Ron threw up his hands and stomped out as Clyde made a slow exit behind him.

A knock at the door startled me and I clicked the close button on the review screen. "Come in," I called.

Clyde opened the door and quickly closed it behind him. "Hey there," he greeted. "Did you get something to eat?"

"I did, thanks. Bernice and I had lunch together and she was nice enough to introduce me around. I was disappointed that I didn't get to meet any of the writers though."

"Let's remedy that after the next taping." He took a seat

on the couch and ventured, "I guess you noticed the rub between Ron and me?"

There was no point denying his question. "Hard to miss."

He nodded, thoughtful. "He's a strong director. I respect him. We've worked together for a long time. Lately he's been more intense than usual. Between us, he's going through a divorce and it's not helping his mood."

I offered a neutral response in the hopes he'd continue. "That's too bad."

"It is. He's been married for fifteen years. He was always a pain in the ass, but it's worse now that his life is in turmoil."

"Oh," I commented.

"Yeah, he's a control freak, which makes him a great director, but as you can imagine since he's out of his element at home, the job is becoming even more important."

I certainly could relate to the feeling of being out of your element. My question wasn't necessarily applicable and I blurted it before I fully thought it through. "Have you been divorced?"

His brows rose. "Yes, a long time ago. It was difficult. The kids were twelve and fourteen. I remember feeling like I'd crushed them by tearing our family apart."

I empathized with him and I knew my curiosity wasn't strictly professional. He was attractive and real. I said, "Me too."

He sounded surprised. "You've been divorced?"

"Yes, also a long time ago. My daughter was nine."

"So, you know how it is."

I agreed, "I do."

"Well, we'd better head out. We don't want to make Ron any surlier."

After several takes, the breakup scene between Rebecca and Manny was finally a wrap. Clyde took me by the elbow. "Let's get you introduced to the voices behind it all."

The late-day sun was sweltering as we walked across the lot and into a building close to the entrance. There must have been twenty desks, all with laptops aglow and people reading or typing furiously on their keyboards.

"Do you have the revision to the fight scene yet?" one person called.

Clyde spoke in a conspiring tone, "Welcome to the writers' room. Maybe one day you'll have a spot here."

His comment excited me. I indulged the fantasy for only a moment, picturing myself at home surrounded by a sea of desks and printers. Lining the wall was an elaborate coffee and tea station but little else.

A lanky woman with dark circles under her eyes approached. "Hi, Clyde. This must be the new PA."

Clyde replied, "I sometimes forget how quickly news travels around here. Yes, Rebba Frank, meet Truth Tuesday."

She smiled, "Now I see what all the talk is about."

We shook hands and I said, "It's an honor to meet you, Rebba."

Clyde explained, "Rebba is our Executive Story Editor."

She smiled broadly, "Trust me, the title is more glamourous than the work. I hear you are an aspiring writer."

The cover was helpful, but my self-doubt rose at her mention of my interest. "I am. I'll be starting class at the film academy in a couple of weeks."

"Great, well, you're in the right place to learn. I look forward to reading your pages when you get going."

I didn't have to act, as it was a most generous and intimidating offer. "That would be incredible if humbling."

"Yep, she's a writer. You can tell by the insecurity."

Clyde chuckled, "If we don't get to the suicide set on time, she's going to be without a job, so we'd better take off. If you don't mind, I'm going to assign her to work with you part-time."

"Great, we can always use the help. Good to meet you, Truth. By the way, that's quite a name. If I didn't know any better, I'd think it was made up."

I shocked myself with the ease in which I found a supporting lie that couldn't have been less likely when you considered my father. "Yes, my parents had quite a sense of humor. I blame the '70s."

"Ahh, my people," she commented.

Clyde commanded, "We'd better go."

"Clyde, do you have time to connect after the taping? I'd like to review the changes you requested."

"Yep, I'll stop by later."

"Great to meet you, Rebba," I said as we departed.

We sat in the dingy bar. A layer of stickiness, decades old, covered everything and the vague essence of vomit wafted. The bartender set two martinis in front of us and Bernice raised her glass. "You made it through your first day. I bet you're thirsty after drinking from that firehose."

I chuckled, "You have no idea."

"Cheers," she chimed.

"Cheers," I copied and sipped. It tasted marvelous, but I knew I needed to take it slow as I was still on the clock and the unwitting Bernice was being interviewed. "So, how long have you worked for Base?"

"Oh, it's been four years now."

"Do you like it?"

"Most of the time I love my job," she said.

"What about the times when you don't," I asked.

"You know how it is. Even if you love your work, there are always some things you don't like."

"Such as?" I pressed.

"A few of the actors are high maintenance and though they have assistants, I end up picking up some slack. One in particular."

She said it as a teaser and I knew she wanted to dish. I leaned in, "Which one?"

"You've already met her: Ms. Mandy Rowe."

I nodded, recalling how miffed she was by the schedule change. "Yes, we were introduced this morning."

She chuckled, "Was she rude to you?"

"Honestly, she acted like I wasn't there."

She took a sip of her drink. "That's her trademark—even when you're doing her a favor. She's quite entitled and the execs feed into it because she's so popular with the fans."

"You don't like her much, do you?"

She looked over her shoulder before agreeing, "No, not really."

"What else can you tell me? Who's been to rehab? Any on-set romances?"

Her expression went wary. "Why are you so interested?"

Shit, I needed to ease up or get her to have another round. "I want to avoid any landmines and you know, writers are curious."

This seemed to put her at ease. "Sorry," she replied, "I hope that didn't sound paranoid. It's not a good idea to gossip when you're in my position."

"I understand," I said and got the bartender's attention. "Can we have another round please?"

I looked toward Bernice and she shrugged, "Why not? I need a stop at the ladies' first."

"I'll be here," I said and when the door closed, I poured

the rest of my martini into my water glass. I'd save the "truth" serum for my unwitting spy.

Three martinis later—half as many on my part—Bernice had slurred through a rundown of most of the staff. I learned that one of the writers was fresh out of rehab, a grip was going through an IRS audit, and several people were either in the throes of affairs or terrible breakups. She was right—the cast and crew of Twist of Fate offered plenty of drama.

We staggered toward the door, she in earnest and I as an act, and when her Uber arrived, I gave her a hug and said, "Thanks for the girls' night and don't worry, your secrets are safe with me."

She chuckled and pointed, "You are the best PA we've ever had."

"Such an honor and on day one. Text me when you're home."

MISS BROWN VISITS

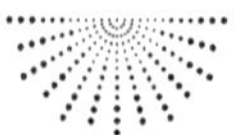

After two weeks of double duty, I was no closer to discovering the leak in the Base Productions staff. The message I—or should I say, Evelyn Snow—received from Jim in IT confirmed the keyword searches and deep dive into the violators yielded little more than the typical infractions. Porn sites and internet dating applications seemed quite popular among the crew, but I wasn't hired to ferret out sex addicts. Even my happy hour gossip sessions with Bernice, though fun, had proven fruitless.

I slid the smart phone into my bag and continued through the exit gates for the walk home. Though I was anxious about the lack of progress on the case, I had plenty of reason to look forward to the weekend. Athena was visiting and nothing could put me at ease like two days with my daughter.

I'd just exited the lot when a voice penetrated my thoughts. "Truth," Clyde called from his car.

"Hi there!" I replied.

"Let me give you a lift."

"Sure," I agreed and got in.

"How's it going?" he inquired.

I assumed he was referring to the investigation so I launched into an explanation. "Unfortunately, I'm no closer to discovering the leak. Jim got back to me and the results were anything but extraordinary, unless you want to know who likes busty babes."

He chuckled, "I hardly think we needed an investigation to uncover that bit of trivia."

"Agreed," I said. "I'm sorry this isn't going faster."

Clyde glanced over, and the late-day light made him squint. "No need to apologize. It's only been a couple of weeks and you warned us this may happen."

I nodded but still felt like I was letting them down. Clyde picked up the conversation. "Any fun plans this weekend?"

I couldn't stop the smile from forming. "As a matter of fact, yes. My daughter is visiting. She's going to be here in a few hours."

"That's great," he said. His smile made me feel like a schoolgirl with a crush. "What are you guys going to do?"

"All the touristy stuff, stroll through Hollywood and daydream shop in Beverly Hills."

"Sounds almost perfect," he said and pulled into the driveway of my home away from home.

"Well, thank you for the ride. I'll see you on Monday," I said.

"Or sooner," he replied and backed down the drive.

I wasn't sure what to think of his comment, but it didn't matter. I had a memo to draft before Athena arrived.

Headlights shone on the driveway announcing Athena's arrival. I stood so quickly, the chair fell behind me. Perfect timing too, as I'd just hit send on the memo that would begin the Base Production computer "upgrade," which was really an activity audit.

I burst out the door and nearly pushed Tommy out of the way as we fought to open the car door for Athena. "Mommy, I missed you," she exclaimed and hugged me tight.

"Baby, look at you," I studied my daughter at arm's length and she looked even more stunning than usual. Her slender frame was highlighted by the simple black T-shirt dress.

Tommy busied himself with carrying her bag inside as we strolled toward the house. "Tommy," I said, "thank you for collecting her."

"You're welcome, Evelyn."

I smiled and relished in finally breaking his nasty habit of using my last name. "Would you like to join us for a drink?"

"Thank you, but I've got someplace to be."

Athena chimed, "Thanks for the celebrity pickup, Tommy. I'll see you on Sunday."

"You will, Miss," he smiled and walked back to the car.

"Come inside and let me get a good look at you." Her hair was pulled into a messy bun and her face, though devoid of makeup, glowed. It wasn't only maternal pride; she was more beautiful than all of the actresses in Hollywood. "You are such a sight."

"You too, Mommy. You're so tan."

"Let me show you why." I took her by the hand and led her down the hallway to her bedroom. "This is your room."

She dove into the bed, tossing pillows with the action. "I'm never going to leave."

"Especially after you see this," I opened the French doors and stepped outside.

She leaned in the doorway. "A house with a pool? Are you ever coming home?"

Her comment struck a chord. As much as I loved my house in Oregon, I hadn't missed being there. The double duty left little time for longing and I wondered how I'd manage once the screenwriting class started next week. The side benefit was I had no time to dwell on my former dating fiascos back home, which was a good thing. "I can't deny I'll miss it here when I go home, but you are a bigger draw than any swimming pool.

"Why don't you get changed? I've got some food ready. We can catch up while you take a dip."

"Done," she agreed.

I yawned involuntarily and Athena said, "Is it sleepy time for Mommy?"

"I guess I am a little tired. My morning started at 5:30AM."

"Well, maybe we should get some rest. There's so much I want to see tomorrow and we don't have much time. Besides, I promised Nick I'd call him before bed."

It warmed me to think of Athena with Nick. "It's going well then?"

Her smile was uninhibited, as was her reply, "I love him and he loves me."

"Oh honey, that's wonderful. I'm so happy for you."

She leaned back, "Me too. I just wish the same for you."

"Stop," I held up a hand. "I've got a full life and more love than I can handle." As I said it my phone buzzed. I tapped on the text indicator and it was a message from Clyde. It read, "Check your email."

It was late for him to contact me and his vague text left me wondering. I opened my Truth Tuesday account and found his message. The subject said, "How about a real Beverly Hills experience?" Since there was nothing further in the body of the message, I opened the attachment. It was an itinerary. He'd booked us facials, massages and pedicures at the Spa Montage in Beverly Hills, followed by an 8PM dinner reservation for three.

My expression was a tell as Athena asked, "What's the matter?"

I shook my head. "Nothing is the matter. Give me a second."

I quickly replied to Clyde's text, "What on earth? I don't know what to say."

Three dots indicated he was about to reply. "Say thank you and I look forward to dinner tomorrow night."

I inhaled and wondered what to think of his generous gift. Instead of overthinking, I embraced it in the spirit of Hollywood's decadence. "Thank you, Clyde. I look forward to dinner tomorrow night."

His reply was swift. "As do I. Until tomorrow."

I looked up to see my daughter's expectant expression and I wondered how I would explain this over the top gift. "What is it?" she demanded.

"Well, it seems my new boss has arranged a spa day and dinner at Montage for us."

"What?" She practically shouted, "Do you know how famous that place is? That's incredible! I love LA already!

As my feet dangled in the lukewarm pool, I agreed, "It does have its perks."

We began our day poolside, taking coffee and sunbathing. Athena's fair skin tanned nicely in the short time we had before our day of indulgence. When we arrived at Montage, we were immediately spirited off to the rooftop restaurant for a late lunch consisting of fresh salads with grilled salmon and açai smoothies. Athena was impressed by it all, particularly the view and the guest list. We tried for nonchalance as a few known actresses shared the space with us.

After lunch we had massages, followed by facials and to finish us, mani-pedis. I hadn't been this relaxed maybe ever, and I had Clyde to thank for the decadent bonding time with my daughter.

We ended the session sipping champagne while lounging on overstuffed chairs, soothed by the Zen tunes that floated through the air. A gentle breeze from the fan above caressed us and dried our vampy colored nails—a shade chosen by my daughter.

"Ms. Tuesday," an attendant came to my side. I looked at Athena and noticed her rolling her eyes at the sound of my pseudonym.

"Yes, that's me."

"Would you and your daughter please come with me?"

I'd thought our treatments were complete but after the day we'd had, I wasn't about to decline. I glanced at Athena as we trailed in her silent steps. "This way," she said and waved to a crimson door which opened automatically at our nearness. "Tanya will assist you from here."

"Thank you," I said, though I had no idea what assistance she was referring to.

We entered the room and were greeted by a tall blonde woman with a Swedish accent. "Good evening, ladies. Are you ready for the final act?"

Athena chimed, "What is it?"

Tanya smiled. "Take a look," she said and waved her hand toward a dressing room, inside of which hung two dresses. "Miss Athena, this one is for you. She pointed toward a black halter dress with a skirt that flowed to the knee. "And Ms. Tuesday, this is yours," she waved to a knee-length and glittery blue jersey with a slit up the side. "But first, hair and makeup."

"This is too much," I exclaimed.

"Mr. Parks insisted and you cannot deny one of our best clients."

Athena didn't hesitate to settle herself into a chair. She spoke to me through the reflection. "You need to tell me more about this Mr. Parks. What's the story with him?"

I took the seat next to her and asked, "What story do you want to hear?"

"Is he married or single?"

"Single."

Her eyes grew large. "Good-looking?"

I couldn't stop the rise at the corner of my mouth. "Yes."

"Are you dating?"

"No."

"Then why is he being so nice to us?"

"I don't know. Maybe it's a movie industry thing. You have to remember, as big a deal as this is for us, in his world, this is the norm."

"You've never had a good radar, Mom. I bet he likes you."

"Athena, your imagination is something I truly love about you, but I don't think so. He's just being nice. People can be kind without an agenda."

She pressed, "Why don't you think he likes you?"

I huffed, "Because he's a famous producer. He probably dates a new actress every week and in case you haven't noticed, I'm not one."

"You don't see yourself very clearly, Mom. You're just as pretty as they are."

"That's enough champagne for you," I kidded.

"I'm looking forward to dinner and meeting YOUR Mr. Parks."

I protested, "He's not MY Mr. Parks."

She smirked in the mirror, "I'll be the judge of that."

We arrived at the restaurant and after a brief wait, were directed to the bar, where Clyde was waiting. As we rounded the corner, I was grateful for Athena's presence, which helped temper my nervousness. Her comments as we were getting ready unsettled me and I wondered if there was any truth in her observations. Quickly we found our benefactor sitting on a barstool.

He noticed us approach and stood to greet us. His eyes danced from me to Athena and back again. "Wow. Look at you two." He said as he hugged me briefly. "This must be Athena."

She was all smiles and said, "And you must be THE Mr. Parks."

"Call me Clyde. It's a pleasure to meet you."

She replied, "You as well, Clyde."

"Mr. Parks," the host commented, "your table is ready."

"Thank you," he said and gestured for Athena and me to go ahead.

We wove through the restaurant with all eyes on us, or should I say my daughter. The dress he'd selected fit like it was made for her. With an open back that highlighted her sun kissed skin and her hair swept into a twist, she looked elegant and so grown up. I wasn't too angry at the ogling men we passed.

We arrived at the table and sat side by side with Clyde facing us. "Your waiter will be over momentarily, Mr. Parks."

He nodded, "Thank you."

Clyde's eyes sparkled in the candlelight as he said, "You look incredible, Evelyn."

He hadn't called me by my real name in so long, it sounded strange. "Thanks to you."

He shook his head, "Oh no, I won't take credit for your

beauty." He turned toward Athena, "And you have turned every head in the place. People are wondering about the new starlet in town."

Her bubbly laugh was music to my ears. "Tell me more," she said.

Before he could reply, a server arrived. "Good evening, Mr. Parks."

"Good evening," he replied.

"Would you care for any wine to start?"

"Yes." He glanced my way, "Is rosé all right with you both?"

I nodded, "It is."

"We'll have a bottle of the Whispering Angel, please."

"Excellent, I'll return shortly."

He left us and I said, "Clyde, we can't thank you enough for today. I'm afraid you've spoiled my daughter beyond hope with your outrageous generosity."

He waved a hand in dismissal. "Please, it's the least I can do. I know how close you two are and you deserve a fun respite after the double-duty you've been pulling."

"The studio is paying me quite handsomely for my efforts and you didn't have to do this."

"It's my pleasure." He turned his attention to my daughter. "Athena, I understand you've just started sophomore year. What's your major?"

"I'm studying business and renewable energy management."

"Really? Brains and beauty. I guess that saying is true: the apple doesn't fall far from the tree."

I was overwhelmed by pride. "She's a smart young woman."

At that moment the waiter returned with the bottle of wine. He poured a small amount in Clyde's glass and he picked it up with a swirl. After a quick sniff and sip, Clyde said, "Perfect."

With one hand behind his back, the waiter poured wine into each glass. "Would you care to order now or shall I let you visit?"

"Would you give us a few minutes?"

"Certainly, sir," he said and departed.

Clyde raised his glass. "Here's to the two most charming dinner companions."

"Cheers," we chimed and sipped the well-balanced wine.

He set his glass down and asked, "Are you only here for the weekend then?"

"Sadly, yes," she joked.

"I'm sure your mom is going to miss you when you leave."

I looked over at my little girl and knew he was right. "I definitely will."

"What has she told you about her assignment?"

Athena glanced my way. "She's been kind of tight-lipped. I know the reason she's here, but we haven't had much time to discuss it." She volleyed, "How do you think it's going?"

"Your mother is doing a fantastic job. Not only is she a terrific PA," he glanced around to verify no one was eavesdropping, "she's homing in on the spy in our midst."

I replied in hushed tones, "We do need to be cautious."

"You see what I mean?"

Athena laughed. "I love her name."

He chuckled and confessed, "Guilty as charged." He turned his attention to me. "Are you getting excited for your screenwriting course?"

I hadn't mentioned it to Athena yet and was met by her questioning gaze as she repeated, "Screenwriting class?"

"Yes," I answered quietly, "I decided to take the class as a cover of sorts. The staff thinks the school referred me to Base Productions as a part of my studies."

"Mom, that's cool I know you journal, but I didn't realize you were interested in taking it further."

I was embarrassed by their attention. "I thought it would give me something to do when I wasn't working."

She glanced at Clyde with raised brows. He replied, "Yes, because two demanding jobs at once weren't enough to keep your mom's attention."

I shrugged and agreed, "I guess I do tend to keep busy."

"It's admirable. Not many people could slip so easily into this world, but you've done a remarkable job. Sometimes I even forget why you're here."

"That's nice of you to say, but I am a disappointed I haven't made more progress."

He stopped me. "I'll have none of that. You're doing everything you said you would and more. I'm looking forward to seeing some pages once you get started on the screenplay."

His comment made me blush and I managed, "Let's hope it's not awful."

He shook his head. "It won't be."

Athena raised her glass. "Here's to my amazing mother and her exciting adventures in Hollywood."

"Hear, hear," Clyde chimed.

My glass joined theirs, which I followed with a gulp of the smooth wine.

<hr>

Though we'd been sitting for hours, the evening passed quickly. It was finally time to leave and Clyde suggested, "Shall we?"

"Yes," I said and we stood and walked toward the exit.

"I'll take you girls home," he said.

We rode the elevator and soon found the valet. As we

drove Clyde pointed out places of interest, which had Athena on the edge of her seat. I noticed her ease with him. Soon we arrived home and I offered, "Would you like to come in for a cup of coffee?"

Clyde refused. "Thank you, but I've dominated enough of your girls' weekend."

He got out of the car with us. Athena wasn't shy about giving him a hug. "Thank you so much for today and for taking care of Mom for me."

His eyes darted my direction and back to her. "I hope to see you again, Athena, and if the environmental studies don't pan out, keep my number handy. You never know."

She smiled. "Thank you again. I'll see you inside, Mom."

I handed her the key and turned back to him. "You made her trip. I don't know how to thank you."

"You already have. She's a delight and this was the best Saturday night I've had in years. Thank you for that."

His eyes seemed to soak in my face and for an instant it looked like he was concentrating on my lips. It was unnerving. Rather than linger, I reached up and gave him a chaste hug. "I'll see you on Monday, boss."

He shook his head. "You know I'm not really your boss. I didn't even hire you."

The org chart had occurred to me, but I played coy. "You are for the time being. Good night, Mr. Parks."

"And to you, Ms. Snow."

We brunched under the shade of the pergola. Athena was wet from her last swim in the pool before returning home. "This weekend went by too fast," I said.

"It did," she agreed. "If it weren't for Nick, I'd stay."

"Wait a minute, I'm glad you're with Nick, but what about school."

"You know what I mean. Besides, according to YOUR Clyde, there may be an opportunity here."

I snapped. "Stop that."

"I'm kidding. I know what I want to be when I grow up. It's kind of funny that you're just starting to figure it out."

"What are you talking about? I haven't changed careers."

"Not yet," she teased, "but after you write the next big screenplay, everything is going to change."

I shook my head, doubtful. "I'm not sure what possessed me to sign up for it."

"I know you, Mom. You don't jump into things and you didn't tell me, which means this really matters to you."

"Listen, I have to tell you something. It's about the case."

She leaned forward, an expectant expression on her face. "Yes?"

"We didn't come to terms."

"What do you mean? They're going to risk a lawsuit rather than do the right thing?"

"They made me an offer."

"Then I don't understand."

"Until I received it, I didn't either. Thing is, it was hush money. The contract they wanted me to sign in exchange, it pissed me off."

"Now what? You can't let them get away with it."

"Trust me, I've considered this and I'm not going to let them off the hook. I can't believe I'm saying this, but I'm telling you because I know you'll hold me to it: I'm going to use my journal entries as an outline for the screenplay."

No doubt the neighbors heard her gasp, "That's brilliant! Wait, won't they sue you?"

I smiled. "Not if it's fiction."

"Can you do that?"

"I think so."

"Wow. That's ballsy, Mom."

"Too ballsy? Will you be embarrassed?"

"Are you kidding? No way! You haven't been the same since it happened and maybe in some ways it's good, but it still makes me furious. I hate that they hurt you. I hope you write the movie and it gets filmed."

"Let's not get ahead of ourselves. This could just be an exercise and even if it is, maybe it will help me get past it."

"Are you going to show it to Clyde?"

I twisted the napkin in my lap. "I don't know. It's so personal and embarrassing. I wouldn't want him to think badly of me."

"You see, that's exactly what they're betting on, that you'll be ashamed and run away. If you're going to do this, you have to give it everything. You have to show how you felt and what they put you though. It's not just for you. It's for all women. We make up more than half the population but we're paid less than men and there are so many double standards that have to go away. Promise me you'll open yourself to this."

"I will try."

"I'm so proud of you and I won't let you back down. This is the best idea you've had in a long time." She squealed, "My mom is going to be a famous movie writer!"

I shook my head in dismay.

18

JUST RIGHT

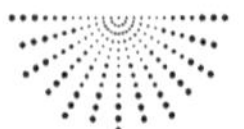

The workweek passed quickly and I found myself grateful for the heavy taping schedule. With Athena back home and little to do before the computer audits began the following week, I busied myself with my day job as Clyde's production assistant. When I wasn't on set, I kept up my running regimen. Though I still despised it, the activity helped my focus. I used the time to think through the sequence of events I'd use for my screenplay and to distract myself from my growing feelings for Clyde.

My phone buzzed and I fished it from my purse. It was a message from Athena: "Good luck on your first day in class. I love you."

I smiled, grateful for the treasure of my considerate daughter. As Tommy pulled to a stop in front of my new school, I quickly scribed, "Thank you, baby. I love you too."

Tommy came around to open the car door and I collected my laptop bag and got out. "Thanks for the ride. I'll see you tonight."

"Knock 'em dead," he replied with a smile.

Victory, I thought. I'd managed to warm the formerly stoic Tommy.

With a deep breath, I opened the door to the building and was greeted by a receptionist. "Are you here for the screenwriting course?" she inquired.

"I am."

"Through those doors." She pointed and I took the last few steps toward an unknown future.

The room was like a high school classroom. There were rows of desks facing the front. A large whiteboard replaced the typical chalkboards of the past and an overhead projector was mounted to the ceiling.

"Good morning." Presumably it was the professor who called, "What's your name?"

"Good morning. I'm Truth Tuesday."

He winked. "Quite an ironic name for a writer. Welcome. I'm Alex Mane. Take a seat anywhere you'd like."

"Thank you," I replied and surveyed the room. Only a few students had arrived, which made sense because class didn't start for another fifteen minutes. I chose a seat in the front row and pulled a notepad and pen from my bag.

As the minutes ticked away, more students filed in and soon every seat in the class was taken. I couldn't help but notice the age and variety of the students I shared the space with. By far I was the oldest and least eclectic appearing of the group.

"Let's get started, everyone. I'm Alex Mane and I've been in the film industry for more than forty years. I started as a grip, then a PA and finally after years of learning, my writing career began. I won't bore you with my accreditations—since you signed up for the class, you already know about me. To get started, I'm going to ask each of you to introduce yourself. Tell us about your writing experience and goals for this course. I know you are writers, so talking in front of a crowd won't be everyone's favorite thing to do, but if you're going to be successful in this business, you need to learn the art of self-promotion. Let's start at the front."

I kicked myself silently for choosing the first row as his hand swept my way. I started, "I'm…"

"Please stand," Alex corrected.

Following orders, I stood and began, "I'm Truth Tuesday and my writing experience was a long time ago in college. I'm unpublished and to be honest, pretty intimidated."

I was about to sit when the professor inquired, "What brought you here, Truth?"

Though I was using a false identity, I somehow let my authenticity out, "I'd like to write something that makes a difference, something that helps me take back my power."

"Bravo," he clapped. "Her name is her motto. Love it and I look forward to hearing your ideas. Next," he pointed to the young woman beside me.

After the thirty or so students finished their introductions, Professor Mane began, "We're going to start out by viewing, in my opinion, one of the greatest scenes in movie history. For those of you who know the film, *The Bridges of Madison County*, that moment when Francesca sees Robert at the intersection is unforgettable.

"The debatable conclusion always left me wondering. The mastery of the writer, his confidence in deciding the character's fate, knowing he wouldn't placate everyone, that's the kind of risk-taking that gets your work discussed decades later.

"Over the next six weekends, we'll explore what it takes to elicit a response and to paraphrase you, Truth, to make an impact. In the end, I hope you are enlightened by the fact that you can't always satisfy the audience, but the best work, just as the best parenting, doesn't necessarily mean we give them what they want. Our job is to help others grow from the controversies and resolutions in our tales.

"To quote one of my favorite writers of all time, the great Arthur Miller, in his work *Death of a Salesman,* 'Why am I trying to become what I don't want to be ... when all I want is out there, waiting for me the minute I say I know who I am.'"

With that, he cut the lights and tapped the start button on the remote. As I sat watching one of the most memorable scenes in movie history, tears shone in my eyes. A palatable fear combined with joy and somehow, I knew I was exactly where I was meant to be.

The scene's dramatic peak leads Richard to honk his horn at the hesitating Kincaid, who idles at the green light ahead. Francesca's hand grips the door and just as she is about to pull the lever, Kincaid pulls forward and the chance passes her by.

Professor Mane stopped the video and turned on the lights. I blinked, inspired by the details and the clarity of choice made by the writer. "Truth," the professor called, "what are your immediate observations about the movie?

I answered him boldly. "Well, I think everyone believes the husband to be a kind and loving man."

He quirked his head. "And you don't?"

"He may be in some ways, but in my opinion, he trapped her."

He nodded. "Jane, can you expand on Truth's statement?"

"If I follow her train of thought, I think she's referring to the fact that he found a daring woman, one who would travel across the world to explore and instead of giving her a life of adventure, he tethered her to a provincial life. He duped her into living his dream and her needs became irrelevant against his way of life."

"Excellent! John," he called. "What prop or object drew your eye during that scene?"

John's deep voice rang, "The obvious choice is the door handle. Her hand clenched around it lent to the suspense and tension of the experience."

"Great. Shawn, what else did you notice?"

"The husband, his expression toward his wife and the fact that he either didn't notice her grim face or he simply ignored it."

"That's right. It lends to what Truth and Jane referenced earlier. He wasn't a selfless man who only wanted his wife's happiness. He would protect his way of life even if it required ignorance on his part. I'm sure many of you can relate to that sentiment, holding on to something that isn't right because it fits our image or society's idea of right.

"Great start, everyone. Now we're going to get into formatting. Take these and pass them around," he said and we followed instructions, digging into page one of the class syllabus.

The hours passed and I found myself enthralled by every second of it. Unbelievably, five o'clock arrived and class was out for the day. "Homework for tonight: Start working on your first scene. Use the formatting example in your worksheets and let's reconvene tomorrow morning at 8AM sharp," Professor Mane said.

Students practically jumped to their feet. Some were already acquainted and people caught up as they walked outside. I'd gathered my things and was about to leave when the teacher said, "Truth, can you hang back?"

I was surprised but agreed, "Sure."

When the room was empty, he spoke quietly. "Clyde Parks and I are old friends. I know what you're doing for the studio, but I have to ask, for my own edification, why are you taking this class?"

His question took me off guard as he was one of the few who knew that I was consulting. My answer would make him the second person who knew my true purpose for wanting to write a screenplay. "I was fired, wrongfully and in a rather disgusting way. I won't call it vengeance, because that's petty and self-serving, but it shouldn't have happened. I have a beautiful daughter who wants to go into the corporate world. If I can do anything to smooth her way, no matter how it embarrasses me, I want to give that to her."

His lips narrowed into a straight line. "Hollywood loves a woman with a past." With a grandfatherly smile, he said, "I look forward to seeing what you have to say."

Monday morning arrived and I found myself at the studio before 6AM. Though the weekend of class followed by long evenings of homework should have tired me out, I found a well of energy I'd never experienced before. I couldn't wait for the days to begin and I pulled myself away from the computer each night only when my eyes could no longer stay open. Adrenaline and caffeine assisted my drive, but it was much more than that. It felt like everything was conspiring to support a future I hadn't fully envisioned.

Since I had the time, I holed up in my trailer and logged onto my business email account. Evelyn Snow replied to Jim Gage's agitated message warning about the difficulty of auditing staff writers' computers.

Good Morning Jim,

I understand the challenge with approvals and auditing the writers' computers; however, this is not a request and with your hesitance we are already a week behind. I've got full authority to advance this plan and I expect the audit to begin as outlined by next week, Monday. If all goes accordingly, the process should move quickly and each writer will be offline for only half a day. This step was approved by executive leadership before my directive to your team.

Please move forward as denoted in the memo and attached, revised schedule and provide me with daily updates of anomalies. Your cooperation is greatly appreciated.

-E. Snow

Another week on set whizzed by and it was finally Friday. I started my daily walk home and Clyde pulled up beside me. "Get in quick," he joked.

I laughed and settled into the passenger seat. "Thanks, Clyde."

He glanced over and asked, "How are you?"

"I'm great. It's been a long week, but I can't wait for class tomorrow."

His tone gave nothing away. "I spoke to Alex."

"Oh," I replied.

"He said he's excited to see your first pages this weekend."

Those familiar doubts came rushing in. "I hope I don't disappoint him."

"I don't think you will. Something tells me you're going to stir things up."

"I'm nervous enough without your added attention."

"Your nerves will only serve you. Besides, overconfident people rarely touch the soul."

"Now I'm expected to touch souls?"

"You're not expected to do anything. This path is of your own doing. The choice has always been yours."

I let his words sink in and finally said, "I know you're right. It's such a leap, that's all."

"And being a double agent wasn't?"

I chuckled, "Good point."

"You fit in this world without fitting in and you are formidable, which will come in handy."

I puzzled, "Formidable?"

His shoulders moved with his laugh. "Yes, you should see the messages that flew after your strongly worded memo to Jim Gage in IT. The guy was in a tizzy, but if you didn't notice, he fell into step with your command. That's the kind of strength it takes to make it here, or anywhere for that matter. I'm impressed."

"I'll be impressed when we find out who has been sharing the storyline with Big Fish."

"May I give you some advice?"

"Of course," I agreed.

"Relax a little. Even the setbacks in life are there for a reason. Learn to roll with the punches and use them to your advantage."

We pulled into the driveway and I turned to Clyde. "Thanks for that and the ride. I'll see you on Monday."

His smile was wistful. "Which seems an eternity away. Have fun in class."

"Thanks," I said and exited the car. His words washed over me and I decided a few laps in the pool were needed before tackling the screenplay.

The long weeks and lack of sleep had finally gained on me and after my swim the previous evening, I fell into a dreamless sleep. Fortunately, I awoke before 5AM, which gave me enough time to edit the opening scene of my screenplay.

Converting my journal entries into scenes gave me a quick start, but it was also like reliving the experiences. At times I was overcome with emotion. Fury, insecurity and even bravery pushed me from every direction. How I perceived the outcome of my first pages didn't matter. I was out of time as the assignment was due by 6AM today. I hit the send button, emailing my work to Professor Mane and wondering if I had lost my mind.

At precisely 8AM Professor Mane called us to order. "Good morning, everyone. I trust your first week as screenwriters went well."

The room fell silent. "We have a lot to accomplish today and as promised we are going to do a live read of three of the strongest opening scenes. We'll keep it anonymous so as not to embarrass anyone. I'll display the scene to be read on the projector and select the students who will run lines. To begin, I'll tap Jane, Ronald and Samantha. Jane, you'll play the part of the female lead, Kara Baxter; Ronald, you'll be Jeff Rand, the visiting VP; and Samantha, read the part of Marge Coleman, the Human Resources Manager."

I nearly vomited in my mouth as they were reading my scene first. Sweat formed in my palms and I wiped my hands down my jeans. The professor said, "Let's begin."

SCENE: Kara Baxter enters the executive office for a meeting with her Vice President. Florescent lights flicker above as Jeff Rand stands.

JEFF: "Hey, Kara. Would you shut the door behind you?"

Kara pulls the heavy door closed and walks toward the oversized wooden desk as Jeff turns to the telephone.

JEFF: "Marge in Human Resources has asked that we conference her in."

Kara is unnerved. She doesn't really know the VP, having only met him a couple of times in the past. They've never had a direct meeting. With adding Human Resources to the mix, in light of the recent restructuring, and her last unsatisfactory experience with the HR manager, she thinks she may be laid off. She knows there is no cause. Her sales numbers are exemplary, but her tenure is short next to her colleagues, all men who have held their positions for decades.

JEFF: "Have a seat."

He waves to a chair beside the desk and makes the outbound call. Two rings later, Marge's raspy voice, attributed to a lifetime of smoking cigarettes, echoes through the connection.

MARGE: "This is Marge."

JEFF: "Hello, Marge. This is Jeff Rand and I have Kara here with me."

MARGE: "Thank you, Jeff. I'll start us off."

Kara wiggles as she awaits their agenda.

MARGE: "Kara, we've had some complaints specific to your actions that I need to investigate."

KARA: "What kind of complaints?"

MARGE: "I have to ask, have you had sex with multiple subordinates?"

Kara's ears ring with confusion. She's certain she's misheard.

KARA: "What?"

MARGE: "Have you had sex with multiple subordinates?"

KARA: pants, "Excuse me?"

MARGE: raises voice, "I need you to answer me. Have you had sex with multiple subordinates?"

Kara shakes her head. Her brain finally catches up and she knows she hasn't misunderstood. From a place deep within, she finds a modicum of courage. Her tone is shocked.

KARA: "What right do you have to ask me about my sex life?"

Anger or possibly satisfaction rings through the line, as Marge persists.

MARGE: "We have an obligation to investigate all complaints, particularly those that are reported on the hotline. Once again, did you have sex with multiple subordinates?"

Kara's mind still can't wrap around the question.

KARA: "What right does any company have to ask about an employee's sex life?"

Marge demands more than states.

MARGE: "It's a policy violation. Please answer me, did you have sex with multiple subordinates?"

Kara does not want to answer and not because she's avoiding the truth, but she is familiar with the company policies as part of her position and training. She knows it contains nothing specific about sexual conduct.

KARA: "No, I did not have sex with my subordinates."

Jeff huffs and grips the edge of the desk.

JEFF: "Why do you think people would make these complaints?"

Kara's anger is barely contained. She is visibly shaking, but checks herself as shown in her steely response.

KARA: "Probably because I had a serious talk with a few of the employees last week. A couple of them are slacking off and it shows in their forecast. If their effort doesn't improve, we won't hit our numbers."

JEFF: "That's true enough. You understand the financial metrics."

KARA: "Who made these complaints?"

MARGE: "They were anonymous and I'll remind you of the company's no retaliation policy. This protects concerned employees who are reporting an issue."

KARA: "Who protects the wrongfully accused?"

Jeff looks blankly at Kara.

KARA: "Do I need an attorney?"

Jeff is silent and Marge's voice fills the room.

MARGE: "For now, we are going to suspend you pending further investigation."

KARA: "Suspend me for what? Holding a bunch of complacent and entitled employees to their work responsibilities?"

Marge ignores Kara's question.

MARGE: "Jeff, will you walk Kara to her office so she may collect her personal effects?"

JEFF: "Yes."

When the call ends, Kara recoils, funneling anger into words.

KARA: "Anonymous complaints of a sexual nature against me are absurd, especially in this boys club where my boss takes my team to strip clubs whenever he's in town. You could have just laid me off. There was no reason to destroy my reputation in the process."

His falsely innocent reply is transparent.

JEFF: "I know nothing about a plot against you. This call was a surprise to me too. We'd better get your things."

As I sat there in class, it felt as if all eyes were on me and the heat surely showed on my cheeks though I tried for a neutral expression. I was not only exposed by having my prose examined publicly, but the most mortifying moment of my life was being replayed before my ears. The little-known VP with a clear tendency toward dismissal and the incompetent Human Resources Manager, who was anything but impartial, attacked the unwitting employee who was disparaged by anonymous complaints. I was once in that chair, facing a line of questioning that crossed every boundary of decency and corporate authority. My heart pounded in my chest until the class began to applaud.

Professor Mane held a hand to quiet the room. "Thoughts? Yes, Wanda."

"This scene, though well written, seems unrealistic to me. No company would ask those kinds of questions of a female employee."

Wanda was in her early twenties and from her appearance—her brow and nose were pierced and her arm was tattooed into a full sleeve—she'd never worked a day in corporate America.

Alex fired, "How do you know?"

"Well," she hesitated, "it's just wrong. Why would a company ever ask those questions? They have no right to know about a person's sex life."

"Your contention is that a company won't do something just because it's wrong?"

"Aren't there rules about things like that?"

"Very good question and I'm guessing you don't know the answer."

She was saying all the things I feared. I didn't blame her for doubting. Although I'd lived through the experience, I was still incredulous they inquired about my sex life, let alone accused me of sleeping with several staff members.

She replied, "No, I guess I don't know the answer."

He set me up. "Truth, what do you think about that?"

My voice broke as I said, "I think people expect a certain political correctness to be present in corporate structures that is more perception than reality based."

He nodded and addressed the man who read Jeff's part, "Robert, how did you feel reading those lines? What was Jeff's motivation?"

"Obviously we were dropped into the middle of the situation so we don't know what led up to the meeting, but he seemed like an ass. Especially when she referenced her supervisor going to strip clubs with her subordinates and he just kind of said, 'I know nothing about that.' It gave me the impression that he not only knew it was a normal occurrence, but he had no issue with the tradition of male bonding over lap dances. He seemed okay with the double standard."

Alex nodded. "And Samantha, what's your take on the HR lady?"

"I thought she was a pawn and probably one of those women who doesn't really like other women. Maybe she was jealous or feared losing her job."

"Very good," he said. "From my standpoint, I thought the scene was executed well. We were dropped into a heated moment that grabbed. The writing was impactful as shown by the comments from the group. The only change I'd suggest is less direction moving forward. Let's move on."

And the Band-Aid was off, ripped from my skin with only a few hairs pulled in the process.

19

THE PLOT THICKENS

As had become my routine, I'd arrived at the studio early Monday morning. With a cup of coffee in hand, I used the time to review the last pages of my screenplay written before nodding off the previous evening. There were a few typos and a line I'd yet to perfect, in the scene with Roman Rossi. I would eventually change his name, because it was true and I wanted to save myself from legal action.

For years I'd been haunted by the VP's warning. Though I was a top-performing consultant at the mega corporation, the inappropriate pressure never ceased. He was careful to say it when we were alone in the car just before we'd entered the appointment with my client. "I'm not telling you to have actual sex with the customer, but eight-hundred locations is a lot of revenue. Do whatever you have to and close the deal." His hawk-like eyes trained in on mine, "Your job is hinging on it."

The resounding opening of the car door as he exited left no time to rebut. There were no witnesses to his threatening remarks, comments that boiled me down to a sex object.

Only the air between us heard the words that should have shocked me, if only I hadn't seen him sexually harass two other female staff members previously. None of us ever reported him. Today he is a VP for another publicly traded firm. I wonder if any women work in his group.

I'll never forget the odd feeling that blanketed me as we entered the meeting where I introduced Roman Rossi to the SVP of Construction at the auto-parts company, nor how apparent it was that my client despised him.

His tired approach at pressuring the customer was pointless, as I already knew. Chris Paul was not one to yield to force, nor was he obliged to succumb to our wants. He was responsible for the business metrics of a giant company and no vendor—however much he appreciated the representative—would cause him to act before he was ready.

Roman said, "You should let us address these locations now before the price increases go into effect next year."

Chris Paul leaned back in his ergonomic chair. His blond-grey hair moved with the action and his hands rested comfortably across his stomach. "If your prices go up, I'll find another provider."

Roman Rossi decided on a new tactic, fake humility. "What can we do to make it easier for you to give us more business?"

"I'm very happy with how Evvy is handling the account. She's done everything I've asked and more. I want to see how the company continues to perform with the number of locations I've already contracted with you. If the service remains at the same level, I'll naturally want to migrate more business her way."

Roman Rossi nearly pleaded, "Still, there must be some way to entice you?"

"I'm afraid I have to cut this meeting short. I've got some

place to be. Thanks for stopping by to introduce yourself." With that he stood and the meeting was adjourned.

Though I walked away from some incredible accounts, a stable income, and vesting, that meeting was the final straw in a series of similar scenarios that assured my resignation. It's too bad my next job proved even more treacherous.

Three raps at the door broke into my memory. I clicked save and closed the document before calling, "Come in."

"Good morning," Clyde announced as he entered. "How was your weekend?"

"Productive, I think. How was yours?"

"Good. I got to see my kids for dinner yesterday, which was fun."

"Remind me, do they live in town?"

"Yes, they both live here."

"And they're not in the movie industry, right?"

"No way," he chuckled. "My son is working on his masters in engineering at UCLA and my daughter is an assistant for a fashion designer in the garment district."

"They sound like smart kids."

"They are," he agreed. "Listen, I've assigned you to work with Rebba Frank in the writers' room for two hours every morning. Since the computers are being audited this week, it might give you some purview into the reactions of the writers and it will help with your other ambition."

"Seriously?" I couldn't keep the excitement from my tone.

"Seriously," he said.

"Clyde, I so appreciate this, but I'm being paid to solve your leak. You don't have to do me any extra favors."

"It's not a favor. I want the person caught. Besides if your screenplay is as promising as Alex thinks, the experience will do you good."

"You keeping tabs on my schoolwork is a little like having a parent in cahoots with my teacher."

He joked, "Until you bring your grades up, young lady…"

"Thank you. I am eager to see how it all gets done."

"Don't thank me just yet. Mostly you'll be making coffee and copies and it's only two hours a day."

"Still, it's very exciting."

"First things first," he admonished. "We're due at the ambulance scene. Grab your mug, Ms. Tuesday."

***

The writers' room was a disorganized haven. Laptop computers glowed against concentrated faces. Some smiled; others tugged at their hair; all were engaged as if nothing else existed.

"Truth, coffee refill," barked Rex Jones, one of the tenured writers. He took his black, which made life easier.

"Me too," chimed another of the team, Jon Rein. He preferred a lot of cream but no sugar.

"Coming up," I called, not in the least bit demeaned by my demotion to snack maiden. I admired their focus and understood the drive to remain seated. They were immersed in their dream job, or what I imagined my dream job might be. What a strong admission I'd made to myself. I was beginning to make peace with the fact that I wanted to be a writer when I grew up.

"Here you are, Rex," I said as I settled a mug on the desk beside him. His nod was barely noticeable.

"Jon, your cream, I mean coffee," I teased.

"Thanks, Truth."

Rebba beckoned, "Copies, Truth."

I walked to her side and accepted the stack she held. After making the duplicates, I returned to her desk.

"Why don't you run through these, edit anything that stands out."

"Will do," I agreed calmly, though it was my first pass at touching the pages.

I found a spot to sit and dove into a vivid scene that would climax at the top of a high rise. A few lines were too dramatic, even for daytime TV. I hovered over the page and ultimately took the liberty of adjusting the phraseology. I not only needed to play the part of an eager writer, I wanted to.

When I was finished, I returned to Rebba's desk. "I made some notes. I hope you don't mind."

"Let's see what we've got." As she scanned the sheets, my pulse quickened. The seconds dragged until she finally looked up. "Good. We'll go with the lines as adjusted."

I was elated by her comment, but was quickly brought to reality when Cherry Adore called, "Truth, latte me."

Rebba smiled and nodded in agreement. "Keep it up and soon you may be demanding coffee."

"Thanks, Rebba."

After I delivered Cherry's coffee, Patty Smite, one of the newer writers, waved me over. "How's it going?" she inquired.

"I'm loving it," I admitted.

"I can tell and don't worry. Not long ago I was delivering coffee. Keep your head down and you'll get your chance to shine."

"Thanks, Patty. I appreciate that."

"Wanna grab a drink after work?" she inquired.

"Sure," I agreed readily. It would be good to dish and I could use a night off from writing and running.

"Meet you at The Gates at five o'clock."

"I'll see you there." I noticed the time and realized I was due on set.

"Rebba," I called, "I'll see you in the morning."

She waved dismissively and didn't look up from her monitor.

The Gates was a tribute to the Hollywood of old that remained unchanged since opening in 1949. Red vinyl booths blended with burgundy and gold-patterned carpeting highlighted by brass light sconces. The dim hideout was a speakeasy of sorts and a local haunt well known by everyone in the movie industry.

I arrived first and asked for a booth in the corner. It would keep us out of earshot of interested patrons and I wanted the quiet after another long day on the lot. "Hey there," Patty announced and flopped onto the bench.

"Tough afternoon?" I asked.

"No, just busy. Did I keep you waiting?"

"Not at all," I replied. "I've just sat down myself."

A cocktail waitress in a French maid uniform arrived to greet us. "Good evening, ladies. Welcome to The Gates."

"Thank you," I said and noted the dress was short for her aging legs, but this was Hollywood.

"What can I bring you to drink?"

Patty said, "I'll have a rum and coke with lime."

The waitress's crinkled blue eyes looked my way. "Vodka soda, please."

"I'll be right back."

As she left, Patty pulled her cell phone out and rapidly tapped the screen. Her face was alight by the glow of her phone and a giant smile. She chuckled to herself and clicked some more. After setting it aside, she said, "Sorry, that was my beau. He's coming over later. I need a little stress relief."

I read between the lines of her not so subtle subtext and a pang of jealousy came over me. It had been so long since I'd had that type of release. "Lucky you," I commented.

"Yes, he's one of the good ones."

"How did you meet?"

"At a writing conference actually. He's a writer too."

"That's great. Do you guys ever compare notes?"

Her reply was stern, "Absolutely not. With my NDA and his, we would be in a world of hurt if we ever did."

I asked, "Where does your boyfriend work?"

"He's the competition. Rob works at Big Fish."

"Oh," I said simply though a shiver ran along my spine.

Our server returned with the drinks. "Here you are, ladies. Will there be anything else or just drinks today?"

Patty replied, "Just these, thanks."

When her fishnet-stockinged legs were out of sight, Patty leaned in and conspired, "Most of the women who work here were B actresses back in the day. It's a museum of relics but I love it."

Though my mind reeled after her revelation about where her boyfriend worked, I scanned the room as if it were my only observation and had to agree. "You have to love Hollywood, don't you?"

"Yes, you have to," she agreed. "To be honest, most days I wake up pinching myself. Since I moved from Kansas, I've never looked back. Life there was nothing to appreciate so I left as soon as I graduated from high school."

"Did you study writing here then?"

"Yes, I went to the same school you're attending. They have a great feeder program and I interned with Base Productions during my courses."

"Wow, so we have something in common."

"We do," she agreed. "What were you doing before you came to Hollyweird?"

"Me, not much. I was a mom and when my daughter left for college, I finally decided to venture out to find myself."

She practically gasped, "Wait, you have a daughter in college?"

"I do."

"How do you do it?" she waved her hand in my direction.

I quirked my head in reply. "Although I hate it, I run, but mostly it's genetics. I have my parents to thank."

"Seriously, you'd better send the biggest arrangement of flowers on Mother's Day."

I smiled, "Thanks, Patty. You're too nice. So, tell me about the writers. What are the backstories?"

She scanned the lounge, quickly verifying there were no familiar faces and after a moment said, "It's a shit show of sorts. The politics and behind the scenes plots are almost as thick as our storylines. I wouldn't know where to begin, but I'll try."

Two drinks and as many hours later, I had a rundown of the entire crew. Patty seemed to know everyone and much of what Bernice already told me was confirmed. The only new information I'd learned was upsetting. I liked Patty and I couldn't imagine her risking the job she so adored, but happy hour was over and I knew I'd do my primary job as agreed upon. Tomorrow I would alert the team about her boyfriend Rob.

"Well," she smirked mischievously, "my booty call is waiting. I'm sorry to leave you, but that man has me wrapped around his…"

I held up and hand and laughed out loud. I realized I liked Patty. "I think I get the point."

"Ha ha," she blurted. "Look at you blushing and adding to my inappropriate comment. I'll see you at the studio in the AM."

The week sailed by and still there were no advances in the case. I was becoming concerned after the first ten writers' computers had passed the audits. With Patty's still outstanding, I worried about what we may find. We'd chosen not to adjust the scheduled "upgrades" so we wouldn't tip anyone off about our true purpose. For the moment, I had to wait. As I settled into my desk in class, I committed to put work aside for the day to focus on my passion project.

Alex began, "Today we're going to start with a scene from one of the students and Truth, I'll ask you to do the reading."

"Okay," I agreed as he handed me the pages.

I began.

Alice Walker is asleep in bed. It's morning and she's alone in the house after her husband, Joseph, has gone to work.

ALICE: "I have to pee."

She tries to rouse herself but her eyes are still closed.

ALICE: "I feel wet."

Her breath is hitched. She struggles to open her eyes, but her lids seemed glued shut.

ALICE: "I have to wake up and pee before I wet the bed."

She thrashes in the sheets, struggling to find movement in her limbs until finally her eyes flutter to reality. Her hand goes instinctively to her swollen belly. Her bladder feels full and there is a dampness between her legs. She thinks she's soiled the bed, knowing a weak bladder was a symptom of pregnancy. She pulls back the blanket and to her horror a pool of burgundy the size of a watermelon soils the sheets.

ALICE: "Oh no, not again."

Her mind races to the inevitable truth: She's losing her. She's losing her baby girl. Her fourth pregnancy is pouring from her womb and she knows it's over. Resolved, she decides what to do.

ALICE: "Why are you taking her from me? This time I'll join my baby in the glorious abyss of nothingness. I can't stand another explanation, or to see their empathy and superiority when I admit I've miscarried, again."

She winces against a harsh contraction of fruitless point

and stands from the bed. Blood pours down her bare legs and drips onto the grey shag rug below.

ALICE: "I won't cry. I won't call the doctor, not Joseph. I'll leave. It's time."

She shuffles against the pain and falls toward the bathroom sink. Her knuckles whiten as she grips the counter.

ALICE: "This fucking hurts."

She reaches past the agony and tugs open the medicine cabinet. After knocking a few items down, she finds the oxycodone. She grapples briefly with the childproof lid—an insulting last act for there are no children in her house—and raises the bottle to her lips, accepting every tablet as it falls to her tongue. Before she changes her mind, she turns on the tap and drinks profusely, choking back the many pills before sinking to the tile floor and her final slumber.

ALICE: "I'm coming, loves. Mommy is coming."

Alex broke the silence, "Nice reading, Truth. Rhonda, what do you think of the scene?"

She hefted her ample breasts and spoke solemnly, "It was intense, visual and very well written. I could feel the pain and though the descriptions were sparse, I was transported."

Alex replied to the class, "Would it surprise you to know it was written by a man?"

The class erupted in ooh's and ahh's, affirming our shock. "This is the goal, people. As writers, you must absorb all of it and find a way to live inside of every depiction. If you can't feel the pain, neither will your audience.

"Let's turn to page sixty of the syllabus."

Class was in session and the rest of the world vanished. Inspired by the scene, I knew now, more than ever I wanted to write something meaningful—to touch souls, as Clyde once said.

THE OUTCOME

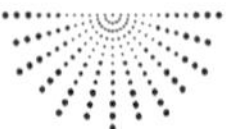

After another week of double duty, my stomach lurched as Thursday morning greeted me. I walked to the studio carrying the weight of unease knowing Patty's computer would be audited by IT today. I'd hoped we would learn something that would point in another direction, but as the days wore on, I had my doubts.

At only six-fifteen in the morning, the studio was just coming to life. I got a cup of coffee from Janice at craft services and headed for the trailer. Clyde stepped through a roll-up door and followed in stride with me. "Good morning," he murmured.

I couldn't smile, for the concern I had prevented it. "Good morning, Clyde."

"How are you doing?" he solicited.

"I'm okay. A little worried."

"Me too," he admitted. "I really like Patty. She's a hard worker and I hired her with Alex's recommendation. I hope it's not her."

His sentiments mirrored mine. I simply nodded.

"Since the audit doesn't start for a few hours, all we can

do is focus on the building fire scene. Shall we get to work, Ms. Tuesday?"

"Yes, boss," I agreed.

"Not for long," he said. "The best thing that came out of this crap situation is that I got to meet you." With that he hooked a right and I followed him to the staff meeting.

His comment unraveled me momentarily and I felt a pang at my chest. He was so damn handsome that I was often distracted by his proximity. It seemed mutual. I shook my head and tried to erase my impure thoughts to concentrate on the day's filming schedule.

It was midday before the results were in. Jim in IT pinged my E. Snow account and we coordinated a phone conversation. As I paced the narrow confines of the trailer, the ring of his inbound call, though anticipated, gave me a start. Clyde's presence only heightened my tension. Answering on speaker mode, I said, "Good afternoon, Jim."

"Ms. Snow," he replied simply.

"I assume you've found something of consequence," I stated.

"We have. It appears as though an external hard drive was used on three occasions several weeks prior to Big Fish's duplication of our scripts. I'm disappointed to inform you that Patty Smite's computer was in violation."

My heart sank in disbelief. I recalled her enthusiasm about working for Base Productions and found it impossible to believe she would jeopardize her dream job, but if had life shown me anything, it proved that many people weren't what they seemed.

"That is upsetting news, Jim, but I hope we've found the problem. Next steps, would you and HR get together in

Room B and call Patty to join you? I'll send a list of questions shortly and will be listening remotely. Be logged into your computer. I'll use instant message."

He grumbled a reply, "Will do. Give me thirty minutes to arrange it."

"Thank you, Jim," I said and terminated the call.

Clyde's eyes met mine and I asked, "Will you be a part of the questioning?"

His gaze was downcast and he raked his hands over his thick hair. "Sadly, it's part of the job. I'll be there."

"I'm sorry, Clyde. It's not over yet. Maybe there is some other explanation." Our eyes met in a wordless exchange. We both knew the chance of another resolution was small.

The room was brightly lit and contained only a large table and chairs. At the head, Jim sat, hands folded at his waist and his laptop computer open. Soon after, Laurie Sands, the VP of Human Resources, entered the room with Patty Smite in tow and Clyde followed shortly behind.

I sat in the trailer, viewing the interaction via the surveillance cameras and with the telephone on speaker mode, but muted. Jim already had a list of questions and I'd message follow-up queries based on Patty's responses.

Patty looked puzzled at the group and in a dry tone Jim began. "Patty, thank you for joining us."

She shook her head slightly and replied, "Of course."

"As you are aware, we've recently had some issues with our storylines being duplicated by Big Fish."

She nodded in acknowledgement.

"It's a serious matter and one that we cannot allow to continue."

"I understand," she said. "I feel the same way about it since it's my team that has been affected."

Jim's expression was grave as he handed Patty a slip of paper. "Do you recognize this?"

She scanned the document and looked up. "I do. It's the NDA I signed when I was hired by Base Productions."

"Do you understand the document and its purpose?"

"I do," she agreed and wrung her hands.

He nodded and continued, "As you know, we've been in the process of upgrading the computers and as an incidental finding, we've discovered some violations of the acceptable use policies and non-disclosure agreement on your machine."

Patty shook her head in denial. Her breath hitched in reply, "No way."

"On February 6th, your computer logged the use of an external hard drive, which is a violation of policy. Do you recall using an unauthorized device on that date?"

She was either an actress herself or was telling the truth. "Absolutely not. I know that's not permitted and I wouldn't do anything to jeopardize my job. I love working here."

He nodded unconvinced. "On April 19th, we found another instance of an external hard drive accessing files on your computer. Do you recall that?"

Her chest rose and she was flustered, "No. I didn't use a hard drive."

He pressed, "What about on June 1st?"

"It doesn't matter what date you ask about, I've never used a hard drive or the cloud or anything like that. You have to believe me. I wouldn't do such a thing."

As I watched the exchange from afar, I felt sorry for her. My first responsibility was to get to the bottom of the matter, but the inquisition was reminiscent of my own termination and from that vantage point, I sympathized.

Laurie spoke next. "This is a delicate question and one that I would normally not pose, but due to the serious nature of the matter, I must ask: Are you dating Rob Marx at Big Fish?"

Patty turned red and replied in a shaky voice, "Yes."

"Have you discussed your work product with him?"

"No, I swear I haven't." Her denial was convincing.

"Did you ever work remotely when he was with you?"

"Never, not once. We've been meticulous about following the rules. Rob and I both value our jobs too much. We wouldn't do that."

I typed a quick message to Jim. He looked up from the screen and inquired, "What about your password? Have you shared that with Rob, even accidentally?"

She started to shake her head but stopped. Her eyes closed and she inhaled deeply.

Clyde, who had been a silent observer until that point, pressed, "What is it, Patty?"

Tears formed in her eyes as she met his stare. "I may have done something careless."

"How so?" Clyde asked.

"We've ordered delivery from GrubHub and I use the same password for that account as my computer."

I scribed a message to Jim and he asked, "You shared the password with Rob?"

"Yes, once he beat me home and we were going to have Chinese. I gave him the login to my account so he could order."

Laurie straightened her shoulders. Any empathy she felt was not discernible. "This is a violation of policy and grounds for termination. We'll have security escort you to the gate and you'll be on suspension pending further investigation."

Laurie's words rang too familiar, but this time, I understood the reasoning.

Patty sobbed an apology, "I'm so sorry. Please know I didn't do this on purpose. I would never risk my job here."

Laurie's succinct reply was simultaneous to the security guard's arrival, "We'll take that under consideration."

The next two days were a blur of legal action and decision. Rob Marx was interviewed by Big Fish Media and he denied any wrongdoing. The studio initially refuted any impropriety until they saw the chain of evidence and scenes written by Patty Smite and the Big Fish group. Upon reading the dialogue, they acknowledged the similarities were too close to doubt. Rob was terminated and the rumor mill would ensure this was end of his career in Hollywood.

As for Patty, though Clyde and Laurie empathized with her plight, her lack of discretion in managing the security of her network credentials was determined to be in poor judgement. She too was terminated with severance and the situation allowed the executives to re-evaluate their previously liberal work remotely policies. Moving forward, all writers' computers were to remain on studio property.

I saw Patty as she left her final meeting with the team. With security following closely behind, I walked her to the gate. She carried a box of her personal effects, and her good luck plant, Harry, flopped with each step. She stood tall though I knew she was crestfallen. "I can't believe I lost my dream job and my boyfriend in one day. It was stupid to use the same password for my network and food ordering account. I feel like such an idiot and I know I got what I deserved."

She still had no idea I was investigating—to her I was

Truth Tuesday. From that vantage point, I commiserated, "I'm sorry. What will you do next?"

"I'm not sure. I always had an idea that I'd write a screenplay of my own. Maybe I'll take advantage of the free time and finally do it."

Her reply was exactly the reason we'd clicked to begin with. She and I were similar creatures, taking misery and turning it into something new. We reached the gate and I turned to her. "I wish you all the best, Patty."

She set the box down and gave me a squeeze. "You too, Truth. I can't wait to see what happens with your career." With tears in her eyes, she collected her box and exited the gate for the last time.

IT'S A WRAP

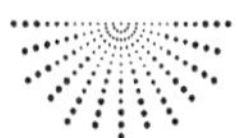

The classroom was silent as I stood at the front and faced my fears. A room of faces as hopeful as mine peered back at me. I gripped the pages with my fingers as if I were holding on for dear life.

Alex prompted, "Truth, you'll read the part of Kara, and Shelly, you're Marge for this scene. You may begin."

I swallowed bile and inhaled unsteadily.

KARA: "Hello, Marge, this is Kara. You requested I call you."

MARGE: "Yes, Kara," Her voice is pinched as if taking a drag off a cigarette. "I've had a complaint I need to investigate."

KARA: "All right. What's the complaint?"

MARGE: "Did you attend a project meeting at the Fine County Jail recently?"

KARA: "I did."

MARGE: "And was your employee Todd Saxon present?"

KARA: "He was."

MARGE: "Did you two drive to the appointment together?"

KARA: "Yes, we did."

MARGE: "I have to inform and remind you of our no retaliation policy and ask that you handle yourself in accordance with those guidelines. We strive to uphold a safe environment where employees can share their concerns without fear of losing their positions or reprisal because they've come forward."

KARA: "I understand the policy."

MARGE: "Great, then I must ask, did you discuss the project as you drove to the appointment?"

KARA: "Yes."

MARGE: "Do you recall asking Todd if you were going to an all-male facility?"

KARA: "I do not."

MARGE: "You don't remember asking him if it was an all-male facility?"

KARA: "No."

MARGE: "Todd alleges that you not only asked that, but when he said it was, your response was, 'It's too bad I didn't wear a low-cut blouse to win the deal.'"

Kara is furious and sickened by his sexist remark, but holds it together, linking logic to her response.

KARA: "Well, it wouldn't make sense for me to ask that question of him. I'd already spoken with my supervisor, Jake, about the opportunity before we agreed to take on the project. Since it was my first time visiting a correctional facility, he wanted to make certain I knew the protocols. We covered the type of facility and rules at length the week prior. Our project manager Robert Lewten was present for the conversation. I was aware it was an all-male facility. Besides, I hardly think the inmates would help sway the contract in our direction."

MARGE: Huffs, "Fine. I'll remind you of the no retaliation policy. This matter isn't closed. I need to speak with leadership and there may be follow-up questions after I redirect to Todd."

KARA: "I understand. Do you have any advice for me as I manage him in the interim?"

MARGE: "Handle yourself professionally and don't have any one-on-one meetings with him. He's obviously uncomfortable enough to complain and you don't want to make matters worse."

KARA: "To be honest, Marge, I think he's complaining because he is struggling with his sales numbers."

MARGE: "I'll caution you not to speculate nor minimize his concern."

KARA: "Of course. You aren't taking these allegations seriously, are you?"

MARGE: "It is my absolute duty to investigate every complaint, so yes, I am."

KARA: "Okay, well, when you speak with Robert and Jake, I'm certain both will confirm the meeting we had prior to us visiting the correctional facility. If they reinforce that I knew we were visiting an all-male facility, will any action be taken against Todd for wrongfully accusing me?"

MARGE: "As I said, we adhere to a strict no retaliation policy. I hope this won't be a problem for you, Kara."

KARA: "It's one thing not to retaliate when a complaint is legitimate, but…"

MARGE: "I'm concerned you don't understand, Kara. You may not conduct yourself in any way other than professionally toward Todd and no, we will not have a meeting to call him out for sharing his concern. I need to conclude this call. Continue business as usual until you hear back from me."

KARA: "I will, Marge, thank…" The line goes silent.

The classroom erupted in claps and I had to blink away the tears. Their validation gave me the boost I'd set out to find. Our final class was like watching scenes from one blockbuster film after the next. I was in awe of the talent that surrounded me and humbled to be a part of such an experience.

Alex sent us on our way with a parting quote by the famed André Gide, author of "The Immoralist," "The most beautiful things are those that madness prompts and reason writes."

I stood and waited my turn to say goodbye and Alex whispered, "It has been a pleasure to teach you, Evelyn. You are quite gifted and I'm sure this is the start of your writing career. I hope you don't mind, but I've submitted your manuscript to the Rise Screenwriting Contest."

My eyes bulged and I was shocked by his compliment. "That's insane. I'm not near that level of accomplishment."

"Your humility is charming, but it's time you took an honest assessment of your abilities. Whatever happened before, it's over and you rose above it. You have a powerful voice, yours to use or squander. Don't waste time fretting that you aren't worthy when you have so much to accomplish. Help the women behind you and change things."

"I don't know how to thank you."

"It's simple," he said, "keep writing."

***

My last day at Base Productions ended with a surprise cake and the good wishes of my temporary colleagues.

Bernice raised a glass in cheers. "Here's to Truth Tuesday, a great intern and fast friend."

Even Jim from IT cheered.

I teared up involuntarily, knowing I would miss them all and the work. Though being a PA wasn't my real job, I found it more fitting than any position I'd held.

"Thank you, everyone. I'm going to miss you guys so much."

Suddenly Clyde arrived by my side. "Truth, may I speak with you for a moment?"

I followed him a few yards away from the group and looked expectantly into his determined brown eyes. "What is it, Clyde?"

"I'd like to take you to dinner tonight. Can you fit that in?"

I responded calmly though my pulse sped under his gaze. "Athena won't be here until tomorrow morning, so I am free."

He looked relieved and replied, "Great. I'll pick you up at eight."

"Eight o'clock it is." I agreed.

The time in Hollywood allowed me a few luxuries, and as I pulled the burgundy Alexander McQueen off-the-shoulder dress from the closet, I knew tonight was the perfect occasion to wear it. The design was impeccable and the frock was the most expensive article of clothing I'd ever purchased. It was my reward for accomplishing not one, but two of the goals I'd set before arriving in LA.

At promptly eight o'clock the doorbell rang. I smoothed my dress and opened the door to Clyde. He wore a black blazer and white shirt unbuttoned at the collar. In his hand was a gorgeous bunch of green roses. "You look incredible," he breathed as I gestured for him to enter.

"Thank you, so do you," I replied.

He extended his hand and I accepted the flowers, taking in their fresh scent. "They're beautiful," I said.

"But they pale in comparison to you, Evelyn."

A frisson of elation came over me, but I managed to say, "Let me put these in water quickly."

He paced to watch as I found the crystal vase and untied the roses, dropping them gently into the water. "Thank you, Clyde. Shall we go?"

His attention was as disarming as the gleam in his eye. "We'd better," he agreed.

We drove silently and I periodically stole a glance at him. He moved with efficiency and exuded confidence as he navigated the roads with ease. His profile was manly, with a strong chin and pronounced nose, and his hands were sure. After weeks of working side by side, I'd gotten to know him personally and professionally. From all I'd learned about him, my admiration was well deserved.

He pulled to the curb of a building thickly covered in plants, so much so the only gap in the wall led to a nondescript brown door. A uniformed valet stepped from the curb and opened my door, extending his hand to aid my exit. "Thank you," I said.

Clyde circled around the car and placed a hand at my back as we moved toward the entry. The sensation of his touch delighted and unnerved me. The door opened and we were transported to a romantic hideaway. Black and white tiled floors bled into a portico where we were greeted by a cheerful redhead in a black dress. "Good evening," she said. "What name is the reservation under?"

"Parks, Clyde Parks."

"Ah, yes, Mr. Parks. Louellen will take you."

In a snap, Louellen arrived with menus in hand. "This way, please."

We followed her through the dreamlike courtyard draped in golden hues. Above us dark exposed trusses seemed to float against the clear roof and the evening light complemented the many votives and light sconces. The main dining area was intimate, with tables down the center, and our final stop placed us at the edge of a tent-like cubicle with red velvet curtains and slithering vines. The table rested against a wall carved with a dozen insets; within each flickered a lit candle.

Clyde stepped inside and pulled the chair out. "Evelyn."

I joined him in the cozy space and as he pushed my seat forward, I looked up. "Thank you."

After he took his chair, Louellen announced, "Here are tonight's selections. Joann will be taking care of you this evening."

"Thank you, Louellen," Clyde replied as she exited.

I leaned forward in my chair. "This is spectacular."

Clyde didn't smile as he answered, "You certainly are."

He made no secret of his intentions for the evening. This wasn't a business meeting. At that moment, Joann arrived.

"I'm sorry to interrupt," she apologized with a smirk. "I'm Joann. May I bring you something to drink?"

"Please. We'd like a bottle of Cristal."

"Certainly," she agreed. "I'll return momentarily."

I took in our surroundings which seemed like one of the elaborate sets we'd worked on at the studio. I couldn't imagine a more romantic setting nor a more compelling date. "Thank you for planning this and for making my time here special. It's been an honor to work with and get to know you."

"I couldn't agree more, Evelyn. I'm going miss you." The suggestion in his comment hung between us. Fortunately, Joann's arrival with the champagne eased the tension.

She expertly uncorked the bottle and poured a small amount into Clyde's flute. He pushed it across the table in my direction. "Will you do the honors?"

I collected the glass and took a tentative sip. Crips

bubbles popped and tickled my nose as the decadent wine teased my throat. "It's divine."

Joann nodded and added more to my glass before filling Clyde's. "As you can see we have a coursed menu with only a few decisions. Would you like to choose your options now?"

Clyde looked my way and I quickly scanned the short list of options. "I'll begin with the little gem salad, followed by the fish of the day and," I hesitated briefly then threw caution to the wind. "I'll finish with a chocolate bombe."

Clyde's smile was childlike. "Tuna tartare for me, then steak-frites and let's finish me off with the toffee bread pudding."

"Wonderful choices. You won't be disappointed. Enjoy your wine while we prepare your meal."

"Thank you," Clyde said as she took her leave.

He raised his glass and met my gaze. "To you, Ms. Tuesday, for illuminating the problem on our team and my every moment since we first met."

I blushed and raised my glass to join his. "Thank you for giving me the chance. Cheers."

The delicate chime of our united glasses left a tiny musical ring. I sipped the spectacular vintage and setting the glass aside, decided now was the time to raise the one topic I labored over. "I'm worried about Patty."

Clyde set his drink aside and nodded. "I get it. I was too. She violated the policy and as innocent as her mistake was, we had no choice but to let her go."

I understood, but still worried about her future. "I know that."

"Don't worry too much. She's a talented writer and I have it on good authority that she's landed a teaching gig."

I quirked my head. "What do you mean?"

"Alex has always had a soft spot for her and he's adding

her to the faculty. She starts next month. With her severance package, she'll end up ahead."

It happened automatically—I reached across the table and touched his wrist. "That's wonderful news."

His eyes shone and his hand twisted to hold mine. "It is. On another topic, your course is finished. How do you feel?"

I shook my head in disbelief. "It all went by fast. I learned so much in that class and Alex was the most encouraging instructor I've ever had."

"He doesn't just hand out praise you know. He told me that he sent your manuscript to the Rise Contest. No matter what, some pretty important people are going to read your work."

"I know. It's alarming. So many people submit, there's no chance mine will surface to the top. Still, I'm honored he thought enough of my screenplay to go to those lengths."

"Alex is a smart man and he's well respected. He didn't do it on a whim. His confidence in you is reason enough to celebrate."

I smiled and raised my glass. "To Alex."

He joined me. "To Alex and his protégé."

We sipped and Clyde posed the question that I'd been tossing around without clarity. "What's next for Ms. Evelyn Snow? Will you continue writing?"

"I'm not sure I could stop now. It's as if I've opened Pandora's box and everything has changed."

"That's when the magic happens. I want to read your work."

His statement wasn't a shock. I knew he was curious about my writing and a part of me wanted him to read my story. In that way I could tell him who I was without saying it directly. From our first meeting, I had the unnerving sense Clyde would change my life. Until that moment, I hadn't given him access. Sharing my story would change that.

My reply was cheeky, "I'm thinking about it."

For the rest of the evening he wooed me over delicious food and luxurious wine, sharing stories about his time in Los Angeles. I felt drawn to him and even my body leaned over the table to get a little closer to his energy. The night was almost over and as we wound through the streets of LA, I grew melancholy knowing I'd soon depart. For as much as I missed my home and being a part of Athena's daily life, I'd found something here that was hard to let go of.

He eased up the driveway and got out of the car, quickly circling to my side. As we took the final steps toward the door, I found the bravery I wasn't sure I had. Removing the large envelope from my handbag, I gave Clyde what he wanted. "Don't be too hard on me. It's my first attempt."

He accepted the envelope and slid the manuscript from inside. The title was, *Dear Men*, and beneath it was typed, *Musings of a Woman in the World. By TN Tuesday*

"You used your stage name."

"I did. Otherwise, it would have been career suicide. I still have a day job to consider."

And in a flash, it happened. Just like the movies he pulled me into his arms and kissed me with the fervor of a man who wanted to leave an impression. He tasted like home and I knew he was my destiny.

ENCORE

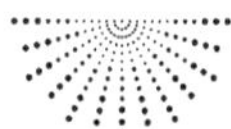

Athena and Nick wrestled childishly on the couch and I had a moment of longing as I recalled the kiss that closed my chapter with Clyde. Like every great movie, I knew it would end. "Hey, I'm running to the store to get more tape. I'll be back in ten."

Athena giggled, "Okay, Mom. See you in a few." Nick pounced and howled like a wolf. "See you, Evvy."

I shook my head and walked the few blocks to the market. The warm day beat down as I crossed the scorching asphalt and made my way inside. My thoughts ran to Clyde and I realized I hadn't heard from him since we parted on the front steps two nights prior. My insecurity was doubled as I was the girl waiting by the phone and the writer who dreamed her story would become a film. I shook myself mentally, knowing both were a long shot.

Clyde was a handsome, eligible bachelor and successful producer living in Hollywood. At every turn women threw themselves at him. Once I was no longer in his sights, he'd forget me. For that matter, there were as many promising writers knocking on his door, begging him to read their work. My story wouldn't stand out against that breadth of competition.

I found the tape and a bottle of vodka and went to the cash register.

A knock at the door interrupted Athena's make-out session. "I'm coming," she called and extracted herself from Nick's seductive kissing.

"Did you forget your key?" she called, but when she opened the door she found Clyde Parks standing there. "Oh, hello, Mr. Parks."

"It's Clyde, remember? It's nice to see you again, Athena."

"You as well, Clyde. Please come in." She waved her hand in gesture as Nick stood up and straightened his wrinkled T-shirt. "This is my boyfriend, Nick."

Clyde stepped forward and extended his hand to shake. "Good to meet you, Nick."

"You as well, Clyde. I've heard a lot about you and that day in Beverly Hills."

"I'm happy it worked out." He glanced nervously. "Is your Mom around?"

Athena replied, "She'll be right back. She ran to the store to get some tape."

He nodded awkwardly. "Can I get you some iced tea while you wait?" she added.

"Thank you," he agreed. "That would be great. It's really hot out there."

"I know. I love the pool, but even I couldn't stay in the sun for long."

Athena filled a glass with ice and tea, then handed it to Clyde. She wondered and since Mom wasn't there to stop her, she asked, "Is this visit business or personal?"

He looked like a nervous suitor and Athena reveled in her ability to unnerve the powerful man who was obviously enamored with her lovely mom.

"It's a bit of both," he replied. Before she could redirect, the front door opened. With the action, a wave of heat from the weather and chemistry between Clyde and her Mom nearly knocked Athena over.

Athena chuckled and said, "Nick, let's take one last swim before we melt."

"Okay," he agreed.

Athena teased over her shoulder, "You kids stay outta trouble."

Though I expected to find Clyde inside—his car at the curb warned me of his presence—the shock was no less. "This is a surprise."

He walked my direction as I set the bag on the table. "A good one I hope."

I agreed, "A good one."

We were feet apart and he finally said, "I can't let you go just yet."

His words pressed the air from my lungs and I was speechless.

He continued, "On a personal level, I am captivated by your every move. From the first time I saw you, I wanted to keep you and that feeling has only increased as I've had the chance to know you."

I swooned at his feet. Still, no words would come.

"And from a purely capitalistic standpoint, I would be a fool not to produce your screenplay. It's disturbing and telling, but most of all honest. The world has to hear what you have to say and I want to help you."

I finally found my voice, and eked, "Some of it is true."

His voice was a whisper, "That's okay. If they want to sue, not only are our pockets deeper, but we're holding the mic."

I knew with certainty what I'd sensed from the start. Clyde was my person. It had taken a long time to find him. A series of disasters led me to his door and I wanted to stay. I asked, "What happens now?"

The world vanished as he reached for me and our lips joined for the second time. Heat from within as searing as an inferno swept over me and I found gratitude for my misfortune. Had I not been dragged through life's muck, I may never have had the courage to seek my heart's desire. Until I was cast into the darkest sea, only then did I find the bravery to be who I was all the time.

TAKE A BOW

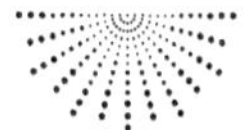

*W*as it the flash of my sparkling new engagement ring, or from the many camera bulbs that blinded me as we made our way up the red carpet? My arm linked in Clyde's and the weight from my crystal encrusted gown helped ground me in this foreign world of excess. "Look this way," one photographer called.

Clyde paused and wrapped his arm protectively around my shoulder. I tried for a smile to replace the inevitable shock that must have shown in my expression. Snap, snap, snap, snap.

The writer in me grappled to find any string of words that could describe the fantastic trice. Surreal came to mind, but that was clichéd compared to the experience. Behind us Nicole Kidman commanded the press with her flawless posture and a smile that could light up the world. Angelina Jolie walked ahead, solitary and unaffected in a tattered black frill of a gown. She glanced at me with the knowing expression and I marveled at my privilege.

Dear Men, Musings of a Woman in the World, was nominated for best original screenplay and I knew casting

Angelina as the lead had propelled the story with an added edge. Athena, though determined to finish university and ultimately devote her life to the earth, took a sabbatical to play the daughter in my story. Tonight, she was ethereal in a cream silken column dress and her dazzling smile. With Nick on her arm, she looked nothing like the baby I'd once held. Surely, I would awaken to find this was only a dream.

Clyde leaned close and whispered in my ear, "You did this. You did this, Evelyn, and you're going to win."

His confidence astounded and embarrassed me. After years of feeling sullied and unworthy, this man saw all of me and loved me anyway. The melt I'd been longing for was finally mine and I couldn't wait to marry him.

Already the corporate world was evolving. Sure, it was forced and reactive, and completely insincere, but that didn't matter. Change was necessary and even corporate America could fake it till they made it. Eventually what we do becomes who we are and that gave me hope.

I was having an out-of-body experience as if floating high above the velvet pews and watching from the rafters. The company I now kept and the opportunities before me were beyond comprehension. Tonight, was a wish come true, not for the notoriety, but for the chance to make a difference.

The moment arrived and as I watched the clips of screenplays from my esteemed colleagues, my head felt light. They chose the car scene for ours and as I watched, I felt enraged all over again. I knew Roman Rossi was watching, like a killer who cannot resist but to take a memento from his victim. I hoped he feared me as I was once afraid of him. The balance of power had shifted drastically and at any moment, I could call him out. It would still be "he said, she said," but now they would believe me.

"And the winner is…"—the drum rolled in time with my

stomach—"…Dear Men, Musings of a Woman in the World by Evelyn Snow."

I staggered to the stage, raising the blush and silvery gown, floating up the stairs and into the brightest lights. The golden statue weighed heavily in my hand and the writer's voice went mute. Tears exploded unchecked down my cheeks, elation warmed me and I looked up to the rafters for divine guidance.

My voice quivered. "Thank you, GOD for weaving a path that lead to a certain doctor, without whom, I may never have written this screenplay. I'd also like to thank the Academy, my parents, my precious Athena, Angelina Jolie, Alex Mane and my love, Clyde Parks for taking this leap with me. I accept this honor on behalf of all the women."

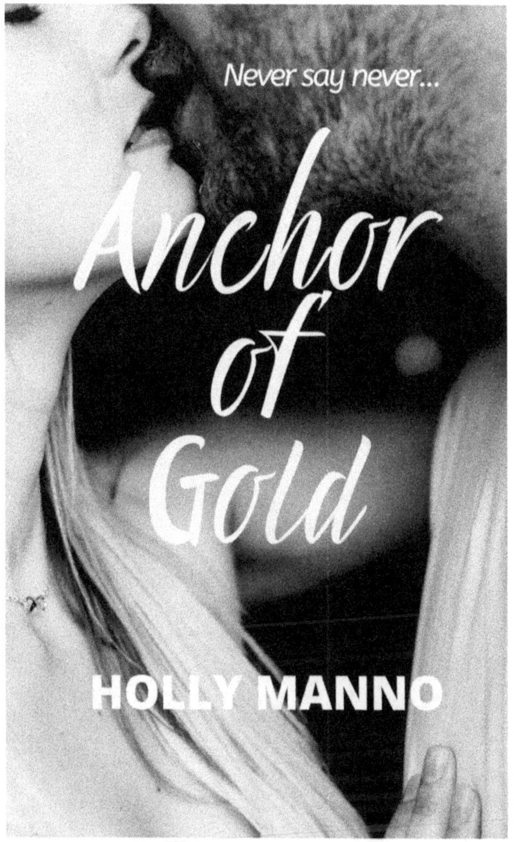

Business, pleasure & chaos send Madeline down a shadowed path where she meets Travis, the man who breaks all of her rules.

LOVE TEST - Online dating while wedding planning? Love doesn't test, but people do...